THE TOWN CLERK

THE
TOWN CLERK

**First Novel by
JOHN SIMMONS**

REPRESENTATION:
Vincent Shaw, Vincent Shaw Associates, 20 Jay Mews, London, SW7 2EP
Tel: 0171 581 8215 (4 lines)   Fax: 0171 225 1079
Compu Serve ID: 100666.2527

PUBLISHER:
Charisma, St Paul's Former Methodist Church, Market Street,
Hoyland, Barnsley, South Yorkshire, S74 9QR
Copyright © John Simmons 1996
ISBN No. 0 9529392 0 7

PRINTER:
J W Northend Ltd, Clyde Road, Sheffield, S8 0TZ
Tel: 0114 250 0331

for Christine

CONTENTS

INTRODUCTION		i
One	*The Town Clerk*	17
Two	*The Mayor-Making*	23
Three	*Mayor's Sunday*	37
Four	*The Opening of Water's Edge Business Park*	45
Five	*The Special Council Meeting*	55
Six	*Yellow*	73
Seven	*Strines Valley*	85
Eight	*Members v Officers at Golf*	95
Nine	*The Lodge Meeting*	105
Ten	*The L.V.A. Cricket Match*	121
Eleven	*Liebfraumilch*	129
Twelve	*The Mayor's Parade*	141
Thirteen	*The Twin Town Visit*	157
Fourteen	*The Conference at Scarborough*	167
Fifteen	*In Memorium*	187
Sixteen	*Committed*	193
Seventeen	*James*	199

INTRODUCTION

One Sunday morning in October 1995, I returned from the communion service at All Saints' Church, Silkstone and announced to my wife that I was going to write a novel, it was to be called "The Town Clerk" and I had already worked out the plot during the service. She didn't think God would quite approve of my mind wandering in church and, anyway, how could I write a novel as I only read non-fiction books? She had two valid points. Firstly, my novel would be quite fruity in parts so it might be considered irreligious to let one's mind encompass such thoughts in church but I considered that perhaps a God-given talent may manifest itself in many a mysterious way? Her second point was equally difficult to counter. We have a library in our home of perhaps a thousand books and 95% of these are non-fiction works, mainly biographies. Each birthday and Christmas I am a willing recipient of another ten or so similar non-fiction works and each holiday I take a clutch of these biographies with me to read whilst stretched out in the sun. Once I was temporarily incarcerated in a prison cell (and that is another story, perhaps for another time) and during this time I read the biographies of Graham Hill, Arthur Askey and King Hussein of Jordan. Other people's lives fascinate me and my favourite part of the Daily Telegraph, after the sports pages, is the obituary page. So my wife had made a very valid point. I can remember reading Great Expectations, one Jeffery Archer novel, one Dick Francis epic and not much else in the fiction field. Well, my answer to this point was that perhaps I would not be influenced by traditional conceptions of fiction and my book might just be something different. Whether I have succeeded or not is for you, the reader, to decide.

So, I started writing "The Town Clerk". Many of the experiences were based on actual incidents during my twenty-three years in local government although I must stress that this is a work of fiction and all characters are fictitious – for example, I have known many Town Clerks in my time and James Pickering-Eaden certainly bears no resemblance to any of them although I suspect that perhaps some – or all – would not mind being him! So I expect no libel writs from that quarter. I am very grateful to Norman Wisdom for giving me his permission – and blessing – to include the scene involving him at the Opening of Water's Edge Business Park. This was based on an actual incident long, long ago when Norman behaved with the utmost decorum and the First Citizen of the borough did not ... the actual incident shall remain a secret between Norman and me.

As the story progressed I got more and more carried away with it. Sometimes I ran into a dead-end but would awake at 3 am with the solution, so I got up immediately and committed it to type lest it disappear from my brain should I leave it until morning. Christmas 1995 came and went with about four pages a day coming from my pen, or rather, my typewriter. It was sometimes difficult because I was working full-time in my antiques warehouse and some days it was impossible to devote any time at all to "The Town Clerk". But things were progressing steadily until one day just after Christmas. It was quiet and suddenly it started to snow quite heavily. I closed the doors, although it must be said that there was a distinct shortage of customers anyway. I decided that I would write until I was sere, dried up, bereft of ideas. I put paper in the typewriter and the words flowed. I did two thousand words and was so fired with genius that I did not notice the hours flying by. To lubricate brain and fingers I crossed the road to the off-licence opposite and indulged myself with a can or two of Special Brew. After three hours I looked at the clock and noticed it was way past my dinner time.

I telephoned my wife and asked her to put dinner on hold as genius had inveigled me into his/her parlour. The words were flowing with Wildean lucidity. I crossed the road and purchased another couple of cans of Special Brew to help the flow. At 10 o'clock the telephone rang and my wife informed me that the mixed grill was gone beyond recall and when would I be coming home? "No problem," said I, "forget the mixed grill, I am concentrating on the mixed metaphors and they are flowing unabated with the help of a can or two of Special Brew." I returned to the typewriter and my fingers sped over the keys like a ballerina on points. At midnight I fell off my chair and found it impossible to regain my equilibrium. I managed to crawl to the telephone and

Introduction

tell my wife that I had committed sixteen pages of literature of unparalleled quality to print and that since I was slightly tired and emotional I had decided to sleep overnight in one of the inlaid Edwardian beds in the warehouse with Lucky, the shop cat, for company. At two o'clock I awoke with a clear mind and clear head but nearly stiff with hypothermia. I telephoned my wife and requested her to carry out duties as a chauffeuse immediately. After what seemed to be an eternity she arrived and I was ferried home through the snow to a warm bed. The following day I eagerly read the sixteen pages I had written the previous evening. It was the biggest load of rubbish I had ever read in my life and I committed the sixteen pages to the waste-paper bin.

In the New Year I eventually finished "The Town Clerk" and was very pleased with it. However, it wasn't long enough as it ran to only 143 pages. I had given little thought as to how it would be published. Naively I thought publishers would be queuing up to dangle untold numbers of pound-filled carrots in front of me for the privilege of publishing my oeuvre. Reality was somewhat different. According to the Writers' and Artists' Yearbook, publishers would like to read the first three chapters. So four publishers were furnished with the first three chapters of "The Town Clerk".

One never replied, two sent the standard rejection slip and the other said he only considered manuscripts submitted by bona-fide agents. So I tried another track. I decided that I had undersold myself. I had heard that a new author had written a story about the collapse of a Merchant Bank and publishers were outbidding each other for his work. I wrote to a publisher telling him that he was the lucky one that I had selected and that I needed £10,000 to fund a civil legal action (see earlier in this introduction about police cells, King Hussein, Arthur Askey and Graham Hill). Despite large capital investment on my behalf of a stamped addressed envelope, the executives at the publishing house were evidently falling about so much in respect of the hilarious demand for an up-front payment that they could not make it to the post-box to utilise the s.a.e.

Next I decided I would get an agent. If publishers were not bothered about "The Town Clerk" then surely agents would be? Wrong again. I tried six. From the first agent that I tried I received the manuscript back by return of post. He neatly encapsulated the chances of acceptance by telling me that he received approximately ninety manuscripts from new writers every week– 4,500 a year and that he accepted only two or three of these. Work out the

iii

The Town Clerk

odds for yourself to ascertain the chances of being set on. The others certainly came up with a myriad of excuses – one was pregnant, three were not taking any new writers and one thought it was great but was going to 'pass' because he was heading in a slightly different direction and couldn't see any avenues for new writers. Pondering on what this meant I was getting slightly deflated but, having spent 23 years in local government, I was used to gobbledegook and circumlocution so I considered he was letting me down gently. It was at that time that Vincent Shaw wrote to me on another matter and "The Town Clerk" came in the conversation. "Send it to me," he said and I did, and he said, "My dear, it's marvellous," which did wonders for my self-esteem. "But it is not a novel, it is a television series and we must get a script written to submit to commissioning editors." Enter Brian Izzard, a respected television producer with a string of strong credits behind him.

He was very encouraging about "The Town Clerk" and suggested immediately restructuring part of it, drawing it up as a post-watershed series (ie after 9 pm) and submitting it to television companies. Very good and away he went to bring "The Town Clerk" into an acceptable format for today's audience.

Vincent said that it was not quite long enough. So in the spring of 1996 I took the manuscript away with me to a family holiday in Keffalonia. Here I extended it by another fifty pages by tidying the thing up and introducing other anecdotal incidents. The night of the snow, cat, Special Brew and mixed grill repeated itself in Keffalonia. One night, fired with literary enthusiasm and armed this time with a bottle of ouzo and inspired by the beauty of a blood-orange Greek sun slowly sinking below the horizon of the Ionian millpond sea, I wrote ten pages of – what I thought – was outrageous and perceptive dialogue for a new chapter. I went to bed with a seraphic ouzo-inspired silly grin on my face. In the morning I read it again and, just like that snowy day in Yorkshire, consigned the lot to a bin. The overall task, however, was successful and when it was extended to the form that it is in today, Val Noble took it in hand and made a marvellous job of presentation, spell-checking and ironing out the many anomalies.

So why are we publishing "The Town Clerk" as a book? Let me veer off on another tangent. Well, in 1973 there was a local government reorganisation. I was Entertainments Manager of Barnsley Metropolitan Borough Council – an interesting job at principal officer grade, responsible for all sorts of

Introduction

entertainment, community centres, Mayor's Parade, writing the Council newspaper, in charge of bars and any other odd job that the Council couldn't find a mug to do.

I was fired with enthusiasm as I had been in charge of a 1,000-seater theatre in the centre of Barnsley and soon after being appointed had designed a suite of rooms on the top floor which lent themselves as the Centenary Rooms to a variety of functions. In the early seventies I had a bit of luck. The Library left the ground floor of the Civic Theatre complex that I controlled, to go to a new purpose-built home elsewhere in the town centre. The way was clear for a major entertainments complex to be built in the centre of Barnsley. The ground floor was to be the hub for visiting bands of international repute – rock groups and orchestral – the first floor was to be a Civic Theatre attracting the best touring and resident companies, the Centenary Rooms were to be arts workshops. Various rooms on the mezzanine could be used for multi-cultural activities. Enthusiastically I threw myself into preparing a working schedule for achieving these aims. I prepared a report (well you can't do anything without a report in local government) – I secured promises of grants from charitable foundations, I identified the catchment area, I listed touring companies, I costed the work and the commitment of continuing expenditure to fund such a dream. Proudly I brought forward my one hundred page report to the Working Committee. "Very good," everyone agreed, "our Entertainments Manager has shown us what Barnsley Council could do," said the Chairman of the Committee. That was the last we ever heard of it. After the meeting I went round and collected copies of the report. Half of the committee had not even bothered to read it, the rest of the copies were either chucked in the bin or put on a shelf where no doubt they are still gathering dust today. Twenty-three years later the Civic Hall complex lies moribund in the centre of Barnsley, unchanged, unloved and unwanted. It costs the Council an absolute fortune in maintenance costs. No-one goes there any more.

So can you understand the analogy between my report to the noble councillors of Barnsley and the reaction to "The Town Clerk" by publishers, agents, commissioning editors alike? Enter Keith Stubley of Northend Printers of Sheffield. Before I was introduced to him via a lovely friend, Karen Thorpe, there was a sporting chance that "The Town Clerk" would join the Civic Theatre Entertainment Complex Report, dusting away on the shelf.

The Town Clerk

"Sod it," I thought, "I am going to go for it and print the thing myself, be my own publisher." Whether the final presentation comes up to standard is for you, the reader, to decide but it certainly satisfies me.

One final aspect. There is a certain amount of sex in this novel. I make no apology for it. Sex is a big part of people's lives and it was certainly a big part of James Pickering-Eaden's life. After all, one cannot live on cocoa alone ..... I must make my apologies in advance for some of the bad language in this book. Notably the tirade by the Mayor on the golf course. Unfortunately, it was not possible to write this without resorting to somewhat basic aspects of our beautiful English language. I can understand if you decide that I may have gone too far but this is how I saw the character and I am afraid that if you are offended you must read no further and take it to the nearest car boot sale or donate it to the next church jumble sale ... perhaps reconciling yourself that by purchasing this you have helped a struggling author achieve some sort of inner satisfaction.

For others who decide to progress further I hope you will enjoy "The Town Clerk". It had its birth in the frustration that I had of not being able to understand or appreciate much of today's offerings of television drama. At least "The Town Clerk" has a beginning, it has a middle and it has an end. Or has it?

I hope you will enjoy it.

JOHN SIMMONS
29 August 1996

CHAPTER ONE

THE TOWN CLERK

James Pickering-Eaden pushed his office chair back eighteen inches and put his feet on his desk. It was the day of the Mayor-making, when the new Mayor for the next Council year was inducted and the old one said his fond farewells and dropped down to Deputy Mayor to act as an elder statesman giving advice to the new man.

He had seen eight of these occasions and each one had become progressively easier to organise. He had been Town Clerk of Middlethwaite District Council for these past eight years and now considered that this was to be probably his last appointment. His whole career had been in Local Government with the exception of a short period after coming out of his articles when he had tried private practice. He had a Second Class Law Degree and a short experience in the Litigation Department of a busy City of London Solicitors had persuaded him that his future lay in Local Government. In the days of the old Urban and Rural District Councils he had been appointed Assistant Solicitor to a small authority in West Sussex. The nomenclature of Assistant Solicitor was a trifle misleading. He headed the Legal, Parliamentary and Ceremonial Department which, in effect, comprised James Pickering-Eaden full-time and the services of a secretary who came Monday, Wednesday and Friday afternoons. The Clerk of the Rural District Council was also a solicitor who had given up practising twenty years before and he delegated anything in this field to his Assistant Solicitor. In the Parliamentary and Ceremonial disciplines there was precious little to concern either officer whilst the duties in the legal field were varied but hardly demanding.

The Assistant Solicitor prosecuted rate defaulters, evicted difficult tenants and with the help of the Sanitary Inspector (as he was then titled), issued

17

The Town Clerk

notices in respect of smelly drains, leaky roofs and rat infestation under the Landlord and Tenant Act. Occasionally the Assistant Solicitor came across something more interesting but, if he did, the matter would immediately be referred to the County Council which had responsibility for anything important in those days. This job of James Pickering- Eaden was safe, undemanding and financially comfortable but did nothing to satisfy him. He looked on this as the first rung on the ladder so after three years he joined a larger Council and then his career took him via another six local authorities, two bouts of Local Government re-organisation until he had arrived in the Pennine Borough of Middlethwaite eight years before as Town Clerk and Chief Executive. The plate on his office door bore the legend THE TOWN CLERK. and, unlike his colleagues in neighbouring authorities he was pleased to emphasise the traditional Town Clerk part of his title and the Chief Executive annotation took a back seat.

He particularly liked the brass plate on his office door and his cleaner took great pride in polishing it every day. The brass plate harked back to Edwardian days when grocers' shops always had a large full-stop after the name on the shop-front and every day he saw his shining brass plate the full-stop seemed to stand out like a pertinent reminder that James Pickering-Eaden had reached the zenith of his career. He was a happy man. He moved across to the drinks cabinet and poured himself a small measure of Glenfiddich. The marble clock on the pollard oak sideboard chimed five o'clock, mentally it struck him that there were still two hours to the Mayor-making so before he could re-cork the Glenfiddich he tilted the bottle again and doubled the measure. All the arrangements for the evening had been tied up so he felt entitled to relax. The drinks cabinet contained suites of good cut glass tumblers, ruby glass decanters from his Victorian predecessors and every kind of beer, wines and spirit. It was safe with him, he rarely visited the cabinet except in exceptional circumstances and drank only as a reward rather than using it to provide inspiration.

He loved working in his office. Each piece of furniture could tell a story and the office was traditionally furnished with only modern machinery such as the fax machine, the computer and the shredder contained in or on an elegant piece of furniture. A large Bokhara carpet covered the whole office, its pile undiminished by sixty years wear giving testament to its quality. No one could remember where it had come from, it had always been there and still retained the vivid colours and the superb symmetry of its patterns. One wall was completely covered by a large mahogany bookcase given by a benefactor to the town of Middlethwaite at the turn of the century when a local glassworks relocated. The Town Clerk had filled it with yards of leather-bound books and the gold-tooled art nouveau decoration of the spines glistened when the sun moved round in late afternoon. On the wall was a Japanese Katana given to the town recently to celebrate the arrival of the Nipponese Ballbearing Corporation from Yamasaka and an Edwardian cabinet of the Sheraton Revival Movement contained many nice pieces of the civic silver. On the walls, in swept gilt frames were sixteen pictures by the Hold family from Cawthorne, mainly birds nests, dead game and naive local views. The Hold family of Ben, Abel, Tom, John and Mary were untutored but talented Yorkshire artists whose work had been collected by the Middlethwaite Art and Natural History Society. This society had closed down in the 1960's and it was touch and go whether they would be confined to the bonfire as was the fate of many Victorian paintings at that time. The Town Clerk at the time felt obliged to keep them as he had been President of the society so they were stored in the large walk-in safe in the Town Clerk's general office. James Pickering-Eaden had found them soon after his appointment, restored the canvasses, re-gilded the rococo frames and hung them in his office. They looked magnificent, complementing the eclectic decoration of his inner sanctum and they satisfied the Town Clerk's traditional conservationist values whilst providing the ratepayers with a capital asset as they were now worth many thousand pounds.

There had not been many peaks in his life, but neither had there been many troughs. He had worked assiduously to ensure that the wheels of the authority ran smoothly and it was testament to his diligence that, in the main, they had. Scores of government directives had given him little cause for concern, he had run a "tight ship" with a good team of officers and – even though he said it himself – he had handled the elected members well, with a mixture of firmness and patience steering them to the direction he wanted them to go and cleverly making them think that they were the innovators and policy-makers when in reality they were following a path neatly laid and labelled by him and his officers. Most of his councillors were Labour members, in fact 57 of the 60 Councillors were, there was one Conservative and two Independents who were returned each election by the skin of their teeth and owed their return to their personalities and not their politics. He had worked for only one right-wing Authority and had not liked it whereas he felt at ease under Socialist masters and although he was a dyed-in-the-wool Tory himself he was happy in the employ of a Labour-run Authority, and had no desire to change it.

And nor could he. Middlethwaite like many Pennine Authorities had seen vast changes over the past twenty years. Once reliant on the coal industry they had been slow to acknowledge the technological change of Thatcher's Britain in the eighties and, despite their favourable location had been left behind in the creation of the new order of Britain's industries. The Town Clerk's predecessor had been twenty years in the job and the last few years had been a steady amble down the path to retirement and not much energy and enthusiasm had been expended in persuading the Labour leaders that Thatcher's premiership had signalled a lasting change of direction. When the Thatcher government had been first elected in 1978 the local Labour party rulers had stoically resisted any notion that Britain was to change drastically, firmly believing that the Conservative government would fall at the next election. Consequently change had been stalled at every turn and Middlethwaite had been left swimming against the tide of the New Britain. It was only when the Tories had commenced their fourth term of office that, rather late in the day, the Socialist politicians of Middlethwaite reversed their Luddite approach to new technology and tried to join the new revolution.

But now James Pickering-Eaden felt that things were getting infinitely better. He had worked steadily in his eight years as Town Clerk and life was getting better now that the inevitable had been accepted. In fact one of the first duties of the new Mayor would be to open the new Business Park along with a Minister of State up from London for the day and a television "personality" to try to get some national publicity and fill some of the many empty units.

So today was the day of the Mayor-making when Councillor Leslie Ullathorne was to be inducted the 108th Mayor of Middlethwaite. He had been on the Council seventeen years and it was customary for Mayors to be elected on a rota basis. This meant that most Councillors had served on the authority for nearly twenty years before it was their turn and it was surprising how many young idealistic Socialists had quenched the fires of their passion when they saw the beacon of the Mayoralty shining in the distance. Les

The Town Clerk

Ullathorne was councillor for the sprawling Sunflower Hill Estate to the west of the Borough and had long since given up work after redundancy from the mining industry. The Town Clerk did not know him well – even hardly at all – for his only claim to fame in Middlethwaite was as Vice-Chairman of the Direct Works Sub-Committee. But, no doubt, he would be a responsible holder of the office and carry out his duties with dignity as had most of his predecessors.

So the Town Clerk was at peace with the world. He took his feet off the desk, poured himself another Glenfiddich from the drinks cabinet, lit a King Edward cigar and returned his feet to the desk. He was 48 years old but felt fit and he wore his years well. He had a full head of hair, greying elegantly at the temples and a slight avoirdupois around the girth but he dressed well and was well-liked by all sections of the community. He had been married to Celia for 23 years but, sadly, no children had come along and as he sipped his malt whisky he reflected that he had set his path well and carefully progressed along the career path, well within his capabilities. Not for him the challenges of the big City Corporations or the Development Agencies. He was happy in Middlethwaite and would probably see out his days there.

He had nearly dozed off when there was a knock on the door and Cheryl Oldroyd, Administrative Assistant Grade III came in. "It's time for you to robe, sir," she said. "The Mayor's Secretary has nearly finished briefing Councillor Ullathorne and no doubt, sir, you will wish to meet them both in the Robing Room." She took out his wig from its powdered box and drew his gown from the lobby. She took his medal case from the safe, ran a light duster over the miniatures and replaced the empty case in the safe. She had finished fussing around, came round behind the desk so the Town Clerk got to his feet and Cheryl (what a bloody awful name, he thought) straightened the wig and dusted some imaginary fluff from the shoulder of his gown. He caught a glimpse of her on tiptoes in the cheval mirror behind her and thought what a lovely girl she was. The thought was fleeting and he looked at himself full-length in the cheval glass and liked what he saw. He wore the black half of his office, striped trousers and patent leather shoes whilst the miniatures of the two medals he had been awarded as an Officer in the Territorial Army set off the sombreness of the official garb. "Is there anything I need to know, Mrs Oldroyd?" he asked, taking another sip of his Glenfiddich and blowing an aromatic cloud of smoke from his cigar, before stubbing it out.

The Town Clerk

"No, sir," she replied. "There is just some formal business to do with the distribution of the Mayor's Charities and the rest of the evening will follow the usual custom and practice just as it has for the past 108 years." She smiled confidently at the Town Clerk and he returned her smile. "If you don't need me any more, sir, I'll be off and leave you to see the Mayor's Secretary."

"No, that's fine, thank you. You seem to have tied up all the loose ends and I bid you goodnight."

"Goodnight, sir," she said, turning on her heels and he watched her go, following her image in the cheval mirror.

You know, he thought, what a lovely bum she has and he recalled the waft of her perfume as she had straightened his wig and it had stayed with him. And didn't she still look crisp and neat even at the end of a long day. Now, Town Clerk, he thought, put thoughts like those behind you..... and he did, crossed his office to the ante-room and knocked at the door of the Robing Room.

CHAPTER TWO

THE MAYOR MAKING

"Come in, Town Clerk," said the outgoing Mayor, Councillor Cairns. The Town Clerk entered and surveyed the scene. The Robing Room was an adjunct to the Mayor's Parlour. A brass track was inset into the parquet floor of the parlour, about one-third the way down. The judicious pressing of a concealed button slowly set in motion a purring motor and, very slowly, a section of panelling metamorphosed from the window-side wall and at a slow rate of knots ran along the track and eventually nestled flush against the opposite wall. Back in its existing position, the oak panelling was a double-skinned wall although an integral door in the panelling actually went nowhere. When the panelling was forming the wall of the Robing Room, the door allowed access to the Mayor's Parlour. It was a masterly piece of Victorian invention, engineered and patented by Aylward of Middlethwaite, Purveyors of Panelling to Queen and Empress as an integral brass plate informed everyone. The Robing Room contained just a scroll-end Victorian chaise-lounge, raised on ball and claw feet terminating in large impressive brass castors, and a dozen or so elegant side chairs donated by the denizens of Middlethwaite over the years. The main Mayor's Parlour had an elegant partners desk, a conference table surrounded by a long set of sixteen Chippendale chairs, a davenport for the Mayoress and various comfortable chairs for visiting dignitaries. At the far end was a serving sideboard groaning under the weight of drinks for the hospitality reception to be held after the installation of the new Mayor. Around the walls were hung photographs of the previous 108 Mayors ranging from the sepia posings of the first Mayor replete with bushy beard and shaggy eyebrows through the passing years of change in the fashion of hirsute appendages to the present day and the lazer image of Councillor Leslie Ullathorne.

The Town Clerk

As usual Robin Armstrong, the Mayor's Secretary, had organised everything well. The Town Clerk knew that he could leave everything to Robin and that it would be perfect. Robin Armstrong had had experience of dealing with Mayors of all shapes, sizes, temperament and intellect. Coming up to sixty he showed no sign of diminution of duty or, indeed, his love of the job as shepherd to the uninitiated. He had left the Royal Air Force as a Wing-Commander and come to Middlethwaite straightaway with only his administrative abilities, man-management and his flair for the ceremonial as his qualifications for the job. And no job could have suited him better – or he it. Every year he was handed by the ruling Labour Party a rough diamond as First Citizen and by gentle moulding and firmness, where necessary, produced a Mayor who had been a credit to Middlethwaite.

Councillor Cairns, the outgoing Mayor, pushed a whiskey into his hand. "Thank you, Mr Mayor," said the Town Clerk, "I think I can call you that for another fifteen minutes or so before you hand over your Chain of Office to Councillor Ullathorne. May I congratulate you on a momentous year of office, magnificently carried out by you and your charming Mayoress."

Councillor Cairns smiled happily, warming to the congratulations and thinking that James Pickering-Eaden was a very good Town Clerk and mentally congratulating himself on the fact that eight years ago he had gone out on a limb as Chairman of the Establishment Committee and had pressed for Pickering-Eaden's appointment ahead of the pedantic old barrister from Bootle and the young whizzkid from Liverpool who had since had a spell in Strangeways for doing strange things with clients' money. "Let me fill you up, Town Clerk," pressing another tumbler of whiskey on him.

"Thank you, thank you," said the Town Clerk, "but this must be my last, for there are many pitfalls that could arise on a night like this. Perhaps I shouldn't have even this one…" the assembled gathering laughed as the Town Clerk sought to put everyone at their ease. He looked around the Robing Room. The Mayor-Elect was sitting on the chaise-longue. Red-faced and swathed in the enormous ermine-clad mayoral robes that swamped him, he cut a somewhat comic figure. Councillor Cairns, his predecessor was an eighteen stone Scotsman of ample girth whilst the new man was seemingly half size, whose perpetual cigarette-in-hand had kept his already slight build down to under nine stone. The tailor had done a noble job in altering the robes but the Mayor-Elect looked lost in them. And the Chain of Office which contrived

The Mayor Making

somehow to contain the names of all 108 of his predecessors seemed to hang heavily on him and he tilted forward. The tricorn hat, fortunately was to be carried tonight, for had he been wearing it, it may have been the last straw which carried the uniform into farce.

He rose unsteadily to his feet. Cigarette ash spilled down his front and nestled within the finery of his lace ruff. The ruff was already discoloured, some beer had been spilled down it. The robes were creased. Councillor Leslie Ullathorne looked like he was wearing a horse blanket that had been thrown over a sweating gelding at the end of a five furlong sprint. From the middle of this horse blanket protruded a gnarled hand clutching a pint of Barnsley Bitter whilst a whiskey-chaser was within reach on a side-table nearby. He exuded nervousness, his pockmarked face was sweating, his eyes were bloodshot and, despite his large liquid intake, his tongue darted over his thin dry lips. Every now and again he said "Kinell" quietly to himself. As the Town Clerk approached the Mayor-Elect rose unsteadily to his feet and, barely audibly, said "Kinell" again.

Christ! thought the Town Clerk, he's nearly pissed, Robin is going to earn his corn keeping this one on the straight and narrow.

Councillor Ullathorne shifted his weight from foot to foot, settled into some sort of equilibrium and fixed the Town Clerk with bloodshot eyes. He extended his hand. "Pleased to meet thee, now let's see lad, tha name's Eaden-Pickering ent it?" getting his surname the wrong way round. As soon as he had greeted the Town Clerk he sunk back onto the chaise-longue, put his head in his hands, shook his head from side to side as if to clear his head and said, "Kinell." The Town Clerk answered him. "Near enough," said the Town Clerk, "that'll do." He felt suddenly a sense of impending doom and his legs felt weak. This man, he felt, was about to upset his cosy status quo. And he was right...

Max Earnshaw, the Mace-bearer entered. "Ladies and Gentlemen, if you would kindly prepare yourselves, it is time for the official party to enter the Council Chamber for the installation of Councillor Ullathorne as the 109th Mayor of Middlethwaite." He was very good, Max Earnshaw, his bearing bore all the stamp of tutelage under Robin Armstrong. He knew how to make the Mayor the most important person in Middlethwaite, Yorkshire, Great Britain, the World.

Les Ullathorne got to his feet again and hauled his Mayoress, Lilian, up

25

The Town Clerk

from the chaise-longue. Lilian was a supermarket cashier and had been granted a year's leave of absence to carry out her year of office. She was used to drinking half-dozen or so half-pints of Tetleys each Friday night at Hollowdene Working Men's Club but was now being plied with Martini, Pimms, Gin and French, Kummel and other exotic chasers and she too was decidedly under the weather. Her stock phrase seemed to be "I don't mind if I do" when offered a drink. Later in her Mayoral Year she was to be known as Mayoress Idontmindifido and it was sometime later that someone told her this and said that it came from ITMA during the War and Colonel Chinstrap had made this a catchphrase during World War II and thereafter she was known as Mayoress Chinstrap. Of such apocryphal happenings are legends made.

At Max Earnshaw's bidding the party started to assemble.The Mayor-Elect looked like an unmade bed. The tailor had made a noble attempt at altering the Mayoral robes but, really, had failed miserably. It happened every year.The current Mayor always hosted a farewell luncheon to celebrate the end of his Mayoral Year and appeared in the full 'uniform' of robes, chain and tricorn hat. The following day the new Mayor was installed and the noble tailor had to alter the Mayoral robes to fit the new incumbent. It wasn't too bad normally but there was a vast dichotomy in the stature of Councillors Cairns and Ullathorne and, despite his noble efforts, the tailor had failed. In truth, though, Councillor Ullathorne did not see himself as a figure of fun and a large lump of vivid scarlet-trimmed ermine shuffled to join the procession into the Council Chamber.

"Ladies and Gentlemen," solemnly announced Max Earnshaw "pray be upstanding for the Mayor and Mayoress of Middlethwaite."

The official party entered the Council Chamber, the current Mayor first, the new Mayor, the time-serving Labour MP and various local dignitaries and friends of the incoming and outgoing Mayor. The Town Clerk followed at a respectful distance for this was the time that Councillor Ullathorne had waited for eighteen years. The Council chamber looked like market day in Middlethwaite, an unhappy pastiche of the elegant and the ugly. The beautiful symmetry of the Council chamber had been lost by the hotchpotch of extra chairs needed to seat all the various official guests at the Mayor-Making. Vivid orange plastic stacker chairs mixed incongruously with the long set of sixteen Chippendale chairs from the parlour. Bentwood chairs from the

The Mayor Making

chapel next door were wedged into every available space and on them were wedged precariously the overflowing bottoms of many of Councillor Ullathorne's friends from the Sunflower Hill Estate. As the Mayor-Elect threaded his way through the Chamber he passed his fellow time-servers, some Mayors before him and some Mayors to come. "Ey up Wally, ow do Charlie, ow are thee Walt?" The supposedly dignified procession was then thrown into confusion when the Mayor-Elect spotted his bookmaker in the public gallery. "As tha got any 'oss tips, Craig?" sotto voce, or so he thought, but everybody heard.

The Town Clerk cringed. He thought that this was pretty basic but it was infinitely preferable to when he tried to speak the Queen's English. As he weaved his way through he came down just about on the majority view that the Mayor was better speaking his broad Yorkshire than having a fist at the Queen's English and putting all the aitches in the wrong place.

The meeting got under way. The Town Clerk relaxed slightly. Councillor Leslie Ullathorne was wedged in a huge ceremonial chair which had once belonged to Baron Middlethwaite. The opening exchanges did not involve him, his turn would come later. The Town Clerk stole sideways glances at him and he seemed to be perking up. Perhaps the whiskey added to the previous intake of Glenfiddich had heightened his emotions – he thought that alcohol induced a whole spectrum of reactions differently into different people. Some people wanted to fight the whole street, some were affected by maudlin lachrymosity, some were suicidal. Perhaps, he thought, alcohol induced pessimistic foreboding into Town Clerks. Robin Armstrong had done his job in his usual exemplary fashion for the formal proceedings were flowing in an uncomplicated manner. The Town Clerk slipped down in his seat. He couldn't imagine how he had had so many trepidations. He remembered five years ago when Councillor Grainger had been Mayor and then it looked like being the disaster of all time but he had done everything Robin had told him and had ended up with an M.B.E. in the Queen's Birthday Honours. The whiskey now seemingly created a roseate glow about him and he now reckoned that by limiting himself to the moderate alcohol intake as he had done it had, in fact, settled him down and he even permitted himself the thoughts of Mrs Oldroyd's breasts within a whisker of his lips as she straightened his wig. And when she had left his office, how he had watched her bottom swaying from side to side and traced with his eyes the pantie lines that obtruded over her haunches... He was brought back to earth by the new Mayor.

The Town Clerk

The meeting had gone its conventional way. Councillor Cairns, the retiring Mayor, regaled the assembled dignitaries with a resumé of his Mayoral Year. He had been delighted to attend the Queen's Garden Party, he had visited the Council's Twin Town of Schleigvighausen in Holland, had been delighted to host the Mayor's Parade at which there had been 63 floats and had visited 37 schools and had escorted 14 others on a tour of the Council Chamber and a lecture on the regalia. He had attended 703 functions throughout the Mayoral Year and had put on 14lbs in weight. The Council Chamber echoed with chuckles. The Town Clerk had heard it all before, especially the one about the increase in weight. If anything was obvious, certainly the increase in the Mayor's girth was. Indeed, thought the Town Clerk, it stuck out a mile. That's rather clever, he thought. He flicked through his minute book and looked at his notes for last year's installation of Councillor Cairns when the then retiring Mayor had been delighted to attend the Queen's Garden Party, had visited the Twin Town of Schleigvighausen in Holland, had been delighted to host the Mayor's Parade at which there had been 58 floats and had visited 42 schools and escorted 9 others on a tour of the Council Chamber and regalia. He had attended 710 functions and put on 12lbs in weight. The Town Clerk added all the figures together and they coincidentally added up to 831, which was exactly the same as the previous year. The Town Clerk thought that if Councillor Cairns had managed to put on another pound in weight he would have won by a short head or large paunch. He had also heard Schleigvighausen, the Town's Twin-Town in Holland, pronounced in the umpteenth different way but then he thought he had heard so many variations that even he was not quite sure of its proper pronunciation.

Councillor Leslie Ullathorne was then installed and was making his speech as to the distribution of the Mayor's Charity Fund of the previous year. The matter was entirely within the gift of his predecessor and had never caused any contention. This year, however, it had been decided to give £5,000 to the Barrowby Squash Club. This did not please Councillor Ezra Redgrave as his vision of charity only encompassed left-wing causes such as crèches for one parent families, lesbian and gay rights groups and similar causes. Councillor Redgrave got to his feet – this caused some consternation to the Town Clerk for it was traditional for this section of the proceedings to be entirely uncontroversial.

Warming to his theme, Councillor Redgrave attacked the grant to the

The Mayor Making

Squash Club. "How could we, as a Socialist Borough, countenance giving hard-earned money to a sport such as squash?" How many of his constituents at the sprawling Leeds Road Estate would benefit from £5,000 being given for squash? His tirade was totally out of order.

It was entirely up to the Mayor as to where he allocated his money and in the 108 years of the Borough had never been challenged.

It was a small point but Councillor Ezra Redgrave would not let it go. "Put it like this Mr. Mayor, if I asked for a grant of £5,000 for my whippet club, you wouldn't give me £5,000 would you Mr. Mayor?"

"No, I wouldn't," replied the Mayor.

He wouldn't let it go, it was just as if one of his whippets had got hold of the hare and was shaking it as if trying to extract some meat from it. Councillor Redgrave red-faced as a ripe tomato bellowed across to the Mayor "Well, why not, Mr. Mayor?" he demanded.

The Mayor got to his feet from within the encompassing confines of the Mayoral ermine "Because," he said looking his interrogator right in the eye, "because, Ezra, thou art a cunt!" The Council Chamber was in an uproar.

The Town Clerk had to think quickly. Seated at the Mayor's right hand he leaned across, switched off the microphone and whispered to the Mayor "Adjourn the meeting for ten minutes."

"What?" said the Mayor.

"Adjourn the meeting for ten minutes." The Town Clerk was speaking like a ventriloquist, his lips hardly moving. Perhaps it was because of this that the Mayor still sat immobile, perhaps it was his near-deafness, perhaps it was the surfeit of pre-meeting drinks.

"Pardon?" he said.

"Adjourn the bloody meeting!" said the Town Clerk, louder, through clenched teeth.

At last the penny dropped and he did so. Robin Armstrong rose, the mace was hurriedly lifted and the Mayor and party swooshed out to return to the Parlour. In the corridor they met a crocodile of neatly clad waitresses bearing the tureens, silver plate and comestibles that were to be the fare for the Mayor's Invitation Buffet to be held after the installation. The Town Clerk broke off from his own procession and sprinted across the marble floor of the corridor to head off the catering party. A few quick words with the Catering Manager, a veer to the left and the waitresses returned, perplexed, to the

The Town Clerk

Servery. The Town Clerk opened the door to the Mayor's Parlour and ushered the men in, led by the shame-faced Mayor. Strong words were needed. The Town Clerk gripped the Mayor by both shoulders and looked straight into his bloodshot eyes. Looking hurriedly to his left he said to the Mayor's Secretary "Quick, pour him a black coffee – strong and neat." He returned to the Mayor's eyes. "You've got to put this right, and quick. If you don't get yourself and the Borough out of this mess, we'll all be sunk. Think what the papers might make of this. In ten minutes time you are going back into that Chamber and you're going to apologise. Neither Robin nor I can write it for you, you are on your own. Look on this as the first challenge of your Mayoral year. Albeit, it has come rather early – only half-hour into your year of office, but there is only you who can get yourself out of it. Understand?" The Town Clerk looked laterally at Robin "Cometh the hour, cometh the man, hopefully, eh Robin?" They seated the Mayor on the chaise-longue, plied him with the coffee and thought of all the consequences and alternatives, none of them attractive and most potentially disastrous.

After a few minutes the Mayor steadied himself. He started to weep, "I'm sorry, Town Clerk," he said. He seemed better. "It must be the gin that's got to me. I should have stuck to Barnsley Bitter. I'll try, and if I get out of this one, I promise you, you'll have no further trouble with me, you'll be proud of me at the end of my year in office." The Town Clerk perked up as the Mayor rose from the chaise-longue.

"There's only one more thing, Town Clerk, before we go back into the Chamber."

"What's that?" was the rejoinder.

The Mayor's eyes filled with tears, "I've fuckin wet missen!"

"Bloody hell," said the Town Clerk. He looked down at the chaise-longue and right in the middle was a large discoloured patch. "You'll have to lay back down again," and pushed him roughly back down again. The brass castors of the chaise-longue threatened momentarily to put the couch into motion but fortunately it stayed immobile. Deftly he swung the Mayoral ermine across the parquet floor as a matador flicks his cape. "Breathe in," he said and released the Mayor's top trouser button and flicked his zip of the fly down. In a second the trousers were down by his ankles but would go no further. The shoes had to come off, the trousers were elevated to the knee and the buckled shoes removed. Off came the trousers as quick as a fireman sliding down the emergency pole. "Get his number two outfit from the wardrobe," he said to the Mayor's Attendant.

The three of them redressed the Mayor in two minutes flat, kicked his stained trousers under the chaise-longue, put his chain back on and settled him back into his voluminous scarlet robes. Then they were off again, in slow procession. The Town Clerk looked at his watch. Eight minutes, twenty seconds from the Mayor's invective against Councillor Ezra Redgrave to the re-entry into the Chamber. Perhaps all the training over the assault course with the Territorial Army had paid off in a most unlikely way.

The party re-entered the Chamber and Max Earnshaw announced "Ladies and Gentlemen, pray be upstanding for the Worshipful the Mayor of Middlethwaite," and under his breath he said "again". Before he rejoined the re-entry, the Town Clerk sprinted down to the Servery and instructed the Catering Manager to reassemble his waitresses. The Catering Manager said nothing but the elevated look his eyes shot at the ceiling said it all.

The Mayoral party wended its way again across the Chamber and decorously filled the top benches. The Town Clerk said a silent prayer and crossed his fingers as the Mayor rose to his feet.

"I am sorry, I was overcome by the heat, Ladies and Gentlemen, and by the majesty of this occasion," (the Town Clerk thought the word 'majesty' a trifle exaggerated) "I've put thirty years down t'pit and sometimes things get said in the heat of the moment that one might regret. I apologise for calling Ezra a skunk," (nice touch, thought the Town Clerk) "intemperate language has never been part of my vocabulary," (liar, thought the Town Clerk) "but I shall work hard to further the status of this town we all love so much and you will find no better man to be First Citizen of this Borough than the man you see proudly standing before you now. When I look at the names of my predecessors on this chain of honour..." his eyes moistened, "I realise that I have a lot to live up to. But, by God, I pledge to everyone here that by the end of my Mayoral Year you'll reconvene here and say 'You know Les Ullathorne did us proud'." He said just enough, he bowed slightly and sat down. "Kinell," he said so only the Town Clerk and Mayor's Secretary could hear.

"Kinell," reiterated the Mayor's Secretary.

There was an awkward silence and then a slight rustle of clapping broke out, an event unheard of in the long history of the Council, it swelled and continued for half a minute. The Town Clerk leaned across to Robin

31

Armstrong and breathed a sigh of relief, "I think he's done it," he said. Timing was important, leaning across to the Mayor he whispered "Get on to the next business... and quick."

The Mayor rose again. "Item number three on the agenda is the motion on the stopping-up of highways and I call upon the Chairman of the Roads Committee to introduce the matter..." In another half an hour the Council meeting was over and the official party adjourned to the Parlour for the Mayoral Invitation Buffet. The Catering Manager had done a good job after his initial difficulties. Each year he had to balance his menu compilation and tread the fine dividing line between providing an impressive Reception whilst guarding against the annual tirade in the local papers alleging a Mayoral gravy train by the champagne socialists.

Fortunately, the Town Clerk was at the head of the procession back into the Parlour. With the deftness of the wing-three-quarter he once was in his rugby playing days, he kicked a trouser leg from a damp pair of trousers that was peeping out from under the chaise-longue back into temporary obscurity.

"Lemonade you'll be on for the rest of the evening Mr Mayor, but if you are good you can have a large scotch at midnight when all your guests are gone," he whispered into the Mayoral ear and, just to be certain, told his Mace-Bearer to serve him lemonade only.

The evening went well. Many disparate personalities were assembled to toast the new Mayor's health. Mindful of the fact that he himself had drunk three large scotches earlier in the evening, the Town Clerk resolved to limit himself for he realised that he could hardly act as the Mayor's minder unless he had a clear head. It was also important for him to circulate during the evening. He had put a lot of work into the new Industrial Park down by the River Dearne and many of the guests were potential tenants. He had put his reputation on the line but, so far, the take-up had been disappointing. So he just had three glasses of Marston's light during the long evening and was thankful that tragedy had been averted. His wife Celia was a charming co-hostess at this function and he thought how lucky he was to have a woman like her at his side. She was lovely; lovely but dull, he thought, but ideal for a Town Clerk's wife and he had never wanted anyone but Celia by his side these twenty years. He was talking to her halfway through the evening when it suddenly dawned on him. He was drinking a glass of Marston's light – why Marston's light? All the liquor outlets at the Council Leisure Centres were

The Mayor Making

contracted to Hebblethwaite Brewery. So, why was he drinking Marston's? He sidled over to the Mayor and asked him. The Mayor gave him one of his knowing quizzical smiles and tapped the side of his nose. The Town Clerk felt unease and he was about to pursue the matter when the Mayor banged on the table and decided to give an impromptu speech. It was very good. In his mixture of a passable attempt at Oxford English and the occasional lapse into broad Yorkshire vernacular he set out his hopes for the coming year, especially the Opening of the Business Park, Mayor's Sunday, Mayor's Parade, Members v Officers Golf Match and many other functions that he knew would put Middlethwaite on the map.

He concluded, "Fun will be my watchword, fun will be my theme and if I may have been slightly hobstroculous tonight, it will be fun from now on."

Sometime later the Town Clerk was buttonholed by Councillor Mrs Eunice Bramble, Conservative member for the East Pennine Ward. This Ward comprised mainly isolated farmsteads, a new upper quality housing estate and a few big houses that had belonged to the mill-owners and coalmine-owners of previous times. She was Leader of the Opposition, comprising just three members, and had been on the Council for nineteen years. Her Ward also embraced part of the Orchard Council Estate but by dint of being an assiduous member and belonging to the Women's Institute and like organisations such as the Footpaths' Society and the Ramblers' Association she had managed to be re-elected at six successive elections. Just.

"Well, he got himself out of trouble, Town Clerk," she said. "that fool Ullathorne. I wonder, Town Clerk, if it had occurred to you that the Labour Party is now scraping the barrel in the quality of its First Citizens?"

Diplomatically the Town Clerk declined to comment.

"And I wonder if it has occurred to you, Town Clerk, that a different Mayor should have been installed tonight?"

The Town Clerk pricked up his ears. Before he could ask why, he was told.

"You see, Town Clerk, I have been a member of this Authority for a year longer than that comic Ullathorne. I should be First Citizen."

The Town Clerk had not realised this but said he thought that as the Mayoralty was in the gift of the controlling party it was highly unlikely that she would be invited. He did, however, sympathise with her and made a mental note to watch out for 'Bramble the Ramble', as everyone called her. She could be a spiteful woman and would need watching. One thing was

33

The Town Clerk

certain, however, there was a deep hatred between the Worshipful the Mayor of Middlethwaite Councillor Leslie Ullathorne and the member for East Pennine Ward, Mrs Eunice Bramble (the Ramble).

Just before midnight the final guest left and the Town Clerk gave a deep sigh, gave silent thanks to Almighty God for his deliverance and poured the Mayor the double-scotch he had promised him for being a good boy. The officers managed to retrieve the Mayoral ermine from the back of Councillor Leslie Ullathorne but only after a struggle in the light of the Mayor's deep protestations. He was fully expecting to travel home in it. Resigned to the ermine returning to the Robing Room, the Mayor extended his hand to the Town Clerk, shook it vigorously and said, "It's been a raight foony day today, raight. Kinell!" A few minutes later Bill Hutchings, the Mayor's Chauffeur, whisked Les and Lilian, the First Citizens back to the Sunflower Hill estate, no doubt to reflect on the events of the day.

The Town Clerk poured himself a large scotch. He had earned it. He poured Robin Armstrong a large brandy. They made eye contact with each other and laughed.

"Don't sit there, Robin," as he hovered above the damp patch on the chaise-longue. They roared with laughter.

"By the way," Robin said, "do you think, Jim, there is such a word as hobstroculous?"

"I don't think you would find that in any dictionary, it's probably a bastardisation of obstreperous. Do you remember that Chairman we had on Leisure Committee who was always 'piturbed.? And, his Deputy, not to be outdone, was always 'incombated'. I remember that it was not long before I was using the words myself and, after a while, they didn't seem at all strange. It was only when I used them at a Society of Town Clerks' seminar that I realised that I was being indoctrinated. But I don't think I was ever hobstroculous! Incidentally, Robin, who's this fellow Kinell the Mayor keeps referring to?"

"Ah, Jim, I hoped that one would fool you. When I was preparing Ullathorne for the Mayoralty he greeted any information he couldn't understand with the words 'fucking hell'. I knew he could not be successfully weaned off in so short a time, so the diminutive Mr Kinell made his appearance. Sorry, Jim, it was the best I could do but if you didn't realise it, perhaps no-one else will?"

The Mayor Making

More seriously the two men analysed the events of the evening.

"I think we have been very lucky to get through this evening without a débâcle. It could have been a disaster. I think we have both got to keep a careful eye on this new Mayor," said the Town Clerk.

It was to prove a very perceptive summing-up of the situation and as the Mayoralty developed it was to need more than just a careful eye to contain the Worshipful the Mayor of Middlethwaite, Councillor Leslie Ullathorne.

35

CHAPTER THREE

MAYOR'S SUNDAY

The following day's papers largely ignored the installation proceedings of the previous evening. There was nothing newsworthy really in mundane Council proceedings but the Town Clerk thought what might have been. He had visions of night editors wrestling with copy from their Middlethwaite correspondents and thinking how they could introduce the vernacular form of a woman's anatomy into their columns. By and large they failed, the nearest they came to it was that the Yorkshire Post referred to some "procedural problems at the installation of Councillor Leslie Ullathorne as the 109th Mayor of Middlethwaite" but that was all and there was no hint at just what these procedural problems had been. The Town Clerk had handled all the press enquiries himself. He had taken Councillor Ezra Redgrave aside along with the Leader of the Council and Redgrave had been warned, on threat of withdrawal of the whip, to limit his comments to "no comment". Redgrave was due, on a seniority basis, to be the 113th Mayor of Middlethwaite and the spectre of this being taken away from him was enough to keep him concentrating on whippets rather than revolution. The Town Clerk had sought out all the press representatives and given his explanation of the "procedural problems" and was pleased that he had managed to iron the matter out. He realised he had been skating on thin ice but he also knew he had got away with it and the Town Clerk resolved to keep a steady eye on the behaviour of the First Citizen and, as the weeks passed, it seemed that, with luck, this could settle down to be another uneventful Mayoralty.

James Pickering-Eaden was grateful for the fact that he was not much concerned with the Mayor's day-to-day activities and that he could leave the Mayor in the capable hands of Robin Armstrong. He had plenty on his plate in the office and with the servicing of the many Committees that comprised

37

The Town Clerk

the Council. He was keen to make a success of the opening of Water's Edge Business Park, a project that he had been involved in for the past five years and had, in fact, been a prime mover in its inception. Truth to tell, Middlethwaite Council had dragged its feet in adapting to change. For years the Borough had been content to rely on rates revenue from the many pits in the area and also content to rely on the coal industry to provide jobs for the workforce through the proliferation of the mines and the many associated satellite industries. However, the Thatcher administration in the early eighties had signposted the decline in the coal industry and Middlethwaite had allied itself with the nearby Borough of Barnsley in supporting Miners' Leader Arthur Scargill and fighting the demise of the industry. Instead, Middlethwaite should have been exploiting its central location alongside the M1 motorway to attract the technological industries of the future rather than fighting to sustain a dying industry. So the Town Clerk knew that Water's Edge Business Park should have been up-and-running at least ten years previously but he had put a lot of hard work into the project over the past few years and the large business park was about one-third filled with new industries, some from abroad. This work had involved long, difficult and protracted negotiations but he could see a light at the end of the tunnel and was proud to drive past the park and see his name on the fascia board. All enquiries to James Pickering-Eaden, MA, LL.B, Town Clerk and Chief Executive it read and he made a mental resolve every time he drove past that he would try his level best to have all the units filled by the end of the year.

Water's Edge Business Park was a slight misnomer for the 'water' in the title was the River Dearne which, at its best, was a murky shade of brown and at its worst, was a stygian black. The Dearne was not quite as black as it was painted. Early in its course it was supplemented by many local becks and springs which emanated or ran through redundant mine workings. These becks were often bright crimson through oxide deposits so even before the River Dearne took delivery of many items of household waste and redundant furniture from illegal fly-tippers and industrial emissions from careless factory owners its early watercourse was anything but crystal clear. The Yorkshire Post had done a feature on the Business Park some time ago and had tried to emphasise the appeal of the Dearne as it wound its sluggish way through the area. It had attempted to highlight the return of wildlife to the River Dearne but had sent a young graduate reporter, fresh out of a trendy

Mayor's Sunday

Southern University and he had turned the publicity potential of the coverage on its head by finding the stretch of the Dearne that meandered through the Water's Edge Business Park had contained no fish but two dead dogs, many live rats, three washing machines, two bike frames and a couple of lice-infested mattresses. But, that was in the past and the Town Clerk was justly proud of the infrastructure that had been created and foresaw a good future. He was not very pleased with the Yorkshire Post and had been tempted to withdraw the Council from the Special Supplement the Yorkshire Post and he were planning to celebrate the opening of the Park, but after careful consideration he persuaded the Editor to have an informal word with the reporter. Perhaps this informal word had borne fruit for it was the same Municipal Correspondent who had been at the Mayor-Making and on whom the Town Clerk had forcibly impressed his version of affairs.

Despite the fact that the Mayor was through an interconnecting door from his office, the Town Clerk did not see much of him. He made sure that the door locked from his side and he had the only key – he had made the alteration a few years back when the then Mayor seemed to think that at eleven o'clock every morning the Town Clerk would welcome a visit from the Mayor for a cup of tea, a woodbine and a talk over the day's racing from Sandown. Tactfully the Town Clerk arranged a hectic round of visits to every primary school in the Borough and Robin Armstrong suggested to the Mayor that the Town Clerk whilst no doubt welcoming a daily visit from the First Citizen of Middlethwaite had other things to do at eleven a.m. The Town Clerk, however, took more practical steps to keep the Mayor out with a changing of the locks.

Councillor Ullathorne threw himself into the Mayoralty with real vigour, mindful, perhaps, that he had almost fallen at the first hurdle. No function was insignificant enough to warrant a visit from the Mayor and Mayoress. The Town Clerk relaxed visibly. Each night following the installation he had woken with a start a couple of times and sat bolt upright covered in sweat. This had followed a succession of nightmares, the central figure of which was Councillor Leslie Ullathorne and which featured murder, corruption and international incidents from which James Pickering-Eaden emerged poorly, dead or dying and Councillor Leslie Ullathorne became an international celebrity fêted worldwide. After a while these nightmares ceased and the Town Clerk, by dint of featuring on the humbling aspect of the Mayor's

The Town Clerk

attempt to sway the mayhem he had caused, began to sleep easier. The way he did it was to focus on the Mayor's slavering visage and to concentrate on the words that spilled from him as the Town Clerk looked him straight in the eyes. Word for word he could recite it. "I promise you, you'll have no further trouble with me, you'll be proud of me at the end of my year in office." Or sometimes he thought of Mrs Oldroyd whose visage was infinitely preferable to the raddled old Mayor.

So the days slipped by and the next function that the Town Clerk was personally involved in was the Mayor's Sunday. Mrs Oldroyd had drawn up the arrangements along with Robin Armstrong and typed out a neat timetable of procedure. Unfortunately, on the Friday that she came into his office to talk him through it, she was wearing that perfume again. She was also wearing the smallest briefs imaginable stretched over her haunches under a pencil-slim yellow skirt that followed every contour of her lower regions. Once again he found his eyes following her from the room, tracing the pantie-lines again and even endeavouring to view the lines of the gusset between the tops of her long legs. The nipped waist under a slightly-scooped neckline excited him also and he felt uncomfortable. He looked at her through slitted eyes. His folio of the Pitchford Report on the Provision of Library Services to the Disadvantaged had no chance of holding his interest. Cheryl Oldroyd busied herself around his office not clad in pencil slim skirt and scooped neckline but, in his eye, was completely naked. Firm breasts bobbed ripplingly like corks on a near-placid sea. The trim waist led his eyes downwards to the rounded curves of her bottom and, as she turned towards him, her flat tummy stretched between two protruding hip bones and his eyes travelled downwards to .... heaven. He was brought back to earth when she dropped her pencil and had to hoist her skirt a few inches higher in order to bend down to pick it up. His eyes followed her right to the door and she knew it too, she looked over her shoulder, tossed her curls and with a light smile said "Good afternoon, sir." James Pickering-Eaden put his head in his hands, aspirated loudly, said 'Kinell' to himself and picked up the briefing sheet. Somehow the list of the organisations due to enhance the Mayoral Procession on the Sunday – the Brownies, the Cubs, the Women's Institute et al did not suppress the vision of Cheryl Oldroyd's tossing curls and the tracery of her gusset. The Pitchford Report on the Provision of Library Services to the Disadvantaged did not stand much chance either.

Mayor's Sunday

Sunday dawned bright and clear and the official party assembled in the Mayor's Parlour. Sherry was served and the Town Clerk's intake was minimal as was the Mayor's – perhaps the Mayor-making was to prove to be a 'one off' occasion and he could be trusted after all. Anyway, the Town Clerk, bewigged again and wearing his medals was at the Head of the procession with the Mayor. The Town Clerk's mind strayed again to his Administrative Assistant Grade III. He was robed and wigged by Celia who, unfortunately for her, was suffering from a throat infection and there was a lingering smell of TCP about her and the Town Clerk compared this unfavourably with Friday's waft of Chanel. He was not being fair, he thought, but these comparisons were only in his mind and no harm was done, he considered. The tailor had done a dozen refits of the scarlet robes and this time, the Town Clerk observed, the Mayor was wearing the robes instead of the robes wearing him. The march-past of a rag-bag of local organisations was its usual shambles but it was charming and the assorted collection of service organisations and voluntary organisations made their way in slow procession to the Parish Church of St Paul. It was usual to play safe and the most popular hymns were always selected and nothing untoward happened until it was time for the Mayor to read the Old Testament Lesson.

Councillor Ullathorne rose and made slow and – let it be said – gracious procession to the lectern. It had always been the practice for the Mayor to read the Old Testament Lesson whilst the New Testament Lesson was read by the Chairman of the Chamber of Commerce and Trade representing the business interests of Middlethwaite.

"The Old Testament reading is taken from the Second Book of Samuel, Chapter 9, Verses 6-12.

6. Now when Mephibosheth, the son of Jonathan, the son of Saul was come unto David, he fell on his face and did reverence. And David said "Mephibosheth!" And he answered, "Behold, thy servant."

7. And David said unto him, "Fear not: for I will surely shew you kindness for Jonathan thy father's sake, and will restore thee all the land of Saul your father: and thou shall eat bread at my table continuously."

8. And he bowed himself and said, "What is thy servant, that thou should'st look on such a dead dog as I am?"

9. Then the king called to Ziba, Saul's servant and said unto him, "I have given unto the Master's son all that pertained to Saul and to all his house."

41

The Town Clerk

The Town Clerk had a sense of unease. Something did not seem quite right with the Mayor and he was getting agitated. Suddenly, the reason occurred to him – it was the name Mephibosheth, which quite unsurprisingly, the Mayor had struggled with at the opening verse. It was a very difficult name to pronounce, particularly for someone unused to reading in Church. The Town Clerk looked round at the congregation but could see no cause for his trepidation. No-one else seemed at all concerned. Most of the councillors were not regular church-goers and were not listening to the scriptures at all. The Town Clerk caught the Mayor's Secretary's eye and he pulled a face. Councillor Mrs Bramble was beginning to smile. The Mayor continued but was looking agitated. His brow was moistening and his teeth were chattering and clicking. At the best of times his dentures were poorly fitting but now the Mayor did not seem to be in control of his mouth.

10. "Thou, therefore, and thy sons and thy servants shall till the land for him and thou shall bring in the fruits, that thy master's son may have food to eat: but Mephibosheth thy master's son shall eat bread always at my table." Now Ziba had fifteen sons and twenty servants."

The Mayor was now getting very exasperated. Every Mephibosheth had been pronounced differently and the Town Clerk glanced ahead at the text and saw to his dismay that there were four more Mephibosheths to come. The whole congregation was by now holding its collective breath. The Mayor put his hand into his mouth as if to firm up the dentures onto the gums and wiped his eyes. He readjusted his glasses and the Town Clerk knew that the Mayor too, was looking ahead to see how many more Mephibosheths were to come. He resumed reading.

11. "Then said Ziba unto the King, "According to all that my lord the king has commanded, his servant, so shall thy servant do." "As for Mephibosheth," said the King, "He shall eat at my table, as one of the King's sons."

12. And Mephibosheth had a young son whose name was Micha. And all that dwelt in the house of Ziba were servants unto Mephibosheth.

13. So Mephibosheth dwelt in Jerusalem: for he did eat continually at the King's table: and was lame on both his feet."

At the final Mephibosheth the Mayor exploded. Each Mephibosheth had been pronounced differently and on the final one, in a welter of accompanying sputum, the Mayor's bottom plate flicked out and shot across the aisle. Everyone looked away as the Mayor descended the pulpit to retrieve it.

Mayor's Sunday

Everyone, that is, except one, the Leader of the Opposition, Councillor Mrs Eunice Bramble. The smirk on her face had been replaced by a broad smile, only partly concealed by Hymns Ancient and Modern. Plate retrieved, the Mayor resumed his place in the pulpit. "Here endeth the first lesson" he said. "Thanks be to God." replied the congregation.

With a face like thunder the Mayor descended from the pulpit and rejoined the other dignitaries in the front pew. As he came down his eyes flicked around to see the reaction of the congregation to his Mephibosheths. There was none. Even Councillor Mrs Bramble was not brazen enough to show her mirth and Hymns Ancient and Modern was quickly elevated to cover her whole face. No other untoward incident occurred and at the end of the service it was then back, in procession to the Mayor's Parlour for light refreshments. Livid, the Mayor sought out the Town Clerk.

"Who fixed me to read about Mephi-bloody-bosheth?" For the first time he pronounced it properly.

Councillor Mrs Bramble was hovering close by, "Perhaps I can help you, Town Clerk," she said, "my nephew is Rector of St Paul's. Didn't you know? I must confess I suggested Samuel 2, Chapter 9, Verses 6-12 – I thought it would be most appropriate for Councillor Ullathorne. Good morning, Mr Town Clerk, good morning Mr Mayor."

CHAPTER FOUR

THE OPENING OF WATER'S EDGE BUSINESS PARK

Mephibosheth became a thing of the past. The Mayor ordered some new dentures and Bramble the Ramble studiously avoided Chief Officer and First Citizen for, having stage-managed what she considered to be a triumphant occasion, she was content to sit back and watch events unfold and to bide her time. She did not have long to wait.

"I've done it, Town Clerk," the Mayor exclaimed as he burst unannounced into James Pickering-Eaden's office. "I've done it," he said, begging the question.

"And just what have you done, Mr Mayor?"

Councillor Ullathorne paused for effect. "Well, do you remember that I have nominated my theme for my Mayoral Year to be Middlethwaite is Fun?"

"Yes, Mr Mayor," the Town Clerk replied, beginning to be bored by the Mayor's attempt to milk the occasion, "please tell me what you're getting at, I really do have a lot of work to do." To make his point he reached across for his copy of the Pitchford Report on the Provision of Library Services to the Disabled. He kept this copy at his elbow for just such an occasion.

At last the Mayor arrived at his momentous climax, "At next week's opening of the Water's Edge Business Park I shall be accompanied by none other than ...... Mr Norman Wisdom!"

The Town Clerk was aghast. He just did not know what to say. He remembered Norman Wisdom from the films of the 1950's when he was Pitkin, if he remembered rightly, and cavorted around in an ill-fitting tweed suit, his peaked cap always askew, always being bullied by Mr Grimsdale. Not much had been heard of Mr Wisdom lately except that recently he had attained the great age of eighty and was still touring his own show and doing all the funny walks and falls that had the fifties audiences falling out of their

45

cinema seats. His humour had become terribly passé in later years but everybody knew his name.

The Mayor was disappointed at the Town Clerk's reception of his momentous news but kept on regardless, "This is what happened, Town Clerk. I saw on television that Norman Wisdom was touring the country with his one-man show to celebrate his 80th birthday and, to my astonishment there was a happy coincidence that he is appearing at Bradford's Alhambra Theatre the week we are having the opening ceremony for the Water's Edge Business Park. So I wrote to him. I wrote personally because I knew he might be persuaded by a personal letter from someone as important as a Mayor rather than through a Secretary. The clinching factor is that one of the units at the Park is a fancy-dress manufacturer. And my theme is "Fun". So, it has all come together, Town Clerk, and I am sure that we shall get maximum publicity value from it. I don't want to tell you how to suck eggs but who is the least bit interested in meeting a stuffy Minister of State from the Department of Trade and Industry? Let him come if he wants to, but I'll bet the press will be falling over – that's a joke, Town Clerk – to see Norman Wisdom." The Mayor was disappointed at the Town Clerk's reception of the news of his tremendous capture, especially as he had done it completely on his own initiative, and returned to the Parlour slightly deflated. But he had his own ideas about the occasion and was determined that it would be a memorable time for everyone. And he was to be proved right.

The Town Clerk reflected on the matter. He had given no thought to the matter of a 'personality' to be invited to the opening ceremony. He himself had arranged for a suitable Minister of State to come up from Whitehall. It only involved writing a letter for the Conservative government were only too pleased to send someone to try to earn some plaudits for the government money that had been allocated to Water's Edge Business Park. Plaudits were really all that could be expected; any votes to be gained were out of the question. That there was an invitation at all could be surprising except that the local Labour party was hoping for some more government money for Phases II and III. The working party had decided that a show-business personality should be invited in order to obtain some national publicity. Quite who this was to be – or what field the personality was to be from – was never quite laid down. Neither did the working party delineate who was actually to do the inviting so, after some reflection, the Town Clerk considered that

The Opening of Water's Edge Business Park

perhaps the selection of Norman Wisdom by the Mayor might not be too bad a choice after all. For someone had to make the decision and the Mayor had gone ahead and done it. Had the matter been left to the working party the suggestions would have ranged from Greta Garbo to Karl Marx, from Geoff Boycott to Aristotle Onassis and they would have ended up with a minor actress from Coronation Street. The matter would have been deferred half-a-dozen times and meeting re-convened ad infinitum so that the councillors could draw their attendance allowances. After reflection the Town Clerk felt he had been less-than-encouraging towards the Mayor of Middlethwaite so he left his office, went next door, knocked on the door of the Mayor's Parlour and told him he was sorry if he had not seemed too enthusiastic and he thought it was a good idea and he deserved great credit.

The arrangements for the opening were well advanced. As there was Government money in the form of grants, a European subsidy and, of course, money from Middlethwaite ratepayers, it was set to become an important occasion in the Council calendar and, with Councillor Ullathorne at its head, it was imperative that everything went off without a hitch.

The Town Clerk had told Mrs Oldroyd, Administrative Assistant Grade III to devote all her time to it for the past three weeks and arrangements were coming along nicely. There was even to be a Russian Trade Delegation coming, for now that the Iron Curtain had come down, the Russians had taken a small unit to make a specialist form of lathe. National, regional and local papers were coming, all the councillors, of course, but not least there would be Mr Norman Wisdom. Perhaps the Mayor was right, thought the Town Clerk and – as the time drew near – he quite warmed to the fact that this unlikely mix just might have the required effect, a full complement of units and, perhaps, even a waiting list for the next phase which was already in the planning stages. Mrs Oldroyd seemed to be flitting permanently in and out of the Town Clerk's office, but, of course, he didn't discourage it and took great interest in all the bodies that Mrs Oldroyd was bringing together. He was also taking great interest in Mrs Oldroyd's body – and she knew it, and whilst she did nothing to positively encourage it, there certainly was an empathy developing between them.

He found himself looking up expectantly when a knock came at his door and felt a sense of deflation if it wasn't her. He tried to analyse the situation but could not. Perhaps he was wrong when he felt her body language was

47

The Town Clerk

aimed at him? Certainly she always called him "Sir," "Mr Town Clerk," or "Mr Pickering-Eaden," no sign of any familiarity there. He was old enough to be her father anyway. But why was he taking off like this? He thought back to the restless nights after the fiasco at the installation and how he had used Mrs Oldroyd to dispel the image of the slavering Mayor of Middlethwaite. How he used to lay on his back fantasising about Cheryl Oldroyd throwing all her clothes off and yelling, "Fuck me, Town Clerk, fuck me." Somehow it didn't quite have a very romantic ring to it and he dropped off to sleep, chuckling.

Unfortunately, the day of the opening coincided with a break in the hitherto pleasant spring weather and it rained continuously from early morning. From all parts, the various personages assembled in the marquee that had been erected for the occasion. They had sent the Mayoral Daimler to Bradford for Norman Wisdom and the Town Clerk took the opportunity to spend some time with him as soon as he arrived. He was a charming man, put everybody at their ease and seemed genuinely interested in the tour of the units that had been let. There certainly was an eclectic range with modern microchip technology vying with traditional potters, painters, the fancy dress manufacturers, of course, the Russian lathe mill and as diverse a combination of trades you could wish to find anywhere. The manufacturer of inshore lifeboats had taken advantage of the deluge and had launched his craft onto an instant lake that had been created in front of his unit. Later he sought out the Town Clerk, said what a fantastic launch it had been (the Town Clerk wasn't aware whether any pun had been intended) and demanded to see the plans for Phase II. The Town Clerk had referred him to Edgar Fox, the Industrial Development Officer and he signed – there and then – for a treble sized unit in Phase II. Edgar Fox, had worked hard to get so many job opportunities for a region ravaged by the diminution of the coal industry and it was to be hoped that the resultant publicity would result in the remaining forty units of the first phase being filled.

The Town Clerk and the Mayor's Secretary put themselves around energetically. The Russians were a trifle dour – they still all seemed to look like Gromykó or Molotov – the token Minister sent up from Whitehall to this Socialist heartland was very effete with a limp handshake and the Town Clerk could sense that he couldn't wait for the whole performance to be quickly over so that he could hurry back to his riverside house in Bray or Shepperton or wherever he lived. The reporters and cameramen had seen it all before and

The Opening of Water's Edge Business Park

were looking for an angle for tomorrow's edition – but in the meantime were giving full attention to the hospitality tent with the food and drink. Two things bothered James Pickering-Eaden. The Mayor was drinking more than he should and Edgar Fox, the Industrial Development Officer, was paying far too close attention to Cheryl Oldroyd, Administrative Assistant Grade III. He made a mental note to have a word with him without, of course, letting on that he was getting slightly besotted with this vision of loveliness with the tossing curls and immaculate bottom. The Mayor had abandoned Barnsley Bitter completely and had settled on gin. The Town Clerk wasn't happy about it but there was precious little he could do. His mind went back to the installation when he had ended up kicking the Mayor's pee-stained trousers under the chaise-longue so he thought he ought to grasp the nettle and he unobtrusively drew the Mayor aside and warned him about his intake of liquor, forcibly reminding him of the near-débâcle at the Installation.

"Don't worry thissen Town Clerk," he said, tapping the side of his nose.

The Town Clerk was rapidly getting tired of this gesture for the Mayor's nose was one of his many unattractive features, being large and bulbous, completely out of proportion to the rest of his thin weasly face and in the first stages of elephantiasis.

"Don't worry thissen, Town Clerk," he repeated, "I've one or two aces up my sleeve – one or two surprises, you understand – and I'm sure they are going to come off."

"Pray tell me, Mr Mayor, what they are. I may be able to help you....." But it was no good. The Mayor had obviously worked everything out in advance and, if he needed any advice at this stage, he certainly did not welcome any from James Pickering-Eaden. Well, thought the Town Clerk, at least he isn't mixing his drinks for having gone through many tasting sessions at the spirit bar, the Mayor and Mayoress had settled on gin.

It was time for the ceremony. Norman Wisdom was going to cut the tape assisted by the Mayor. He had changed into his ill-fitting suit and the Mayor in full robes was now wearing them with dignity after further attention from the tailor. Norman Wisdom made a few jokes which were well-received and the Mayor tried one or two that were not. Robin Armstrong, the Mayor's Secretary, passed the comment to James Pickering-Eaden that had Les Ullathorne been in his pre-alteration robes then the combination of the Unmade Bed and Mr Pitkin might have been ready-made for a Whitehall

49

The Town Clerk

Farce. The Town Clerk offered the opinion to his Mayor's Secretary that although Robin Armstrong might think this comment to be amusing, it was too near the truth to make the Town Clerk laugh.

But nothing untoward happened and the Mayor was about to have the major triumph of his year so far. After the introductory speeches and a terrible effort by the plum-voiced Minister of State for Trade and Industry, who spoke 'terribly far back' and got the name of the Borough all wrong, it was time for the Mayor to respond. He thanked Norman Wisdom for helping put Middlethwaite on the map, thanked everyone for their best efforts and succeeded in not missing anyone out at all. Truth to tell, Robin had crossed all the t's and dotted all the i's but with a mixture of his broad Yorkshire and a plummy imitation of the Minister's accent the Mayor succeeded beyond anyone's expectations and the opening ceremony ran like clockwork.

Then came his tour de force. He turned finally to the Russian Delegation, none of whom could speak a word of English, and with a superb guttural accent said "Dàor krap ekorb dik, retseh-cor yaw dna teerts yesd Nomreb. Doownoclaf noitats dna drahcro Esir t-sew."

He had made great play of putting his prepared notes aside as he launched into his gutteral accent. The 'Russian' was delivered quite impromptu and with superb delivery and annunciation. Every syllable could be heard perfectly by the large crowd.

The Russian Delegation were enthralled, they clapped the Mayor, nodding happily to each other and every other member of the platform party. The applause swelled, everybody was clapping everybody else and when the applause finally petered out the Mayor led the official party into the hospitality tent with an aura surrounding him. The Mayor had obviously rehearsed this moment and had taken just about the right quantity of gin on board to carry the plan to fruition.

He was surrounded by a phalanx of media personalities hanging on his every word, pencils poised, notebooks trembling. He led them Indian-file into the hospitality tent where he held court and revelled in the fact that the media seemed in awe of him.

Scotch in hand, the Town Clerk buttonholed the Mayor's Secretary and shook him warmly by the hand. "Congratulations, Robin, how the hell did you manage to get some Russian into him? What a wow he was, he was magnificent, however did you manage it?"

The Opening of Water's Edge Business Park

"I don't know where he got it from," replied a perplexed Mayor's Secretary, "I just wrote all the rubbish that came before. The Russian bit was pure Ullathorne. Didn't you notice that he lobbed my notes away before he launched into his Russian. But what I can't understand is that he was so good. He couldn't have been inventing it because the delivery was so perfect. I didn't know he could speak English let alone any of the Baltic languages. Now, Town Clerk, I think we should sit back and bask in a bit of reflected glory for a change."

The Town Clerk agreed and glasses were filled and refilled. The journalists and photographers had commenced their post-prandial freebies and all was sweetness and light. The Mayor, although drinking a bit too much was the perfect host. Refilling the glasses of all the VIP's he was enjoying being the centre of attention. Sometime later the Town Clerk and his own Secretary managed to get him alone in a corner. In unison they said, "Mr Mayor, that was a superb performance. Wherever did you learn that smattering of Russian that obviously enthralled our Soviet guests?"

The Mayor grinned widely and tapped the side of his nose. This was a newly acquired gesture which he seemed to be using more than ever. The Town Clerk thought that if this action proliferated that by the end of his Mayoralty, Councillor Leslie Ullathorne would be pushing his nose ahead of him in a wheelbarrow. The Mayor was enjoying being surrounded by a sycophantic Secretary and Chief Executive so he gave his nose six more blows and said, "That wasn't bloody Russian. I learned it when I was working temporarily in south-east London on the building sites. I had no money and had to cycle everywhere. To occupy my mind I used to read all the place names backwards. 'Dàor krap ekorb dik, retsehcor yaw dna teerts yesd Nomreb Doownoclaf noitats dna drahcro Esir t-sew' is 'Bermondsey Street, Kidbrooke Park Road and Rochester Way, Falconwood Station and Orchard Rise West' backwards!" He bowed slightly, "I knew the Russians didn't know any English and the English couldn't understand Russian so I was on safe ground really ...." and was off again to mingle with his guests.

For once the Town Clerk and the Mayor's Secretary were speechless. But happy. There was no point in returning to the Town Hall just yet, they might just as well enjoy the success of the occasion.

"Come on, Robin," said the Town Clerk. "Let's do a bit of canvassing. We've got lots of possible leads here today and perhaps we can offer a few

51

sweeteners to get them to make up their minds to come to locate at Water's Edge. I know Barnsley and Wakefield are making overtures at just about the same contacts as we are, so let's try to strike whilst the iron is hot. Round up Edgar Fox – he's trying to get too friendly with my Administrative Assistant Grade III as it is, and let's see if we can come up with a few inducements such as six-months rate free, or landscaping frontages of the units. Let's tell them that they have got to sign up today or they'll lose the opportunity. But, most important, get that Edgar Fox away from my Mrs Oldroyd ...." he stressed in exaggerated exasperation.

They did just that and the small coterie of Council officials canvassed the visiting industrialists in a way that they had never been canvassed before. The Mayor appeared slightly squiffy and getting worse but who could begrudge his milking every bit of credit from the occasion. Hardly anyone had left over an hour later and the Ratepayers' Hospitality Fund was getting a bit of a trouncing from the assembled coterie. The function – similar ones had previously been so boringly predictable – was fast becoming one of the social events of the calendar. Even the Minister of State from the Department of Trade and Industry was still there and enjoying himself. But just when everyone was thinking that the event was winding down one more unexpected surprise was waiting to top the bill.

The Mayor had disappeared into an ante-room to get out of his robes and similarly, Norman Wisdom had been provided with facilities to change from his ill-fitting stage suit that he was well-known for, into his normal day wear. It seemed that the stress and pressures of the day could now be relaxed but, by his disappearance, the Mayor had increased the tension. The Town Clerk felt that he was able to control his Worship if he could have him in his sights. And he hadn't seen him for sometime. The Mayor and Norman Wisdom had seemed to have been gone for some time and the Town Clerk and Mayor's Secretary fresh from their canvassing which was beginning to bear fruit, were getting worried. Then the débacle occurred. Into the imbibing throng a loud entrance was made.

"Pray silence for the Mayor and Mr Wisdom," came the voice. The trouble was, it was the Mayor's own voice that was making the announcement. And through the curtains at the end of the room burst the two men. The Mayor was dressed in Norman Wisdom's ill-fitting stage costume and Norman, albeit looking slightly abashed, was wearing the Mayoral gown, chain and tricorn

The Opening of Water's Edge Business Park

hat. Worse still, the Mayor was trying to do an impression of the Norman Wisdom laugh that had featured in the record he had made with Joyce Grenfell in the fifties.

An embarrassed silence was instantaneous. But only for a few seconds as the photographers snapped into action.

They had got their pictures for tomorrow's papers.

The Town Clerk looked at the Mayor's Secretary. The Mayor's Secretary returned his glance. "Kinell," they said in unison.

CHAPTER FIVE

THE SPECIAL COUNCIL MEETING

Councillor Mrs Eunice Bramble rose early. It was only half-light when she left her cottage in the foothills of the Pennines and strode out purposefully for the Upper Ridge. Rather theatrically she gulped large helpings of the frost-laden air and dug her walking boots into the springy turf. She had made this her morning ritual for more years than she cared to remember. She was seventy and had lost her husband many years ago. Despondent at his death she had thrown herself into community work and was connected with a dozen local good causes.

She had been elected to the Council nineteen years ago and was now the sole Conservative on it. She sometimes felt like a lost voice in the wilderness and was treated as an irrelevance by most of the ruling Labour group, although intellectually superior to most of them. She enjoyed her Council work and had kept her seat for such a long time despite the vagaries of politics, by assiduously looking after her electors and making sure she was in the public eye by attacking Labour-party policies and personalities. That she had a vitriolic hatred for the current Mayor was because she felt that he usurped her rightful position as Mayor on a seniority basis. She did not blame the Town Clerk for his ruling that the Mayoralty was the gift of the majority party but she certainly did resent "that fool Ullathorne". Although she was always happy to promote Middlethwaite she did not enjoy the fact that the Mayor had made such a success of the opening of the Business Park yesterday and had only stayed briefly at the official reception afterwards. She knew that the Mayor liked his drink.

She had been at numerous functions with him and noted that he had always been one of the first up to the free bar and one of the last when it had been a pay-bar. She had kept a surreptitious eye on Leslie Ullathorne at

55

The Town Clerk

yesterday's opening of Water's Edge Business Park and had noted that he had been caning the gin bottle. She had hoped that he would have made a faux-pas of his speech and was disappointed that he had carried it off so well. But what she really resented was the way he had enthralled the Russian delegation and was annoyed that there were many councillors who previously had been critical of him were now sycophantic towards him.

She had stood at the back as the applause resounded around the marquee, peering through gimlet eyes and resenting every ripple. No-one noticed her, or paid her any respect, yet it should have been Councillor Eunice Bramble, the Worshipful the Mayor of Middlethwaite. So after the speeches she had had a brief word with the Government's representative, the Minister of State at the Department of Trade and Industry, but he was a bit of a wet anyway and seemed as anxious as she was to depart the reception. She did not understand how the Mayor had learned to speak Russian for she felt he had a difficult job departing from his broad Yorkshire to speak English. She never thought that Ullathorne would have carried it off as well as he did, let alone enhance his reputation, but she was sure that there would be another occasion, she just had to be patient.

So Eunice Bramble gazed down on the reservoir glistening in the early morning sunrise and began retracing her steps. She had carried out this ritual each morning for many years. She knew that everyone called her 'Bramble the Ramble' but she did not care and – anyway – a lot of people were called a lot worse and she certainly felt incredibly fit for her three score years and ten. If only she could have capped her career by becoming Mayor of Middlethwaite, life would have been so much better but as there was more chance of Labour capturing Weybridge than Conservatives capturing Middlethwaite she would have to put this thought to the back of her mind. Besides, the moors were beautiful in this early springtime and she felt well as she contemplated the distant view of her cottage from the top of the ridge. Away to her left were sweeps of wild primroses and the late daffodils waving in the early-morning breeze created a shimmering effect which slid like treacle down the valley to Maciag Woods. The woods were awash with bluebells and the banks of blue slid away from the woods as if to meet the different shade of daffodils and primroses that were seemingly coming towards them. This quirk of nature only happened for a few days in the spring before the colours died or were overtaken by new vegetation and Eunice

The Special Council Meeting

Bramble stopped to watch this apparition and tried to think if any recent years it had been bettered.

This early morning communing with nature covered all of five miles. She rarely varied her route and such was the level of her fitness that the five miles were covered in almost exactly one hour. She would pause for the same amount of time to take in the panoramic views at several different vantage points and if she stayed momentarily too long at any one point she would quicken her pace to compensate. The walk took the same time winter or summer, exactly one hour. On the ramble she collected her thoughts and planned the day ahead.

She loved the bracing Pennine air and she liked the full range of colours that nature laid out before her, especially in the spring. She stepped lightly along the escarpment above Maciag Woods and as she did so her eyes veered from the serenity of the greens and blues and she glanced up at the wind farms dominating the Ridge and thought how obtrusive they looked. Some time ago she had sat on the Planning Committee that considered this installation and she was lobbied by many quarters. So many quarters in fact, that she did not know quite where she stood. On the one hand there was the anti-nuclear lobby, then there were the acid-rain environmentalists complaining about the local coalfired power station. Then there was the dichotomy that many of these protesters were attacking the Government for closing the coalmines. Then there were the advocates of the wind farms who were strident in their opposition to advertising hoardings saying they were a visual intrusion in the countryside. Somehow, as she looked at the vast concrete windmills and heard their eerie hum, she wondered if anything could be quite as visually intrusive as these monsters perched on High Ridge. She had been with a Council working party to Cornwall to view these wind farms and had been ashamed of herself that she had bitten her tongue back and had been afraid to condemn them. She thought how inappropriate they looked on the Cornish peninsular, she also was aghast when she read that there were wind farms planned for the Brönte country. Where next she thought – Loch Ness or her beloved Peak District perhaps? So she concluded that she did not know quite where she was on the matter of provision of electric power. Perhaps this was one occasion when she was glad to be in opposition, she could be all things to all people and gather a sympathy vote for her triennial struggle for re-election.

The Town Clerk

As these thoughts were filling her mind she found herself home again earlier than expected. It had taken a mere forty-eight minutes to cover the five miles and 188 yards. She had borrowed a pedometer from Colin Turner, the Borough Engineer and measured it exactly. Why had she been so fast this morning? She analysed it and concluded that it was that bloody idiot Ullathorne who had got under her skin. She had failed to fully appreciate nature's changing moods this morning, she still resented the Mayor's tour de force of the previous day. She collected her Yorkshire Post from the box at the end of her lane and stuffed it in her kagoule. As the warmth of her kitchen hit her she threw the newspaper on the old pine kitchen table, put the kettle on, shoved some toast under the grill and then kicked off her wellies and hung her kagoule up. She then poured a saucer of milk for her cat, by which time the kettle was singing and her toast was brown. She made the tea, buttered the toast, drew up her Windsor chair, tucked her leg onto the chair and sat on her leg and opened the Yorkshire Post. It was the same ritual every morning, timed to the second. This morning something was different. She flicked the Yorkshire Post open and there on page one no less was the Worshipful the Mayor of Middlethwaite Councillor Leslie Ullathorne, dressed in an ill-fitting tweed suit with his arms wrapped around Norman Wisdom who was enveloped by the Mayoral crimson and was also replete with chain and tricorn hat. She was apoplectic but at the same time she instantaneously realised that this could be her opportunity to capitalise on a situation that she thought had slipped away. She was no football enthusiast but she had a basic appreciation of the game and she likened the situation to a team being outplayed for ninety minutes and then equalising with an own goal in the time added on for stoppages. She liked the analogy and was determined to score the winner in extra time. So she picked up the telephone and dialled the Town Clerk until she realised that it was only just after seven thirty in the morning so she replaced the receiver. She began to think of the political capital she could make of this and as she had her breakfast her mind was veering in a dozen different directions at once.

The piece in the Yorkshire Post was very cleverly written, implying that Old Time Music Hall was returning to Middlethwaite thirty years after Moss Empires had closed Middlethwaite Empire, but this time would be located in Water's Edge Business Park. Its first variety bill would be headlined by the new comedy duo 'Wisdom and Ullathorne'. Rather late in the day maybe, but

The Special Council Meeting

show business had at last found noble successors to Morecambe and Wise, Jewel and Warris and the Crazy Gang, also known as Middlethwaite Metropolitan Borough Council – it was not quite libellous, but only just not quite. The piece had been written by the same reporter who had done the preparatory report of the creation of Water's Edge Business Park, the same man who had been amused by the Stygian gloom of the River Dearne and the dead dog floating thereon. There was no mention of the Mayor of Middlethwaite's splendid linguistic skills neither were any statistics culled from the briefing sheets compiled by the Town Clerk and the Industrial Development Officer. Probably the reporter had commenced his article using this information but mentally spiked it when Wisdom and Ullathorne burst upon the stage.

Eunice Bramble poured herself another cup of tea and pondered her tactics. That the Borough had been brought into disrepute was, in her mind, beyond dispute. Here was a chance to get the throne off that fool Ullathorne or, at least, get that fool Ullathorne off the throne. But how was she to do it? She took down a copy of the Council's Standing Orders from the library shelf and flicked through the index until her eyes alighted on "Notices of Motion" for a Special Council Meeting. That was it. She would put down a Notice of Motion expressing 'no confidence' in the Mayor. She read on and immediately hit a snag. "A Notice of Motion," she read, "must be signed by not less than ten members of the Council." Well she could muster only three, herself and the two Independent members who usually did what she suggested although, it must be admitted, did not share her enthusiasm. Where was she to get the other seven? Well, there was Ezra Redgrave, he of the Whippet Club whom the Mayor had publicly insulted at the Mayor-Making. She thought that he could be persuaded to support a motion of 'no confidence' but where were the other six?

By the end of the day she had them. It was rather cleverly done, she thought. She could not ring up and say something like "Let's get this Mayor out of office." That would only harden attitudes. Her tack was, "I think the Borough has been let down by this escapade, especially the cruel reporting of it by the Yorkshire Post. I think that if the Mayor were to be tested with a vote of 'no confidence' and won it, he and the Borough would come out of it all the stronger." However trite that sounded, it worked. She trawled her mind for instances over the past nineteen years when Ullathorne had been in

59

The Town Clerk

controversy. She got the first lead from Ezra Redgrave. Redgrave had taken more persuading than Mrs Bramble had reckoned. She was unaware that the Leader of the Council and the Town Clerk had taken him aside and warned him his Mayoral turn might be at risk if he had commented on the events at the Installation. He decided to back Mrs Bramble's motion of no confidence after she had reminded him how he had been publicly insulted by the Mayor. He told Eunice Bramble that Councillor Maud Turnbull had once shared a bingo jackpot with the Mayoress (commonly known as Mrs Chinstrap) who had refused to split the prize with her, although she contended that there had been an agreement. She "would be willing to sign the motion." Now we are five and with this base she just about managed the others.

The following morning she was at the Town Clerk's office bright and early. She first made contact with the Town Clerk's Administrative Assistant, Grade III. She had known Cheryl Oldroyd most of the young lady's life and had, in fact, fallen out with Cheryl's husband, Darren, over some rights-of-way through the Upper Haugh Quarry where he worked. She claimed that he had extinguished a footpath during some blasting that he had been carrying out. She thought that this Darren Oldroyd was a bit coarse and he had used some ripe language when she tried to persuade him to restore the path which had been slightly diverted since the original path lay under several hundred tons of rock since the blasting. She had had a confrontation with Darren Oldroyd which was never quite resolved. Cheryl Oldroyd was placed in a rather invidious position during the dispute, being married to Darren but also being employed by the Town Clerk's department whose duty it was to uphold the law regarding the diversion of the path.

So, Mrs Oldroyd listened to 'Bramble the Ramble's' demands for instant access to the Town Clerk and went and put her case to him. She had no appointment but the Town Clerk agreed to see her. James Pickering-Eaden was a clever man. His office was no fortress. It was not exactly an open door to councillors but he had learned over the years to grant them reasonable access if they came knocking at his door. This way he had attained a tremendous reputation with his members and over the years had acquired a happy knack of running with the hares and the hounds and could cheerfully maintain that he was a friend and confidant to all of them. It was, however, with some trepidation that he agreed to see Councillor Mrs Eunice Bramble after she had made the necessary overtures via his Assistant, Mrs Cheryl Oldroyd.

The Special Council Meeting

What she had to say took the wind out of his sails and rendered him temporarily speechless. "I am disgusted with the Mayor, Mr Town Clerk," she said, "especially after the pantomime at the opening of Water's Edge Business Park. And, Mr Town Clerk, I use the word 'pantomime' advisedly." The Town Clerk knew that she had left early but did not labour the point and assumed she had read what had happened in the local and national press. Even the Daily Telegraph had featured the item and had a big picture of Norman Wisdom wrapped around the Mayor of Middlethwaite.

"I want you to call a Special Council Meeting, Town Clerk," she said "and I hereby give you Notice of Motion." She paused for effect, "That this Council deplores the behaviour of the Mayor of Middlethwaite, Councillor Leslie Ullathorne, and demands that he relinquishes the appointment forthwith."

The Town Clerk pushed his swivel chair backwards and was about to put his feet on his desk when he remembered, with propriety, that he was on official business and 'Bramble the Ramble' deserved respect. "I am afraid, Councillor Mrs Bramble, that in accordance with paragraph 3, sub-section iv, of the Standing Orders of the Council of the Metropolitan Borough of Middlethwaite," (he did not like to be so pedantic but he could quote this section from memory), "you need a minimum of ten signatures to demand a Special Council Meeting and that I would be unable to go ahead unless you could provide ten signatories." Rather out-of-character a superior smile flitted around his lips. He knew the balance of the Council was 57-3, but he had reckoned without the political skill of Councillor Mrs Eunice Bramble and he was brought down to earth immediately.

"No problem, Town Clerk," Councillor Mrs Bramble said. "I have them here – ten signatories, three of the opposition plus Councillors French, Grainger, Lomas, Scourfield, Pepper, Redgrave and Mrs Turnbull."

The Town Clerk was mute in his respect for 'Bramble the Ramble'. Not only had she done everything by the book but she had acted quickly and, in 24 hours, had convinced seven members of the ruling Labour Party to set down in a motion against their democratically elected Mayor. The Town Clerk could smell trouble. He rang his intercom and a 'vision of loveliness' appeared. At this time the Town Clerk was inured to her charms. "Two coffees, please Mrs Oldroyd – how do you like yours Mrs Bramble? – and please see that I'm not disturbed for twenty minutes." Mrs Cheryl Oldroyd, Administrative Assistant Grade III, returned with the coffee and closed the door behind her.

The Town Clerk

"Tell me, Mrs Bramble," the Town Clerk whispered although no-one else was in the room, "how did you manage it?" He rapped out their names staccato fashion, "French?"

Just as rapidly came the reply, "Ullathorne refused to back the appointment of his daughter in the Social Services Department and accused Councillor French of hedonism – I think he meant nepotism," she sniggered. "It was twelve years ago but he had always harboured the grudge and wanted to get back at him."

"Grainger?"

"He got the M.B.E. for his Mayoralty and reckons Ullathorne has demeaned the office of Mayor."

"Lomas?"

"Eighteen years ago Ullathorne pinched the nomination as Councillor for Sunflower Hill Estate by nefarious means and Lomas had to look elsewhere. Some people have long memories."

"Scourfield?"

"Found out that Ullathorne had been a Trotskyist when he worked in Greenwich, south-east London," she replied, quick as a flash.

The Town Clerk thought that this must have been around the time that the Mayor-to-be was pedalling around south-east London reading the street names backwards, but only he and Robin Armstrong knew this. "Pepper?"

"The old bugger is a bit senile now. He didn't like Ullathorne but couldn't remember why, but he said he couldn't stand the little squirt and was delighted to be of help!"

"Redgrave?"

"He was called a skunk – or worse – at the Mayor-Making. He took a bit of persuading, I thought he would be the easy one. I think Pat Sage, the Leader of the Labour Party had had a go at him."

The Town Clerk knew more about the disciplining of Councillor Redgrave than he cared to admit and wisely decided not to comment.

Finally, the Town Clerk read the last name, "Mrs Turnbull?"

"The Mayoress, 'IdontmindifIdo', fiddled her out of half of her bingo winnings."

There was nothing that the Town Clerk could do. He said farewell to Councillor Mrs Bramble and immediately nipped round to the Mayor's Parlour to give the Mayor the bad news.

The Special Council Meeting

He did not take the news at all well. "Kinell," he said, turned away from the Town Clerk and stared through the windows across the commercial district of Middlethwaite. His fingers were tightly clasped behind his back and the Town Clerk could hear his fingers cracking and see the knuckles gleaming white. He wheeled round after a minute or so. His eyes were moist and his bulbous nose was visibly throbbing like that of a hippopotamus emerging from a mudhole. "The fucking bitch, the fucking old cow," was all he could say and there was no comment the Town Clerk could make about the Mayor's summation of the Leader of the Opposition. Moments later his flared nostrils had returned to normal.

"What are we to do, Town Clerk?" said the Mayor. There was a humble manner about him and the Town Clerk momentarily felt sorry for him.

"We'll have a word with the Leader of the Council to decide how to play it but the Special General Meeting will have to take place in three weeks time – there is nothing that you, I, God or Walt Disney can do about it. Councillor Mrs Bramble has done everything democratically and you'll have to face the music. I'll give you all the help I can, but I fear you may have overstepped the mark this time, Mr Mayor," he said.

Of course the papers picked up on the Notice of Motion and had a field day. A few days before the Meeting the Town Clerk received a visit from Robin Armstrong, the Mayor's Secretary. He was bearing a letter – without a word he handed it to the Town Clerk and said "Read this." It was his resignation.

The Town Clerk cupped his head in his hands. "Please, Robin, don't do this to me. Not now," he said.

"I can't go on any longer, Jim," explained the Mayor's Secretary, "the man's mad. He's on the bevy every morning. He touches up the waitresses who bring him his morning coffee, he pings the bra-strap of the typists and I can't stand another nine months of this – he's an absolute megalomaniac. He's a ..... shit! I had a few hairy moments whilst I served in the Royal Air Force and I learned to cope quickly – well, when you are flying at the speed of sound you don't have much time to consider things. Later on when I was in administration I dealt with all kinds of people and situations. But I don't think I've ever met anyone like this Ullathorne. When he was first appointed it was not too bad after we had weathered the first altercation on opening night with Councillor Ezra Redgrave but since then power has gone to his head. He was alright whilst he was on the Barnsley Bitter but he has found a taste for gin

The Town Clerk

rather late in life and he can't handle it. He still drinks it like Barnsley Bitter. He pours himself one when he first comes into the Parlour in the morning and unless I can keep him occupied he's at it all day. I'm on a knife-edge all day with him. He hasn't taken to ordering me around yet but I fear that is next and I don't want to be humiliated by him. I think resignation is the only way out ..."

The Town Clerk thought quickly. He would be sunk without Robin Armstrong. He might even be sunk with Robin Armstrong but, it was for certain, that the Worshipful the Mayor of Middlethwaite would destroy everything he had built up and he might not be able to steady the ship without Robin Armstrong. He replaced Robin's letter in the envelope and fed it into the shredding machine. He leaned forward, "Look, Robin, PLEASE see it through. I promise this, I'll have a word with Alan Brannan, the M.P. of my former authority. He has a few avenues he can explore in Westminster," he tapped the side of his nose, just like Councillor Ullathorne, "I'll see if he can get you a C.B.E. in the next Honours List. If I can't – I'll accept your resignation then."

The Mayor's Secretary was taken aback. He was unprepared for this instant riposte by the Town Clerk. He had not considered it, but as most men would be, was flattered by the proposal. He was also unprepared by the look of desolation in James Pickering-Eaden's face as he had read his letter.

The Mayor's Secretary was swayed, "Alright, I'll stick it, Jim, I'll stick by you. But, it's you not the C.B.E...."

The Town Clerk shook his hand, "Thanks, Robin, but a C.B.E. will look fine alongside your other gongs, won't it?"

The two men shook hands and, in a rare show of affection, hugged each other.

A bond had grown between the two men and they were both sad that the new Mayor threatened to undermine that bond. The Town Clerk was relieved that he had managed to dissuade the Mayor's Secretary from resigning and when he was done he put through a personal call to Alan Brannan.

The Town Clerk had to give much thought to the impending Special Council Meeting. He had to act even-handedly as custodian of the ancient office of Town Clerk. He was honour bound to allow Councillor Mrs Bramble every opportunity to pursue her motion against the Mayor although he considered it malicious, which indeed, it was. On the other hand he owed it

The Special Council Meeting

to the First Citizen of the Borough a duty of care, a duty of care that had evolved over the centuries and was enshrined in local government custom and practice. Mrs Bramble did not have to show her hand as to how she intended de-throning the Mayor, it was enough for her to have acquired the necessary ten signatories, itself no mean feat, which had drawn a measure of respect from the Town Clerk. He did consider, though, that this was distinctly harmful to the Metropolitan Borough of Middlethwaite and to him personally. He was due to be the next President of the Society of Town Clerks but he did not consider, for one moment, that his candidacy would be endorsed if he were to be the Chief Executive of an authority in which the Mayor had been the subject of a motion of 'no confidence' and had been ditched from office so soon into the Mayoral year.

So, he swung his legs onto his desk and gave the matter deep thought. He came up with the solution in a matter of minutes and rang for his Administrative Assistant Grade III. "Mrs Oldroyd," he said, "I want you to spend some time with Edgar Fox, the Industrial Development Officer. Get as much information for me about the progress of Water's Edge Business Park so that I have it for the Special Council Meeting." Almost as soon as he had evolved his tactics he regretted it. Hadn't he seen his 'vision of loveliness' in close conclave with the Industrial Development Officer at the opening of the Park? And, here he was, sending her into the lion's den. A smile flitted across his mouth. He should not be putting any credence at all to the thoughts of the legs and tossing curls and beautifully rounded bottom of Cheryl Oldroyd when the future of Middlethwaite, the Mayor and the next-President of the Society of Town Clerks was at stake. However, he did decide to safeguard his position so he put a call through to Edgar Fox. He wanted to liaise with him about the progress of the Water's Edge Business Park. He had several leads himself that he felt could be pursued and he had also come up with various other sweeteners that might be carrot-dangled to firms to make them locate to Middlethwaite. Along with the rent-free periods and the landscaping outside the factories he had also explored the possibility of some obscure Government Grants and had also found that there was a possibility of European money being available to certain trades. He had gone into it in minute detail for he knew that his rival authorities in Wakefield and Barnsley and Kirklees, as well as the larger authorities in Leeds and Sheffield, would similarly be looking at these avenues for they also had enterprise zones alongside the M1 that they needed to fill. He felt confident as he outlined these to Edgar Fox, who was pleased to be lent the Town Clerk's Administrative Assistant Grade III to further the hopes of expansion. Edgar Fox was not sure what the Town Clerk meant when he told him that, "Mrs Oldroyd has a big, strong husband, as wide as a gable-end, so be careful you do not give any wrong impressions..."

Edgar Fox had taken it as a joke. Had he any designs on Cheryl Oldroyd he certainly did not pursue them after he had met husband Darren. Was there a slightly threatening tone in the Town Clerk's warning? The Industrial Development Officer thought there had been but gave little thought to it.

The day arrived. The public gallery was packed out and local, national and regional papers had sent reporters to monitor the proceedings. The Town Clerk entered the Robing Room, bewigged as usual and met the Mayor, whose face was like thunder. "Best wishes, Mr Mayor," was all the Town Clerk had said.

"Kinell," was the rejoinder.

From the top of the building could just be heard the Town Hall clock striking seven so at the cessation of the chimes Max Earnshaw led the official party into the Council Chamber.

"Pray be upstanding for the Worshipful the Mayor of Middlethwaite," announced the Mayor's Attendant, deftly swinging the mace onto his shoulder.

The Mayor threaded his way some steps behind Max Earnshaw, his gimlet eyes darting from side-to-side, seeking the seven defectors who had caused this evening's proceedings. Gone was the "Ay-oop Walt, Ow are thee Stan," to be replaced by "Good evening, Judas, good evening Quisling, good evening Blunt," as he passed three of the dissenting Labour Councillors.

What a nice touch, thought the Town Clerk, voice perfectly weighted, just above a mutter and not quite loud enough to reach the eager ears of the Yorkshire Post reporter who was obviously looking to write another tongue-in-cheek piece that might elevate him into a contender for 'Yorkshire Journalist of the Year', after his tale of the resuscitation of Music Hall at Water's Edge headlined by Wisdom and Ullathorne, the new comedy duo and his previous piece about the dead dog, the washing machines, the lice-infested mattresses and the stygian gloom of the River Dearne.

The meeting got under way. It was taken by Councillor Cairns, as Deputy

The Special Council Meeting

Mayor, since the motion was directly aimed at the current incumbent. Councillor Ullathorne just sat there glowering and did not seem to be listening too intently as his bête noire, Councillor Eunice Bramble, outlined her views on his unsuitability for office after the events of the Mayor-Making, Mayor's Sunday and opening of Water's Edge Business Park. Particularly she sought to emphasise the events of the Business Park with the cavorting of the Mayor. After a short, pithy but hard-hitting speech she reached her climax.

"The borough has been ill-served by Councillor Leslie Ullathorne. Mr Deputy-Mayor we don't need a comedian to be our First Citizen. We don't want people to invite the Mayor to functions and sit back to be regaled with knock-about comedy. We need a Mayor of dignity, a Mayor with a presence, a Mayor who will instil a sense of awe in the proceedings. This we have not got with our present incumbent, we have got a man who looks on himself as a reincarnation of an amalgam of Tommy Cooper and Mac Sennet. The events at the opening of Water's Edge Business Park were disgraceful. The only way the borough can put this behind it is to support my motion of No Confidence in the Mayor and for Councillor Leslie Ullathorne to step aside and make way for a new Mayor of dignity and decorum."

There was complete silence in the Council chamber. The Mayor bristled but kept silent and then there was an uneasy embarrassed rustling as papers were shuffled and a few nervous coughs eddied about.

The motion was opposed by Councillor Pat Sage, Leader of the Labour Group on the Council. The Mayor pricked up his ears as he rose. Not everyone would know that his name pronounced backwards was E. Gas Tap, harking back to his years pedalling between the building sites in south-east London. His predecessor had been Councillor Charlie Gabbitus. In order to keep his mind active he thought about old Charles Sooty-Bag who would have been useless in these circumstances. As Councillor Pat Sage rose the Mayor thought he would rather be represented by a gas tap than a sooty bag. He slipped further down into the magnificent armorial chair, his elephantine nose proudly aloft from a pile of ermine. Pat Sage was very good, even though he had no time for Ullathorne and was concerned solely with party unity and the image of Middlethwaite.

"Our Mayor is a one-off," he told the meeting. No-one could disagree with that. "He has his own way of doing things." No-one would disagree with that either. "But success dogs his footsteps – yes success, Mr Deputy-Mayor –

success. I want you to consider the following. The Water's Edge Business Park is our largest investment in this Borough and, one might say, the future rests on its success. Last month the Mayor opened the Park and carefully considered how best he could enhance its future. And he decided on a unique plan of action. He masterminded a plan to get maximum publicity from all the media that would undoubtedly be covering the opening ceremony. He thought that they would not be too interested in seeing a Conservative Minister of State somewhat reluctantly travelling north of Watford," (this certainly hit home with all the Councillors who were convinced that Government grants and sympathies were definitely diluted the farther north you travelled), "so, our energetic and enterprising Mayor hit upon the idea of inviting a national celebrity to join him at the opening ceremony. And what better national figure than Mr Norman Wisdom," he paused for emphasis – but, the Town Clerk thought that perhaps this theatrical pause may have been a little ill-conceived as, no doubt, many present could think of many better national figures than Norman Wisdom. "What better nationally known figure than Norman Wisdom would get us the national publicity for which we crave and, indeed, which we deserve here in Middlethwaite?" He paused for effect and the Town Clerk thought that he was perhaps going over the top or speaking tongue in cheek. "and the success of that plan of action," he continued, "is contained in this dossier that the Town Clerk handed me just prior to the Meeting tonight. I am pleased to announce that the Business Park is now full to capacity. Since the Mayor's momentous and – may I say courageous – decision to put his reputation at stake, enquiries have flooded in from all over the world. Twenty three single units have been let, five doubles and Marley's Cycles have taken six units, Celestial Computers have taken ten and the Russians are expanding their lathe manufacturing works seven-fold. Ladies and Gentlemen, the Water's Edge Business Park is now known throughout commercial Britain and I am happy to announce that soon the first sod will be cut for Phase Two of the Project. There is one man to be credited with this – Councillor Leslie Ullathorne, the Worshipful the Mayor of Middlethwaite..."

As if orchestrated, cheers broke out and agenda papers were waved. The Mayor, carried away with the euphoria of the occasion rose and took a deep bow that would not have disgraced Sir Malcolm Sargent at the last night of the Proms. As the Mayor elevated himself from the ermine to acknowledge

The Special Council Meeting

his salvation so Bramble the Ramble sank into her chair. She was livid. She had lost. She had lost ignominiously. The seven dissenting Labour Councillors red-faced and trembling, stared embarrassingly at the floor.

The Town Clerk was alive to the timing of the moment. As the cheers subsided he leaned across to Councillor Cairns, the Deputy Mayor who was in charge of proceedings and, giving his impression again of a ventriloquist, hissed "Move that the motion be put – QUICKLY."

The Deputy Mayor did as he was told, the motion by Councillor Mrs Bramble was lost by 46 votes to 10 and the amendment framed at the Town Clerk's suggestion "That this Council heartily endorses the Mayoralty and, indeed, congratulates the Mayor, Councillor Leslie Ullathorne" was carried nem. con. The official party was on its feet, the mace was lifted onto the shoulder of Max Earnshaw and the party swept out of the Chamber only forty five minutes after it had come in.

As the Mayor passed Councillor Pepper, one of the signatories of the motion, he looked him straight in the eye and said, "Nem. con., nem. con. you Judas bastard!" This time he said it just loud enough for the Yorkshire Post reporter to hear, although the reporter knew that there was no way he would be able to use that. He was also pretty sure that the Mayor did not know what nem. con. meant but it certainly sounded impressive.

Within ten minutes the Town Hall was deserted. No after-meeting drinks and light refreshments had been planned for this meeting as no-one was quite sure if there would be anything to celebrate. The Mayoral Daimler had departed packed with the Mayor and his cronies to Hollowdene Working Men's Club, but not before the Mayor had been de-robed, de-tricorned and de-chained by Robin Armstrong, for had he not, the Mayor would have worn the lot for his triumphal visit to the Working Men's Club. Some years ago Robin had had trouble with the then incumbent who had insisted on wearing his chain-of-office at all times and even went to the toilet wearing it. This evening, however, the Mayor went to Hollowdene without any mayoral trappings although sometime later the Town Clerk learned that the Mayor had treated forty of his cronies to a fish and chip supper and had sent the Mayoral Daimler to collect the food.

In his rush the Mayor had not thought to give his thanks to the Town Clerk but that did not concern him. Pat Sage had read word-for-word the speech the Town Clerk had written for him. The Industrial Development Officer had

The Town Clerk

worked tremendously hard to get the 100% occupancy that was needed at Water's Edge to make tonight's rebuttal of the vote of censure a success. As his footsteps echoed along the marble corridors of the Town Hall he made a mental note that he must make a gesture towards Mrs Cheryl Oldroyd, his Administrative Assistant Grade III, who had contributed as much as anyone to tonight's successful conclusion.

James Pickering-Eaden walked slowly back to his office through the darkened corridors of the Town Hall and gave himself mental congratulations for getting the Mayor out of trouble again. He let himself into his office, poured himself a Glenfiddich, swung his heels on his desk and lit the largest cigar that he could find in his desk drawer. He took his wig off and chucked it across the office towards the bentwood hallstand in the corner. It was a trick he tried often and it missed ninety nine times out of a hundred. This time it nestled around one of the bentwood spears and he raised his glass to it as it quivered and settled. "Equilibrium has been maintained," he said to no-one in particular especially as he was the only person in the Town Hall, "equilibrium has been maintained," he repeated. "Equilibrium has been maintained," he said for the third time and filled his glass with another Glenfiddich. He was in no hurry. He had his own keys to let himself out of the Town Hall. He had often worked late in the past and had established a ritual with Max Earnshaw, the Mayor's Attendant, who lived in the penthouse flat that he would buzz him to let him know when he was leaving. He was tired, he was as tired as they would be now at the only surviving pit in the Borough, but he had been stretched by the mental stress of the occasion and felt drained as if he had done an eight hour shift at the pit.

To savour the occasion he closed his eyes and took a long, deep pull on his King Edward. His lungs filled, he kept inhaling until his lungs filled to bursting point. He kept the smoke in his upper body as long as he could and then exhaled so slowly that he nearly passed out. There was a resultant fug of thick blue smoke, as thick as a 1950's London smog. Through this smog he took another long thick sip of his Glenfiddich and then shot up in his desk as he thought he heard a knock at the door. He looked through slitted eyes and could not believe it as he saw Cheryl Oldroyd strolling purposefully towards him. Saying nothing she swung her voluptuous hips and pendulous breasts across the room, came round him and kissed him lightly on the cheek.

"Congratulations, sir," she said.

The Special Council Meeting

He swung round in his swivel chair to face his Administrative Assistant Grade III and the thought flashed through his mind of an appropriate gesture that could be made towards Mrs Cheryl Oldroyd.

CHAPTER SIX

YELLOW

Cheryl Oldroyd woke earlier than usual. It was a typical spring morning and she could hear larks twittering, a long way off a cuckoo sounded and she could feel nature – and spring – awakening. It had been a long winter, the snows had fallen deep, half-melted and then a hard frost had created a surreal atmosphere with ugly frozen slush carvings which had lasted for two months during which time the temperature never got anywhere near melting them. But now, spring at last was here. She stirred, realised it was earlier than usual, felt for Darren but as her fingers tiptoed the empty space near her, she had some kind of expectation ahead, some trepidation even. She couldn't put her finger on it, there seemed to be some latent force oppressing her but she had had this feeling before and nothing had come of it.

It was the day of the Special Council Meeting and Cheryl Oldroyd was quite intimately involved in it. Although she was quite a way down the responsibility ladder in the Town Clerk's department she felt that today was an important day for her. She had done a lot of work in respect of the Special Council Meeting but she had been pleased to do it because she felt that James Pickering-Eaden was forever picking up the pieces scattered by the Worshipful the Mayor of Middlethwaite and she was glad to help him in his latest crisis, which as usual had been instigated by the Worshipful the Mayor, Councillor Leslie Ullathorne.

Her husband, Darren, had left an hour since – he was Under Manager at the Upper Haugh Stone Quarry, about twenty miles into the North Yorkshire Country Park. She had been married to Darren for eight years and they had established a comfortable home in one of the new houses on the Pickstock estate about three miles from Middlethwaite Town centre. It was a comfortable existence but she felt unfulfilled. She had been a bright pupil at school and had set her heart on a career in law. She had attained the requisite 'O' levels and 'A' levels and had started work in the Legal Department of the Town Hall with aspirations of becoming an Articled Clerk. Then she had met and married Darren and she felt that she could not give the necessary dedication to mastering the examinations that she needed to becoming articled and ultimately qualifying as a Solicitor. So she had scaled her ambitions downwards and embarked upon the somewhat easier road of being a Legal Executive. There was plenty of scope for progression through the career network at the Town Hall as a Legal Executive – for there was important and responsible work to be done in relation to Compulsory Purchase Orders and jobs of that nature. However, it was when she was at the crossroads of this career that she had married Darren whom she had met some five years previously.

Darren was a big loveable softie. He was enormous. Large pectoral muscles, short haircut, a chest as big as a barn door and thigh muscles that rippled through the skin-tight jeans that he always wore. He was an Adonis and she was smitten the moment she met him. If the ardour had cooled over the years of their marriage it was because they had different aims in life. Darren had worked hard in the Quarry and become Under Manager. His was a hazardous job with dynamiting new faces a continual hazard, as was the quality of the slate they were mining. In the early part of the year they had lost a valuable Italian contract due to the poor quality of the stone that was coming out at the time and the workforce had to open new seams and find new markets for their product. That they had turned the corner was due, in no small measure, to Darren Oldroyd.

However, there had been sacrifices. Cheryl had already scaled down her aspirations to be a Solicitor or Barrister and, because Darren was heavily committed at the Quarry, she had missed lectures in her bid to re-route into being a Legal Executive. So she had quit that course also and been appointed an Administrative Assistant in the Town Clerk and Chief Executive's Department. Darren was earning a good salary and deserved every penny but she was unfulfilled. They had no family. This was not planned and both she and Darren were laissez-faire about the matter but somehow children had not come along. They had gone to a clinic four years ago and the Consultant had found nothing wrong with the sperm counts and reckoned it was just a matter of time before they conceived. But now, four years later they still had

Yellow

no children, Darren was Under Manager at Upper Haugh Quarry and she, at the age of 28, was Administrative Assistant Grade III in the Town Clerk and Chief Executive's Department. She felt that she was going nowhere but there were many women infinitely worse off than her in Middlethwaite so she was reasonably content. Subconsciously she blamed Darren for her lack of progress up the 'litigation ladder'. When a man has been working in the open air for twelve hours he was entitled to a large steaming dinner when he came home. Cheryl accepted that a dissertation on Crossley's "Contract and Tort" was not an acceptable substitute so she had reluctantly scaled her expectations down.

She was also besotted with James Pickering-Eaden, Town Clerk and Chief Executive of the Metropolitan Borough of Middlethwaite. Unfortunately, he did not know she existed beyond being at the end of a buzzer when the Town Clerk needed an Administrative Assistant Grade III. Darren had only met the Town Clerk once. In the early days of their marriage, Darren had taken to picking up Cheryl direct from his early shift at the quarry. He had waited for her in reception. He was completely covered in dust and wore large denim overalls. He looked like the Abominable Snowman waiting for his wife Cheryl in the reception area of the Town Clerk's office. The only trouble was that there were ratepayers – some in pin-striped suits on official business like checking the Electoral Register or Planning Applications or objecting against the Town Plan and they did not like seeing Darren Oldroyd lounging against the counter waiting for an Administrative Assistant Grade III. One had remonstrated with Darren two years ago and Darren had threatened to "Push the front teeth down the throat of you – you pin-striped pratt." The Town Clerk had been involved personally for the then Mayor, Councillor Gillespie, had objected to this "Shaven-headed oaf in his dirty rags despoiling the dignified surrounding of the Mayor's Parlour, Council Chamber and Town Clerk's Office." He persuaded the Town Clerk to have a quiet word in his ear but the Town Clerk thought this was rather obtuse as Councillor Gillespie was a Rodent Operative in neighbouring Barnsley Metropolitan Borough Council and the Town Clerk had, at this time, noticed some ripe smells coming from the Parlour sometimes when Councillor Gillespie had come straight from work. The Town Clerk had smoothed the matter over rather well, he thought, and felt a degree of sympathy for Darren and Cheryl Oldroyd. It was about this time that he had thought about the nomenclature

The Town Clerk

of Darren and Cheryl. But, he concluded that names went in cycles and today's twenty-to-thirty year olds who were named Cheryl, Darren, Lee, Craig, Debbie etc had now been superseded by the old Victorian names of Sophie, Charlotte, Henry and George that had now come back. But still, Cheryl was a bloody awful name.....

Cheryl Oldroyd slung her long legs over the bedside. A jumble of thoughts pervaded her mind. Town Hall life was outwardly boring but many feuds interlaced around and she felt excited by her involvement in these intricacies. She did not bother with any breakfast beyond a bowl of muesli and a glass of grapefruit juice. There was still the smell of bacon and egg and fried bread from when Darren had cooked himself a breakfast an hour ago but this turned her stomach over. She had a quick shower and towelled herself off in front of the cheval mirror of her bedroom. She looked at herself from all angles. She placed herself at ninety degrees square to the mirror and she swivelled round on a fulcrum so she was lateral to the mirror. She was now in silhouette. The sun just creeping over Murray ridge threw spears of crimson lasers onto the mirrored glass and the rays bounced off and caught her elevated nipples in profile. She felt that she was encouraging the voyeur in her inner self and she was embarrassed by her lesbianic thoughts as she admired the symmetrically swept elevation of her breasts. For just a minute it was there, then the sun shifted a fraction and the sun's rays heightened different and unattractive features of her body. She was pleased, her guilt had been assuaged and she now had a flat two-dimensional image reflecting back at her. There was not an ounce of fat on her. Her slender shoulders tapered to a neat waist passing pendulous breasts replete with small nipples, cherry pink and slightly elevated by the late spring frost. The slight feeling of self-consciousness returned as she admired the steady sweep of the lines of her hips. Her thighs were just right also and she thought as she looked at herself in the mirror that she just might be wasted as an Administrative Assistant Grade III.

She sat naked in front of the integral mirror of her wardrobe. She assessed her life. She was married to a good man, even if he was a trifle rough. She had always been satisfied in her sex life with Darren although she sometimes dreaded the Friday nights when she "went round Middlethwaite" with Darren and they returned to energetic sexual romps which often left her unfulfilled whilst Darren fell asleep after their frantic cavortings. His loud snorings bore

Yellow

testament to his satisfaction whilst Cheryl often lay awake for hours staring at the ceiling. She thought about unfulfilled sex. Darren always seemed satisfied by these energetic gyrations. In fact, Darren seemed to think there must be a degree of hard physical stimulation in the sex act. Not for Darren any subtle manoeuvres or whispered phrases of love, he thought Cheryl appreciated his large torso and muscular technique and his lovemaking mirrored his rough-as-an-uncut-diamond approach to life. But Cheryl Oldroyd longed for a more subtle and educated approach to life and love, and over the years she had started to notice the latent sex appeal of James Pickering-Eaden, Town Clerk of the Metropolitan Borough of Middlethwaite. She often fantasised about him. But in the confines of the office he was always the perfect gentleman and gave Cheryl Oldroyd no hint that any reciprocated passion for her stirred beneath his pin-striped trousers.

She was looking forward to today's events. Although on a smaller scale the machinations of local government were every bit as devious as the political life at Westminster's Houses of Parliament. She knew James Pickering-Eaden was teetering on a knife-edge. Through no fault of his own he had been saddled with a Mayor of no culture, no breeding and no appreciation of the duties and obligations of office. She felt desperately sad for the Town Clerk. All the office knew that the Mayor's Secretary was considering resigning to take early retirement and leave the sinking ship to the Town Clerk. She felt angry with the Mayor's Secretary who was planning to buy a retirement home in Cromer, Sutherland, Lytham St Annes, Totnes or wherever it was, and leave the Town Clerk to try to steer Councillor Ullathorne through the coming maelstrom that looked certain to engulf the whole department. Yes, she felt desperately sorry for the Town Clerk but had an ill-concealed admiration for him, especially for the manner he had rescued the Mayor from his "Thou art a skunk (or worse!)," and "Mephibosheth" and the "Norman Wisdom" episodes. It had been a hard time for him for he had been so busy with other Council duties that she felt it unfair for him to be saddled with problems that were not of his making.

She tried hard to analyse why she felt the way that she did for the Town Clerk. Mere sorrow would not engender sexual thoughts about him. No, it was his inherent bearing that she admired, the way he had to cope with pressures from councillors above and officers below and yet he still kept a calm equilibrium and nothing seemed to divert him from this straight path that he himself had set out ahead of him. Just why this serene yet steely demeanour of the Town Clerk should engender sexual awakenings within her she could not explain but they were there. No-one else knew they were there and she thought she could handle them but she was not sure. But as the possibility of her feelings being tested were extremely remote she did not dwell on her position for any length of time.

She had played a significant part in events leading up to today's Special Council Meeting. The Town Clerk had seconded her to the Industrial Development office with a brief to try to generate interest in the Water's Edge Business Park and she had also spent many hours along with the Town Clerk exploring grant possibilities. He had confided her tactics to her and she was determined to give it her best shot. If she and Edgar Fox could make inroads into the vacant lots at the Business Park it would give the Town Clerk ammunition to rebut the malicious Notice of Motion by Councillor Mrs Bramble. So she had practised the telephone sales voices so beloved by the times-share sales- ladies and the small-ad salesladies of the evening paper – and by dint of smooth-talking and pushing herself somewhat she had managed to convince a few waverers to bring their business to Water's Edge. It had been hard work but it had been worth it. The only drawback was that when she told Darren when he returned from work he was not the slightest bit interested and did not look upon the Town Clerk's job as a proper job. Darren thought that if you didn't sweat, you didn't work. It was as straightforward as that.

A few days before the Special Council Meeting Cheryl knew she had won. She and Edgar Fox had succeeded in filling the last Units at Water's Edge Business Park. The Russians had fallen for the Mayor's obsequiousness to them at the Opening and had responded well. She and the Industrial Development Officer had managed to convince the waverers. She never realised that it would be such hard work. She had lots to offer prospective clients in terms of incentives but, once or twice, she felt that some industrialists felt that her body should come into the equation as well. She had been sworn to secrecy but she and Edgar Fox had been able to go to the Town Clerk and report that it was now a take-up of 100% with a few definite and many possibilities for Phase II of Water's Edge Business Park.

She went to her underwear drawer. How was her mood to be translated into today's events? She picked up the maroon Charnos set. It comprised bra,

Yellow

pants and long slip. No, that would not do. The white was a non-starter also. She looked at the brown set and thought that did not reflect her mood. She felt excited as if she was on the brink of something momentous. She was not unduly impressed by this – she had felt excited before but had returned from work to a fish and chip supper and a husband who had expired from surfeit of Barnsley Bitter as soon as they had reached the marital bed. She settled on the vivid yellow which was the latest Charnos colour and slinked herself into it. The French knickers hugged her waist although the gusset tended to get lost in her labia and feel uncomfortable. She squeezed her breasts into the brassière which was slightly small for her but her eager young breasts frothed over the cup edges. She stepped into the matching slip, put on her outer garments and went to work. She felt excited for she knew about the one hundred per-cent take-up of the availabilities at Water's Edge and if the Town Clerk's tactics succeeded she knew she would get some reflected glory.

It was her turn to take the coffee to the Town Clerk.

"Put it there, please, Mrs Oldroyd," he said. He seemed far distant this morning. She felt that the Town Clerk did not know she existed and he certainly had no perception that the Charnos French knickers were cutting into the soft hairy triangle at the top of her thighs. The Town Clerk was thinking about Council procedure. In the outer office she was thinking about the Town Clerk replete in his black half, striped trousers, mink-coloured waistcoat, patent leather shoes and a soft attractive manner unruffled by the unsettling events around him. The Town Clerk's bell sounded again and again she responded.

"Pop out for a bottle of Glenfiddich, Mrs Oldroyd," he said, "I think I may need it tonight." He gave her £15.44 – it seemed parsimonious but how could he give her a tip for going? "Have you got the latest on Water's Edge?"

"I have nearly collated the latest but I am waiting for a fax from the Russian Delegation."

"Is it encouraging?" said the Town Clerk, "I've missed you these past few days whilst you've been with the Industrial Development Officer – I hope it's been worthwhile," he said. Quite purposefully he had distanced himself from the minutia of filling the park. Although as he liked as much Oldroyd proximity as possible he had given his Administrative Assistant Grade III and his Industrial Development Officer the brief to "Fill the park by any means legal ... deadline is late afternoon on the day of the Special Council Meeting ... see me then."

79

"I think you'll be well pleased, sir," she said, "I think you will be well pleased," she reiterated.

The dossier came to her about an hour before the Council Meeting. It showed an occupancy of one hundred percent. She was ecstatic. She tidied up the details and took them into the Town Clerk. She could feel the tension as the Town Clerk read the dossier. One hundred percent take-up, all contractually tied up. He was so pleased he permitted himself a punch into the air like a football supporter.

"You know, Mrs Oldroyd, this is wonderful. I think I may survive to be your Town Clerk in the morning. Thank you." Quickly he finalised the speech he had prepared for Councillor Pat Sage. "E Gas Tap" he thought to himself. Realising that the Mayor had got him reading everyone's name backwards he mentally admonished himself for letting the Mayor influence him. "Kinell," he said, barely audibly and realised the Mayor had done it again. The Town Clerk put wig and gown on himself and poured a tot of Glenfiddich from the bottle that Mrs Oldroyd had delivered. Mentally he was ready for the fray. It was just a question of tactics.

Darren was working the a double shift and would not be home until ten o'clock. He had commenced a large contract that would secure the future of the quarry for some time and had been awarded a large bonus. But it meant working long hours which had left Cheryl many evenings alone.

Cheryl Oldroyd saw the Town Clerk go into the Robing Room to join the Mayor for the 'entry of the Gladiators' and looked at her watch, there was ten minutes before the start of the Special Council Meeting. All the staff of the outer office were ready to leave. Their job had been done – they had compiled the Town Clerk's dossier and the ceremonial part of the occasion was now down to him and him alone. Slowly she fixed her make-up and sprayed her perfume into her hair. She put on her outer coat and prepared to put the light out as last one to leave. She opened the outer door and saw the milling of people – Councillors, public and press going into the Chamber and Public Gallery for the Meeting. There was an unlikely conclave of Councillors huddled in a corner outside the chamber. She recognised some of them, especially Councillor Mrs Eunice Bramble for she had come across her many times when she had visited the Town Clerk. There was also the unpleasant incident of Darren dynamiting her right of way, an occasion that still brought a smile to her lips. She guessed that this was the 'gang of ten' that had forced the Special Council Meeting. She was intrigued, so intrigued that her step shortened and she wheeled around and returned to the General Office. She took off her top-coat, smoothed her skirt, applied another coat of lipstick and decided to watch the proceedings from the Public Gallery. It was an about-turn that was to have momentous consequences for many people in Middlethwaite.

She was looking down on the Town Clerk and she could feel his hackles rising as Councillor Mrs Bramble began her attack on the Mayor. She had eyes only for him and she felt that she was almost inside him as he chose his moment to force the Deputy Mayor to "Move that the motion be put." She could see his neck redden but – just as suddenly – the meeting was over. The news that the Water's Edge Business Park was now oversubscribed climaxed the short meeting and it was over, the Mayor swept from the Chamber and, just as quickly, quit the building along with his cronies. The Public Gallery emptied instantaneously. There was an air of euphoria as the sycophants sought to congratulate the Mayor whilst the other factions were in disarray and Cheryl Oldroyd saw Councillor Mrs Bramble slip away alone and unheralded. In a matter of moments the officials were gone and in five minutes a pall of silence hung over the Chamber. She was amazed. The Town Clerk had timed the action like the dénouement of an Agatha Christie thriller. So she returned to the General Office, put her papers into the file and was just about to put her top-coat on again when she heard a clink of a glass from the Town Clerk's office. He had returned to the Glenfiddich, she was not the last to leave the Town Hall, there were two people left, the Town Clerk and his Administrative Assistant Grade III. She put her topcoat down, strode across the office and knocked at the Town Clerk's door. Without waiting for an answer she entered and looked straight at the Town Clerk, tumbler in hand and half-submerged by a cloud of cigar smoke. She swung across the office and kissed him lightly on the cheek. "Congratulations, sir," she said.

His reaction was instantaneous. He smiled at her, skipped past her and went across the office and dropped the latch of the Yale lock to his office. He returned to his desk, drained the Glenfiddich, stubbed out his cigar and leaned against his mock-Chippendale desk, drawing Cheryl into him. He said nothing. Neither did she as she nestled close to him. He put his hands around each cheek of her bottom kissed her passionately, his tongue flicking inside her mouth seeking hers. As they kissed she pressed herself to him. His hands sought the zip of her skirt and the sway and shrug of her hips ensured that as he pulled the fastener down, the skirt slithered gracefully to the floor. The cheval mirror was perfectly positioned. It was as if fate had decreed that it should be in just the right place for him to see the lovemaking unfold before his very eyes. In the reflection he could see her long legs topped with French knickers under a diaphanous slip. The slip went the way the skirt had moments before, followed swiftly by the French knickers. She was now naked from the waist down and within seconds he was too. He inserted himself into her and froze. This was bloody paradise, he thought. She felt him thrusting into her. This was bloody paradise, she thought. They stayed locked and immobile for just a matter of seconds before James Pickering-Eaden deftly slipped the bra catch of his Administrative Assistant Grade III and her young breasts were out pressing into the muscular hairy chest of her refined lover. Looking again into the cheval mirror over her shoulder he could contain himself no longer. He watched her buttocks heaving as he pushed into her, slipped down and almost out of her, pushed up again, slipped down and almost out of her again and then with a final thrust came into her at the same time feeling her labia vibrate with a lunge that made him happy to know that they had climaxed together. They stayed in the same position for some three minutes, the man with legs apart leaning against the desk and the girl pressing between the muscular thighs before the combination of his detumescence and the amalgamation of their bodily juices washed him from her. But they stayed tightly together, faces pressed close and each tingling with excitement. It was only after half-an-hour that the Town Clerk felt cramp in his back and reluctantly abandoned the clinch. Not a word had been spoken, but they both thought plenty. It had been a truly spontaneous happening, no amount of rehearsal could have brought this union to such fruition.

He dressed. She slipped into the yellow matching underwear that had so hastily departed from her person sometime previously. What could he say that would not sound trite?

"Glenfiddich, Mrs Oldroyd?" he said quizzically.

"Please," she said, realising that for the first time she had not said "Sir."

He poured two large measures of Glenfiddich and handed one to her. He glanced round the room, the antique furniture looked magnificent in the half light of falling dusk, the magnificent russet colours of the Bokhara carpet added to the completeness of the occasion. The best of the Abel Hold pictures had caught the last sparkle from the downing sun. A pair of pheasants in rural setting, the cock strutting in his magnificent plumage with the hen in the foreground, preening herself. Perhaps the Town Clerk only imagined that they both looked fairly satisfied with life? Peeping out from a mahogany Canterbury was a yellow half-slip that the Administrative Assistant Grade III had omitted to re-dress into. Chuckling the Town Clerk retrieved it, speculated what would have happened had the cleaners found it in the morning and then told the story of kicking the Mayor's trousers back under the chaise-longue after the installation débàcle.

They sat together and spoke nonsense and rubbish. They were awkward in each other's company but things eased after a while. They had had three large tumblers of Glenfiddich each and neither were fit to drive. She said to him that she thought he had never noticed her but he refuted this.

"You know that tight beige skirt of yours?"

"Yes," she said.

"I could tell exactly what pants you had on underneath. I used to have a competition with myself as I drove to the Town Hall in the morning, whether the imprint of your pantie lines were the French knickers, the briefs, the cutaway fuller panties or the ones with the little legs in them. I was an expert on your underwear Mrs Oldroyd and I am pleased to say I have now graduated in Lingerie Studies.." he laughed.

She sniggered and he drew her to him again. She kissed him full on the lips and the kiss stayed and fulminated. His urge was rising again.

"Wait a moment," he said, opened his top drawer and took the key to the interconnecting door to the Robing Room. He unlocked the door and returned and gathered up the girl in one action, carrying her through to the Robing Room, now in complete darkness. Within moments they were both naked again and she lay, legs spread wide on the Mayoral chaise-longue whilst he lunged into her. Again they climaxed simultaneously – this time he was sad not to have watched the action on the cheval mirror but continuously thinking that this day that he had entered with trepidation had finished with consummation and he had had a day that would stay in his memory forever. And so had she.

As they both slipped from the chaise-longue the brass castors eased it forward slightly and they both fell off, landing in a heap at one end. They

The Town Clerk

laughed as they both remembered to check if any underwear languished there.

"I'd better ring Mr Earnshaw," the Town Clerk said. "It's nearly ten o'clock and whilst he is used to my working late, it's imperative I tell him I am leaving soon or he'll be commencing his security rounds. We don't want him to find us, do we?" he smiled mischievously.

At the mention of ten o'clock Cheryl Oldroyd froze. Darren would be home soon and she must be in before him. The Town Clerk let her out as if Cinderella was returning to Baron Hardup. As he watched her slip into her car he thought of the words the Mayor had said recently, "it's been a raight foony day." His attempt to mimic the Yorkshire accent was pathetic but as he tried his mind went back to a joke he had heard some thirty years ago. He could not remember the joke but the punch-line was "fucking is in its infancy in Barnsley ..." Well, he thought, it's progressed quite considerably in nearby Middlethwaite.

The Town Clerk got into his own car. He carefully drove the short distance to his own house mindful of the fact that he was probably at just about the limit. He parked his car only slightly at an angle and let himself in. Celia was in the kitchen making cocoa. She did not ask him why he was a bit late, assuming that the meeting had overrun. She was wearing her winceyette nightie and the unmistakable smell of Musk perfume.

"Shall we have an early night, dear?" she said. Thrusting a steaming mug of cocoa towards him. "Kinell," thought the Town Clerk.

CHAPTER SEVEN

STRINES VALLEY

There was a new spring in the step of Cheryl Oldroyd. That she was in love with the Town Clerk there was no shadow of doubt. But there was an increasing feeling that there was absolutely no future at all in this relationship although she was content to let things ride along and to try to get maximum enjoyment from the affair. For his part, the thrill of seeing Cheryl Oldroyd every morning more than compensated for the increasing workload brought about by new Government legislation and the watchful eye he had to keep on the Mayor. He felt that he was due for another crisis, but weeks slipped by and the Mayor seemed to have calmed down and was showing a degree of dignity in the office so perhaps the Town Clerk's forebodings were misplaced. As to his affair with his Administrative Assistant Grade III, he was ecstatic at the sexual aspect but wished that they could spend some social time together without arousing suspicions. They managed to make love once or twice a week, often on the Mayoral chaise-longue in the Robing Room. Browsing around the local antiques market he had bought a nice set of porcelain castor-cups which he had placed under the brass wheels of the Mayoral chaise-longue. He told the Mayor that they added to the decorative appeal of the fine piece of furniture but, of course, they had the practical effect of creating immobility when he used it to make love with his Administrative Assistant Grade III. But the Town Clerk also had uneasy feelings about the outcome of the affair. He had taken to leaving little coded messages for the girl and giving her small gifts but they had both to be careful that no-one suspected their involvement together.

In early summer he arranged a day out in the Strines Valley in the Derbyshire Peak District. Cheryl had taken the preceding two days off so that their joint absence would not be noticed and the Town Clerk convened a

The Town Clerk

'shadow' meeting of the Northern Branch of the Society of Town Clerks which he mysteriously 'forgot' to inform his colleagues. The two met in the Strines Valley, just over Langsett Reservoir and Cheryl left her car parked in the Waggon and Horses pub car park. The Town Clerk had enjoyed stuffing a picnic hamper full of good things, although he would have infinitely preferred to have had a lunch at the Strines Hotel deep into Derbyshire but, of course, they could not take the risk of anyone seeing them together. Some way up the valley they stopped the car and set out on foot into the beautiful Peak District looking to find lesser-known paths which would not be on the maps of the Ramblers Association for obvious reasons. England was at its best as the couple, arms around each other and with just the wicker picnic hamper to carry, meandered off the beaten track heading for a small inland lake that not many people knew about. They walked slowly savouring each other's company. It was their first time that they could really relax together without having to watch what they said, instead of brushing hands unobtrusively together as they had in the office they could squeeze each other's hands very tight. They walked at a funereal pace. They picked cowslips and he put some in her hair. As they walked with arms around each other his hand slipped round her hip and travelled down her outer thigh, she put her hand in the back pocket of his trousers. They stopped often and kissed passionately, nature was with them, they had made an early start, the day was warm and set fair and hours of pleasure stretched before them. They were in no hurry and they both relished every moment of still balmy air. They climbed a stile, followed an overgrown trail and skirted a small hillock.

Eerily, they heard voices which seemed close by. The Town Clerk's Territorial Army training came into play. He threw himself to the ground and snaked on elbows and knees through the bracken until his eyes peeped over the hillock and surveyed the valley below. Just like his army training he swivelled round for his "men" to follow and his "men" (Cheryl Oldroyd) did just that although she found it hard to refrain from laughing and spoiling the solemnity of the military operation. In the balmy stillness of mid-morning they could see a line of walkers, all of three miles away whose voices were amplified by the wafting eddies of zephyr-like breezes and so clear was the atmosphere that, even at such a distance, they could almost make out what they were saying. The line of walkers wore waterproofing and kagoules of every colour and hue but all of them bright. Walking in Indian file they bobbed like corks and flies on a fisherman's line standing out vividly against the verdant green backdrop. Save for scattered cows and sheep, they were the only occupants of the magnificent cyclorama and the two lovers lay on their stomachs and watched their slow progress.

"Are you thinking what I'm thinking?" said the Town Clerk.

"Probably," was the reply.

"It would be funny if we bumped into 'Bramble the Ramble' so far off the beaten track, wouldn't it?" They both laughed at the thought of confronting their bête-noir but the day was to pass peacefully and the line of walkers, three miles away, was the nearest they came to seeing any other human being. An eagle-eyed kestrel circled overhead watching a family of young rabbits playing in a field and Cheryl threw a stick at it, lest it should swoop on its prey. At the other side of the covert a big dog-fox was also watching the family of rabbits with similar designs on breakfast. The kestrel was replaced in the skies above by a courting couple of noisy crows telling the world about the illicit union being enacted below by the Town Clerk and his Administrative Assistant Grade III.

The wicker picnic hamper was just beginning to feel heavy when the couple arrived at a fold in the hillocks and there before them was the lake, barely fifty yards by ten and just about six feet deep. The clear water was freezing despite the fact that by now the day was warm with a bright June sun shining down from a cloudless sky. The cold water was no detriment for the Town Clerk had brought four bottles of wine, a bottle of Liebfraumilch, a light Sauternes, a bottle of Laurent Perrier champagne and – just for contrast – a bottle of Hungarian Bull's Blood. If they managed to consume all that between them it might be a repeat of their first time together when they quaffed Glenfiddich and had driven home probably over the limit. So the white wines were laid down in the cold clear water, the Bull's Blood was laid out in the bracken to be served at room temperature and the Town Clerk unpacked the Art Deco hamper, early bakelite and plastic crockery in garish shades of yellow, green and red.

"Same shade as the yellow French knickers," said the Town Clerk, "are they on display today?"

"No," she said, "but no doubt you'll find your question answered later," as if to forestall his anticipated enquiry as to the colour of today's Charnos set. She had never quite come to terms as to why the colour of underwear

The Town Clerk

fascinated the male species but she knew that it did and she liked the fact that it was so admired.

"We'll need a fire," said the Town Clerk, "so, if you'll search for wood, I'll build a range from these rocks here." He was tempted to sing a few lines of 'Mountain Greenery' but resisted as it may have emphasised the generation gap between them. He lifted a few large rocks and dragged them into a covert out of the slight breeze, by which time Cheryl was returning hidden under an enormous armful of brushwood.

"Till Burnham Wood do come to Dunsinane," said James Pickering-Eaden.

"No, you've lost me with that one," came the rejoinder and the Town Clerk had to explain his quotation from Macbeth which he had thought quite cleverly summed up the apparition of Burnham Wood on the move. He was not sure that Cheryl quite understood the epithet but he did not labour the point as he did not want to appear to be too clever. And, he thought, when you consider the position of a Town Clerk and his Administrative Assistant Grade III behaving like young lovers in the country, it wasn't being very clever at all.

Despite his best efforts the fire failed at first so Cheryl had further searching to do to find drier tinder. The rocks had to be reconstructed and they both laughed as, once again, the fire roared into life only to die as quickly as before.

"I think the fire is suffering from detumescence, Mrs Oldroyd," said the Town Clerk. "It seems firm and strong and excited and roars into life but once the initial energy has been expended it suddenly falls flat and is a withering limpid mess with no spark at all."

Cheryl Oldroyd understood the analogy perfectly, "Forget the fire, talk dirty to me, Town Clerk," she said, her dark eyes dancing enticingly and playfully.

Momentarily James Pickering-Eaden was embarrassed. "At some later time, perhaps," he said, "but at this moment let's concentrate on the fire ..."

Off she went again to find some more dry tinder and she laughed out loud as she could hear the Town Clerk cursing and swearing and the lighting of several matches, each fizzling out before the fire could get hold. It was incongruous, she thought, here was a man who had repeatedly earned her admiration by the skilful way he dealt with problems litigious, and social and human that came the way of his office and he couldn't light a bonfire. So she told him so.

"Alright," he said, "let's talk dirty instead, let's give up on the fire. You've got me thinking of other things."

She ignored him. "Let me try," she said. She took a few paper hankies from her bag, inveigled the flame to spread to some dry bracken and gradually introduced some larger sticks and soon the fire was roaring.

"I can see you were never a Boy Scout, Town Clerk," she said, "fortunately, I attained high office in the Girl Guides and had an armful of badges to prove it. I had badges from wrist (she tapped her wrist) to shoulder." (She flicked up her sleeves and playfully pushed her shoulder strap up, flicking her bra-strap down.)

"Come here," said the Town Clerk.

"Wait," said Cheryl Oldroyd "the fire is the most important thing at the moment, I'll takeover the fire."

He deferred to her greater prowess as a firelighter and set off to replenish the woodstock. As he came down the hillside peeping behind a double armful of bracken she said, "Touché. Till Burnham Wood do come to Dunfermline."

"Actually, it's Dunsinane, but good try, Administrative Assistant Grade III."

They both laughed again, they were supremely happy in each other's company and soon the smell of woodsmoke was subjugated by the sizzle of bacon and steak and mushrooms and they both ate a hearty meal for their hours in the open air had given both a good appetite. They had started with the Sauternes which had cooled well from its time submerged in the chill waters and, like two gastronomes had enjoyed the Bull's Blood with the red meat of the best steak that James Pickering-Eaden had bought. Cheryl was no vegetarian and her sturdy limbs and breathtaking figure gave full evidence of a hearty intake of a full and balanced diet.

"I'll wash up," said the Town Clerk, "but we'll leave them to soak whilst we go exploring," and put the whole lot of implements into a shallow puddle at the side of the lake, "not very hygienic," he said, and when they returned from their exploration everything was just as greasy as when they had left.

By now it was well into the afternoon and they had been together since early morning, just happy in each other's company. There was a pinkness on both their faces as they had been exposed to the early summer sun for some hours.

"Hey, we'd better be careful," said the Town Clerk, "I'm supposed to be at the Society of Town Clerks' meeting at Leeds. Somehow I don't think I'd get this kind of tan there. Where are you supposed to be?"

"Shopping at Harrogate – perhaps Darren will be pleased when I come home with a virgin credit card?"

They had found a bothy at the other side of the ridge and had played 'house' in it like a couple of children. They had climbed trees, they had found a nest of a meadow pipit with a mother sitting on it and the bird cocked its head at the two lovers and seemingly winked, knowing that they would leave her undisturbed. They saw the dog-fox again, his magnificent red coat standing out against the verdant green of the hedgerows, they had gazed down on the shimmering magnificence of Langsett Reservoir some ten miles distant and they had cultivated every moment of their time together. All the problems of Middlethwaite and the guilt and ramifications of their affair seemed to belong to another world as they lay under the sun which was beginning to go down under the nearby hillock. The girl lay on her back and the Town Clerk's head was on her chest, nestling between her breasts.

"Do you realise," he said, "we have been together – alone – for eight hours and we have not made love? Who could say that I wanted you just for your body? We have had the opportunity to consummate our relationship far away from the Mayor's lumpy chaise-longue and all I have had to admire is your firelighting skills and your tree-climbing. Eight hours and I don't even know the colour of your knickers ... well, I suppose I do, if they match your bra strap. You know that drives me wild," he said.

"Yes," was the simple rejoinder.

They both laughed, marvelling at their moderation but the celibacy of the day was soon to be broken as he gently elevated her short skirt and sighed as he looked at her brief pants covering the silky hairs that had made him crazy in thoughts. He put his finger into her, gently drawing the elasticity of the gusset aside and felt her quick intake of breath as he immediately stickied up. She opened her blouse and unhooked the front opening of her bra, her breasts spilling out so that he could suck her nipples. He was astride her in a moment, and her skirt was rolled under her buttocks to give her some cushion on the thorny grass.

"Shall I take my pants off?" she said.

"No need," he said as he drew aside the gusset and inserted himself into her. It was all over in a moment, they both came mightily, fuelled by their attraction and love for each other, the two bottles of wine that they had consumed and the fact that they had waited eight hours for this moment of love to arrive. He said nothing as they lay together but, trawling through his forty-eight years of memories he thought that that had been the best fuck he had ever had and would not wish to have a better one.

"So fucking is in its infancy in Barnsley, is it? Kinell! It's quite well advanced in Langsett, that's for sure." Of course, she wanted an explanation of this so he told her the long tedious joke which he had since been able to remember. Just for good measure he told her who or what "Kinell" was and thereafter she couldn't stop using it either.

"A celebration," he said as he popped the cork of the Laurent Perrier champagne and incongruously poured it into two plastic beakers from the picnic set. Now he was getting slightly drunk, he was also getting emotional. They toasted each other, they toasted Glenfiddich, they toasted the Mayor's chaise-longue. They even toasted Mrs Bramble, they toasted the Mayoress, they toasted Elton John, they toasted Councillor Pepper, they toasted Blur – although the Town Clerk was not quite sure who they were so he toasted them again just to make sure. After each toast they said in unison "Kinell," and their laughter echoed across the valley. They were being very silly and enjoying every moment. They then made love again and by now it was dark. Her pants were in a mess for the Town Clerk was very virile. She searched in her bag for her spare pair.

"Give them here," he said and, obediently, she threw them to him. "Not these," he said, throwing them back, "the mucky pair."

"Why should you want those?" she said, but obeying him nonetheless.

"There's something about women's secretions," he said, "that turns men on. I'll tell you a story. I've always enjoyed the smell of soiled panties. I thought that perhaps I was strange – I almost said queer, but that seems to have a different connotation these days – but one day when I was Clerk to the Leisure Services Committee at my former Authority, I made friends with Duggie Smart, who produced our pantomime that we put on in the Town Hall Theatre. When he first came to my office he produced his card to my Administrative Assistant Grade III, it was Mrs Jeanette Hall in those days, and on it it said 'DUGGIE SMART pantomimes, summer seasons, touring shows, old time music hall, variety shows, bar mitzvahs, birds pulled, bras burnt, knickers sniffed', well, I thought there are at least two of us." He took the pants and gave a big sniff. Theatrically he convulsed with asthmatic coughs,

The Town Clerk

gathering sputum from the bottom of his lungs and acting as if he was suffering from the miners' chest disease silicosis. "There, look what they've done for me, Mrs Oldroyd!" he wheezed.

"What will you do with them?" she said.

"I'll put them in the safe with the sealed tenders as I have the only key for that safe and each morning, especially the days when you are not there, I shall take them out, take two lungfuls of Middlethwaite air and give them a good sniff!" he replied.

She had never known anything like it but was pleased that the Town Clerk wanted a keepsake. Surely he would not do that? Black jacket, striped pants, mink waistcoat, patent leather shoes and sniffing soiled pants?

It was now nearly dark and the walk back to the road was fraught. They hugged each other closely.

"It's been a lovely day. Bring me back here someday, Town Clerk. Please," she said.

"Well, we've got an excuse," he said, "there's still a bottle of Liebfraumilch laid down in the chilled department," he replied.

"You think of everything, Town Clerk," was her rejoinder.

Not once had she called him James or Jim. She had studiously avoided this method of address in case it had become endemic and she had used it in the office and had given the game away. In fact, on one passionate occasion on the Mayor's chaise-longue she had moaned "Fuck me, fuck me, fuck me ..... sir," and he had immediately lost his erection and dissolved into fits of laughter. But they made light of the matter and Mrs Oldroyd was never 'Cheryl' to the Town Clerk. Early on in their relationship they had resolved the question of contraception as the Town Clerk had had a vasectomy some years ago when Celia had reached forty and they had reluctantly concluded that parenthood was not mapped out in God's plan for them. Or, if it was, neither of them wanted it at forty-something. So Cheryl Oldroyd could relax about this aspect of their lovemaking although she was not aware of the Town Clerk's "snip" when they first made love after the Special Council Meeting.

The journey back was difficult. A path gently meandering between thorn and gorse was easy to follow under a bright sun but in half-light it was difficult and limbs were scratched and ankles turned. More than once they stepped into cowpats but this did nothing to diminish the strong bond between them. As they stumbled over the rocks littered around they thought they could hear

Strines Valley

the big dog-fox chuckling. They eventually reached the Town Clerk's parked car. They were very much in love and neither of them wanted to return home to their divided loves. In the car park of the Waggon and Horses, they kissed passionately and went their separate ways, albeit reluctantly. It had been a lovely day, it was a day that would stay in their memories forever. Perhaps their sunburn and scratched legs may need a bit of explaining after their respective visits to the Society of Town Clerks and shopping in Harrogate.

Very circumspectly Mrs Oldroyd drove home. She had consumed one-and-a-half bottles of a combination of Sauternes, Bull's Blood and Laurent Perrier champagne, but drove carefully. The house was in darkness and Darren had not arrived home from his double-shift at the Quarry. The Town Clerk drove similarly, very carefully, and arrived home without incident. As he turned the key of the door he heard the bubbling of cocoa and the smell of 'Musk'. "Kinell," he said to himself.

CHAPTER EIGHT

MEMBERS v OFFICERS AT GOLF

Some years ago when Middlethwaite was a prosperous industrial town, a group of mill owners got together with a conglomerate from the local glassworks and formed a Citizens' Party which was Conservative in all but name. They never quite came close to taking control of the Council which had been Labour-held since time immemorial but at one time they formed quite a large caucus on the local Council. Some of the few cultural aspects of Middlethwaite are down to their influence and one thing they did institute on the Council was an Annual Golf Match between the councillors and the officers. It had been played at the Municipal Links for sixty years save for the war years and the prize was the Sidney Hebblethwaite Trophy in honour of the Leader of the Citizens' Party, whose idea it was to try to get the town away from its whippets and woodbines image. It had not really succeeded but this rather anachronistic challenge had lasted through the years and in early summer the ritual was duly re-enacted. It was usual for the officers' team to be comprised of the eight Chief Officers, most of whom were passably competent with the clubs whilst the Members' team comprised the Mayor, the Leader of the Council (E Gas Tap) and his selection of six others. Of the sixty Councillors there was usually a few who could 'play a bit' and some years the tournament was keenly contested and closely fought. To assuage the ratepayers' complaints, a sum of about a thousand pounds was usually raised by means of a tombola, lottery etc and the sum went into the Mayor's Fund for distribution at the end of the Mayoral Year.

The Town Clerk was not very keen on playing in this year's match but in recent years the result had been close with the officers just about getting the upper hand. In fact the Sidney Hebblethwaite Trophy was on the chiffonier in his office at the moment, if the members won the match the trophy merely

95

moved twenty yards up the corridor and spent the year on the ormolu credenza in the Parlour.

The teams assembled in the Club House around mid-morning and it was traditional that the opening match was the Mayor v the Town Clerk and it was also traditional that the Mayor won. The Leader of the Council then lost to the Treasurer and thereafter they were proper games and the result of the match often hinged on the last game of the afternoon fourballs. It was going to be quite some feat this year for the Mayor to win, for the Town Clerk was quite a passable player with a handicap of eight whilst the Mayor's experience was limited to a round of putting each year at Mablethorpe where he and the Mayoress went on holiday every year. The Mayor also had another large handicap in that, despite the early start, he had had several large gins to fortify himself in the Club House beforehand and was swaying quite considerably as the two teams gathered at the first tee to start the match.

The officers had won the toss and the Town Clerk got ready to drive off. He took a few practice swings and cut a few divots which caused the Mayor to say "Careful, Town Clerk, there are men working under there." This raised quite a large round of laughter but as it had been said every opening match for the long duration of the Sidney Hebblethwaite Trophy it was more apocryphal than original.

The Town Clerk played a good drive straight down the middle and everyone prayed that the Mayor's opening shot would follow the Town Clerk's and not be hooked into the bunker or pulled into the trees. There was an audible sigh of relief when the Mayor did indeed make good contact and the ball followed the Town Clerk's straight down the middle. The photographers from the local papers got their picture and went off to cover the local baby show and the Women's Institute tea, for they obviously thought that there was no chance of a repeat of the Wisdom and Ullathorne Show. At one time there had actually been men employed under the first hole, for the Municipal Links had been built over the workings of a redundant local colliery and many a golfer in recent years had been frustrated when his ball, apparently heading for the centre of the hole, often took a wide detour, courtesy of some shale bits from the spoil heap working their way to the surface from under the thin covering of topsoil. St Andrew's or Wentworth it was not, but it was well used and well appreciated by the working (and not-working) class of Middlethwaite, whilst the businessmen and wealthier residents played at the private golf club to the west of the borough.

As the morning progressed the matches got strung out but by dint of playing himself into the bunkers on purpose a few times and kicking the Mayor's ball out of a bad lie, the Town Clerk and the Mayor came to the end of the outward half all square. The Town Clerk then lost the next hole and went one down by helping the Mayor's lie on all five strokes and deliberately slicing his own ball into the water. The Mayor did not appreciate that the Town Clerk was helping him so much and when he went one up the Mayor got quite arrogant.

"You know, Town Clerk, I didn't realise that this game was so easy. I should have took it up years ago, I'd be a professional by now. Look at it this way, Town Clerk, if you play off eight after all the years of practice that you've had yet I'm ahead of you this morning, it stands to reason that I'm a natural for this game ..... try to do a bit better on the next eight holes."

The Town Clerk looked away, "Kinell," he thought.

They had become separated from the other matches and the Town Clerk formed the impression of impending doom. There was something in the Mayor's demeanour that he could not put his finger on but did not like it. There seemed to be a build-up of atmosphere and he was uneasy. It was something he could not figure out. The Town Clerk thought he could read the Mayor's mood swings but this morning he was unable to analyse the situation. He felt that there was a Sword of Damocles hanging over him and, as the holes slipped by, his trepidations were transmitting down to his golf clubs and he was playing now as badly as the Mayor. His fears were to be realised at, appropriately enough, the thirteenth hole. He played three conventional shots to the green whilst the Mayor hit a cataclysmic drive which hit two trees and landed into the pond. He was out of the rough in six strokes and down in eleven. The Town Clerk holed in par-four and the Mayor was down in bogey-seven.

"We'll call that a half," the Town Clerk gratuitously said to the Mayor with a smile.

The Mayor was not amused. He had a face like thunder as if blaming his playing partner for his eleven shots. He reached into his pocket and took out a hip flask. Throwing his head back he took a large swallow of gin and handed it to the Town Clerk.

"I don't think I will, thank you, Mr Mayor," said the Town Clerk, "it's a bit

The Town Clerk

early for me, but thank you all the same."

The Mayor took off his cap, threw down his bag of clubs and sat down on the fairway. "Sit thissen darn, I want to talk to thee," he said in broad Yorkshire.

James Pickering-Eaden knew that this was it. He had felt uneasy all morning but what he was to experience now outdistanced his worst fears. The Mayor got straight to the point. His eyes darted around as if to check that they were on their own.

"I want to talk to thee, Town Clerk, about sealed tenders," said the Mayor. "The sealed tenders in respect of the new Sports Centre."

He had been trying to guess the Mayor's point of attack and had considered several things, but the sealed tenders for the new Sports Centre did not even make the short list. The Town Clerk was quite unprepared and was taken aback. What should this have to do with the Mayor, he was not even on the Leisure Services Committee and had never shown any interest in sport, as witness his eleven at the thirteenth hole. In a way he was relieved. He knew that the Mayor wanted to assail him with something but he was certain that he was not the slightest bit vulnerable on the subject of sealed tenders. He was wrong.

The Mayor got straight to the heart of the matter, "There are six tenderers invited to price the contract for the building of the new Sports Centre. I want you to open the first five that come in and tell me the figures that have been bid." He was so calm about it despite his large intake of gin that morning that the Town Clerk rightly surmised that he had been rehearsing what he was to say all morning and had been biding his time to drop the bombshell. He had waited until they had got two holes ahead of the following match and they were on their own with no-one around.

"I can't do that, Mr Mayor," he replied after a few moments consideration. "You know I can't do that. Privacy in sealed tenders is at the nub of local Government law and the sealed tenders are kept in my safe, of which I alone have the key and I deliver them to the appropriate Committee to be opened by the Chairman in front of the Leisure Services Committee who then decide who to award the tender to. It's a procedure laid down in Standing Orders and is sacrosanct. It's a procedure designed to ensure that everything is far and away above board, it's a procedure that has been followed in Middlethwaite by successive authorities from the Board of Guardians, the ancient boroughs, the old County Borough Council and it's a procedure that is enshrined in the annals of Middlethwaite Metropolitan Borough Council, it's a procedure ....."

The Mayor was getting het up and interrupted loudly, "I know all that, Town Clerk, I have been on the bloody Council for eighteen years and I know all about the custom and practice of sealed tenders. I'm not a bloody idiot, tha knows..." he said lapsing into broad Yorkshire dialect.

The Town Clerk got up and fixed the Mayor with a look straight between the eyes, reminiscent of the way he pulled him together at the evening of the Mayor-Making. "What you are asking me to do is illegal. I cannot do it and I will not do it and it ill-behoves a man in the position of First Citizen of the Borough to make such demands on his Town Clerk and Chief Executive." For the first time in a long while he used the full nomenclature of his office. He was furious, he knew exactly why the Mayor wanted the tender prices, it was because he would be getting a kick-back from the sixth tenderer if he could find out the other five prices. He was on his high horse now. He took the Mayor by the shoulders and fixed him with another steely stare and said, "Just what do you think I am? For what reason do you think I should reveal these figures to you?" he said in measured tones.

The Mayor returned his stare and surprised the Town Clerk with his equilibrium. After a theatrical pause the Mayor said, "Because, Town Clerk, thou art fucking Mrs Oldroyd."

The Town Clerk's breath was taken completely away, his head swam and he struggled to say something. Eventually he sat down on a hillock and said, "Mr Mayor, I think I'll take you up on that offer of a swig from your flask." As he took a long deep draught he considered his next move. He must discover exactly how much the Mayor knew. He did not have to wait long and what he heard did not assuage his fears but was a lot worse than the worst scenario he could ever have envisaged. What the Mayor had to say next made his knees weak and he could feel his bladder weakening and a few globules of urine leave his uncontrolled sanitation department. The Town Clerk descended to a mood of deep gloom.

The Mayor was not in the least mollified by the Town Clerk's somewhat demeaned approach. He launched into a vicious and unremitting invective against the Town Clerk, his class and the supposed inequalities that had been visited upon him by the upper class, to which he saw the Town Clerk as a standard-bearer. The next pair of players in the Sidney Hebblethwaite Trophy

The Town Clerk

were nowhere in sight as the Mayor launched into his invective, "Sithee, Town Clerk," he began alternating his delivery in the stilted way that had been the hallmark of his Mayoralty since his installation, with a poor attempt at standard English, "a few weeks ago I went into the Robing Room and noticed something strange about the Chez Lon Gue," he began. He pronounced chaise-longue in three syllables as if it were the name of a Chinese laundry or restaurant. If it had not been for the gravity of the occasion the Town Clerk may have likened the delivery of Chez Lon Gue to the difficulty the Mayor had with Mephibosheth at Mayor's Sunday. But these were serious times and things got blacker and blacker as the Mayor's tirade progressed. "So I looked close and what did I see, Town Clerk?" he paused for effect. He was relishing every moment. "Spunk stains, Mr Town Clerk and 'pewblic' hairs, Mr Town Clerk."

The Town Clerk put his head in his hands as he considered how desperate his position was and what a fool he had been. He must think quick. He was far more intelligent than this fool whose only claim to fame is the fact that he is very versatile at pronouncing words backwards. He must be confident, there is no way that Councillor Leslie Ullathorne, Mayor of Middlethwaite could outwit James Pickering-Eaden, Town Clerk and Chief Executive.

But the Mayor was no-where near finished. "I knew right away what you had been up to for you were the only keyholder of the Robing Room," he said.

The Town Clerk looked at him. The adrenaline of the situation had sobered up the Mayor. He was as clear as a bell, his sway had gone and he was in full control of the situation.

The Town Clerk sat on the hillock taking the matter in. He would deny everything, he would brazen it out, no-one would believe this fool Ullathorne after his escapades at the myriad events that had comprised his tenure so far. That is what he would do – he would brazen it out. The Mayor's next salvo made this course of action impossible and caused James Pickering-Eaden to have an even longer draught at the Mayor's hip flask. The Mayor was enjoying it and he stuck the knife in further and gave it an almighty twist with is next revelation.

"Do you know what I did next, Town Clerk?"

The Town Clerk shook his head, he was shell-shocked. He couldn't say anything that would not sound trite so he did not say anything at all. The Mayor looked at him, his elephantine nose was seemingly redder and more bulbous. He had not expected an answer to his question but the stage pause seemed to last for an eternity before he spoke again.

"Well, do you remember a few meetings ago we were considering surveillance cameras for the Middlethwaite Town Centre and we had a very nice chap from Spy Control Limited to give us a demonstration? Well, I put a 'phone call into him and he very kindly lent me a camera, recording video and all the technical equipment. It set up very nicely in the Robing Room and it only had to wait three nights for its little surprise to be revealed to me the next morning." He looked across at the Town Clerk who was squirming. "You know, Town Clerk, I quite looked forward to viewing the action when I came to the Parlour," he paused again for effect, "you know, that performance you and Mrs Oldroyd gave on Tuesday evening was ...... a classic! Wasn't that underwear of hers a lovely colour? When I looked at her in your office I didn't realise that she was such a raver." He slipped back into his broad Yorkshire dialect, "Dus tha know, Town Clerk, I used to know a joke that finished 'fookin is in its infancy in Barnsley' – I'll tell it to thee one day. Ha, ha, ha!"

"Now, Town Clerk," he said again, "I want to discuss sealed tenders with you. There is only one copy of the video and it is lodged with my Solicitors and marked 'Council Business (funny business)'. My solicitor has been given certain instructions as to what to do with it and I won't bore you with the details. Suffice to say, Town Clerk, you are in a rather delicate position. The sort of delicate position that Mrs Oldroyd was in on my Chez Lon Gue." He was enjoying every minute and then he got decidedly crude. "She looked a good fuck, eh Jim? Can she gobble, Jim?"

The Town Clerk seethed at the thought of the Mayor watching the video.

The Mayor knew he was making the Town Clerk uncomfortable and could feel him squirm. He felt no gratitude towards the Town Clerk for extricating him from the mess he made of the Installation. His glee subsided and he was businesslike again. He came close to the Town Clerk and breathed gin fumes all over him.

"Now don't say anything. This is what is going to happen. You will open the sealed tenders and you will let me know the five bids so far on the Sports Centre. This you will do by next Wednesday which is the cricket match, as you are no doubt aware, of the Council versus the Licentious Villains, the annual match against the team selected by the Licensed Victuallers' Association. You will be in my team and we shall take the opportunity of a

The Town Clerk

walk around the boundary when we shall discuss the matter. It will all be done in the open air so don't think you can get up to any funny business. Now I think we should play the fourteenth hole. My tee-off I believe."

The Town Clerk was abject. He thought what a fool he had been. Fancy placing himself in a position like this. Fancy placing Cheryl in a position like this. His future looked bleak and he could see no way out. If he attempted to force the Mayor into a corner he would simply get the video back from his solicitors and publish it.

As they played the next hole the Mayor was reading his mind, "The Sun would pay me a fortune for the video. Perhaps I should send it to them and we could forget all about the sealed tenders. What do you think Jim?" He was turning the screw and it hurt.

The Town Clerk was in a dichotomy. If he did not respond to the Mayor in relation to the sealed tenders, it would be a sudden and immediate debacle hastened by the Sun. He was unhappy about the cricket match as it was because he thought it was not wise for the ratepayers to see press pictures of golf one week and cricket the next.

He had not intended to play the following week against the Licensed Victuallers' Association but that was to be the only way he could buy time. And what if he revealed the tender prices, what would be the Mayor's next demand? He was in the Mayor's pocket and he knew it. He had one week to come up with a solution to a problem that looked insoluble. He looked for a crumb of comfort in the situation but he could find none. Certainly he had had his last shag on the Mayoral chez lon gue – well it was getting lumpy, but that's not much consolation is it?

As they played the eighteenth hole the Mayor saved one more tirade for him, "You know, Town Clerk, it is a pleasure to see you squirm. Your class from a privileged background doesn't know what it is like to be poor. It would do you and your piss-elegant pals good to do a double-shift down the pit. It would do thee," he was slipping back into broad Yorkshire as he mounted his invective, "bloody good to do a ten hours in front of the ovens at Stocksbridge Steelworks or the Redfearn's Glassworks at Monk Bretton. You wouldn't fucking last five minutes you and your Architect pals and your Treasurer pals and the pansy Town Planners and the Borough Engineers. The engineers and surveyors should be made to dig a fucking road not just draw the bastard thing on a piece of paper and then let the real workers break their backs with

102

their shovels." He was getting his metaphors mixed now but continued his tirade unabated. "And those Social Workers. All of them on £25,000 a year whilst the poor of the Borough don't have enough to bring their kids up or buy a decent loaf of bread. And librarians – who reads books these days? All the sodding librarians have got fancy names like local historians and reference consultants whilst the only ones who do any work are the poor kids who stamp the books out."

The Town Clerk thought that if nobody was reading books then there couldn't be anybody stamping them out, but he let it pass without comment.

The Mayor returned to his invective "And that ponsified Cultural Officer. £30,000 a year and what bloody culture does he put on for the youngsters of the Sunflower Hill Estate? He once brought the Royal Shakespeare Company for one performance in Sunflower Secondary but they couldn't wait to fuck off back to Stratford. Meanwhile he swans round wearing those skin-tight trousers of his, always followed by half-a-dozen poofs in even tighter trousers and white sweaters. And those bloody teachers all on good money. They only work for about three weeks and then they're off for half-term, Baker Days or some other bloody excuse for not teaching the poor little buggers. You talk to them and they tell you they are the hardest working people in the world. Bollocks. They make out that as soon as they get home they shove a quick sandwich down their throats and then they have to work until one o'clock the next morning preparing lessons. Who the bloody hell do they think they are kidding, what a fucking load of bollocks. No wonder so many of the little sods turn to crime, the teachers all driving their swanky cars to the best estates outside town with their double garages and their la-di-da cocktail parties and fishponds in the gardens whilst the little buggers in the Sunflower Hill Estate mooch around the street corners with nowt to do except get up to vandalism and sniff from glue cans. And it's all thy fault, Town Clerk. Thee and thy cronies, all conspiring to keeping the working class down. Tha going to have to pay for it. Tha'll regret the day you ever went a-shagging on my Chez Lon Gue! Now let's play the last hole and get back to the bar and another bottle of gin."

The Town Clerk thought that it was inconsistent with his class that this paragon of socialism was not looking forward to a proletarian pint but a sloane gin. It was a small point and he got no comfort from it. The Town Clerk's mind was a blank. Somehow he got through the prizegiving and the speeches when

The Town Clerk

the Worshipful the Mayor of Middlethwaite was at his expansive best mixing his metaphors. The Town Clerk was in a daze. He couldn't even remember who had won the match, whether the Sidney Hebblethwaite Trophy would be returning to his chiffonier or gracing the Mayor's credenza. All he did know was that he was in deep trouble and could see not the slightest light in what seemed to be a very dark and very long tunnel.

What he did not need was for Robin Armstrong, the Mayor's Secretary, to sidle over to him and say "The Mayor's in a good mood, Jim. Whatever have you been up to to get him like this? Whatever you've done, please do it again. I like him like this, ha ha ha!"

The Mayor's limousine glided slowly past the two men but the Mayor did not notice them. He was berating his chauffeur Bill Hutchings, "Tha knows, Hutchings, thy are about as much use as a one-legged man in an arse-kicking contest. I've bin up and down like a prostitute's knickers looking for thee ....."

The Mayor's Secretary looked at the Town Clerk and said, "You know, Jim, I'd say our First Citizen suffered from mood swings, wouldn't you?"

Philosophically the Town Clerk nodded.

CHAPTER NINE

THE LODGE MEETING

A couple of days after the momentous events of the Sidney Hepplethwaite trophy match it was the turn of the Town Clerk to be installed as Worshipful Master at the local Freemason's Lodge. That he did not consider himself fit for office need hardly be emphasised, neither did his upcoming installation as President of the Society of Town Clerks give him the sense of pride that it would have done had circumstances been different. He had to try to behave as if everything was normal so he threw himself into his Council work and sorted out some dreadfully dull legislation that he had delayed tackling.

He was in his office taking stock. He had managed to have some time alone with Cheryl but it was not satisfactory and she could feel that he was nervous. He debated whether to tell her about the Mayor's bombshell but decided against it as no useful purpose would be served, so he would shoulder the burden on his own. The physical side of their relationship had to be put on hold but it forged a stronger bond between the couple. The Town Clerk had to find a reason as to why the Robing Room was out of bounds so he hurriedly decided to have it redecorated and recarpeted and they had to resort to fumbling in the car which was unsatisfactory and dangerous. But he was very much in love with his Administrative Assistant Grade III and she with him. So far as either of them knew, no whiff or scandal had permeated to other members of the Town Clerk's staff but this was unimportant when considered alongside the one person who was in the know. And his video of the affair was securely lodged with his solicitor if the Mayor could be believed – and the Town Clerk felt that, unfortunately, on this occasion he could be believed.

So the Town Clerk took stock. He could resign but then the Sun threat would come into play so this would not be an option. He could flee with Cheryl and give up everything he had established over all these years. Was

The Town Clerk

that an option – would Cheryl be willing to devote the rest of her life to a man twenty years older than herself, who had had a vasectomy and could not father a child with her? That was hardly an option either. He could go on the offensive against the Mayor but how? He could go to the Police but he knew that this would end up with him getting the sack, Cheryl humiliated and perhaps the Mayor thrown out of office although with his capacity for survival as instanced already many times in his Mayoral Year, this was by no means certain. He could have an unofficial word with Chief Inspector Murray who would be at the Lodge meeting that evening. This had to be ruled out also as the police nowadays did not take kindly to unofficial approaches in case the whole thing rebounded on them later. Although a fellow member of his Lodge he did not think Chief Inspector Colin Murray could be trusted so this idea was a non-starter. So the Town Clerk pushed his chair back, put his feet on his desk and said out loud, "Jim, lad," with a passable impression of Robert Newton as Long John Silver in Treasure Island, "Jim, lad," he reiterated, "the Mayor's got you by the balls – or, to put it into the Mayor's vernacular – he's got thee by the fookin' knackers." He even permitted himself a hollow laugh at the quality of his Robert Newton impersonation. This laugh grew to a near-hysterical guffaw which aborted peremptorily when his Electoral Registration Officer entered and said "Pardon, sir?"

"No matter, it's not important..." he said, minimising the situation somewhat.

His policy of throwing himself into his work was paying good dividends in that the efficiency of the Council was being streamlined by his energies. Unfortunately, it could have no effect on tackling his underlying problems but he got on with his work and the second phase of Water's Edge Business Park was filling up well, he had got on top of the new government legislation and he had carried out a review of the Council's establishment giving it a more up-to-date look. He had dotted every 'i' and crossed every 't' in the name of efficiency. It succeeded in that it filled every moment of every day but as the Robing Room adjacent was being redecorated he could see the chaise-longue – or 'Chez Lon Gue' as the Mayor called it – standing out as a beacon to his folly. But not for one moment did any regret trigger his emotions and he thought of the wonderful times cavorting on it with his Administrative Assistant Grade III, thoughts of which naturally progressed to the wonderful day out in the Strines Valley when there was no-one else in the world apart

The Lodge Meeting

from the two of them.

It was time for his annual medical with Dr Joshua Slack, the Council's Medical Officer of Health. He had arrived in Middlethwaite about the same time as Josh Slack and their friendship had grown, as it had with all the other Chief Officers. He had a first-class team and he was proud to be at the head of it.

"Any problems, Jim?" said Doc Slack.

"None at all," replied the Town Clerk, although he did consider asking to have his head examined. He was given a full medical which he sailed through and Doc Slack pronounced him fit for another year as Town Clerk.

"There is just one thing, Jim, it is a few years since I performed your vasectomy and I think we ought to check your sperm-count. It should be nil but sometimes things are not always one hundred percent so will you let me have a specimen so that I can send it to the lab?" The Town Clerk smiled and said that he hoped he would not be expected to produce it immediately in such sterile and uninspiring surroundings.

"I can let you look at the few copies of Health and Efficiency from the 1940's," said Josh Slack, "but I don't think they would excite you as all the pubic hair has been brushed out and they are all matronly women anyway. Look at this, Jim," he handed the Town Clerk a yellowing copy dated 1949, "all the men look like librarians with little Hitler-type moustaches and they are all holding strategically-placed books or tennis racquets. Isn't it amazing that bookshops used to keep these under the counter?"

The two colleagues shook hands and the Town Clerk promised to let him have the specimen later after "he had had sufficient inspiration." He did not tell Doc Slack of the inspirational mucky pants he kept in the safe and he did not take with him the proffered copy of 1949 Health and Efficiency. He certainly did not consider having an Armitage Shank or Jodrell Bank (or whatever they called it these days) on the Mayor's 'Chez Lon Gue' in case the video was still switched on.

Roundabout mid-day the Head Messenger brought him sealed tender number 5 in respect of the new Sports Centre. This was duly placed in the safe for which he had the only key. The sight and the smell of the translucent pants of Cheryl fresh (hardly the right word, he thought) from the day out in the Strines Valley leapt into his fingers when he was placing the sealed tender in the safe. Cheryl had taken a few days off and was touring Cornwall with

107

The Town Clerk

Darren her husband. He was missing her terribly and only had the comfort of one quick, hastily-convened telephone call from Mousehole to sustain him. He placed the sealed tender in the safe, took the pants out, dropped the Yale latch on his office door and within seconds Doc Slack had got a specimen for analysis. He took it along the corridor to the Medical Officer of Health's office.

"Come in, Worshipful Master," said Doc Slack in mock homage, referring to the coming evening's rituals at the Masonic Hall.

Without a word James Pickering-Eaden handed him the specimen.

"Still warm, Town Clerk," he said, his face impassive as he received it. "However did you manage it? I see you managed to resist the charms of the 1949 Health and Efficiency. Didn't pop out for a copy of the Sun, did you and scrutinise page three?"

"No, I didn't," said the Town Clerk. He was feeling slightly embarrassed by the Medical Officer of Health's question about the derivation and delivery of the specimen and the doctor's joke about The Sun spelled an entirely different aspect to him. He was thinking more of page one than page three. "And anyway," he continued, "I thought your profession was trained to put people at their ease and not dwell on unsavoury matters such as sperm counts."

"Quite so," said his colleague, hardly able to keep a smile from flirting round his lips, "I am sorry if I embarrassed you. Worshipful Grand Master Elect, I look forward to seeing you again this evening. Let's hope we shall have an evening to remember."

The Town Clerk returned to his office and was not pleased to see the safe wide open with five sealed tenders at view, replete with a certain item of lady's underwear, but thankfully he had remembered to drop the Yale lock so his macabre fetish was safe. He did not really want his Deputy Town Clerk, a pedantic old failed barrister by the name of Roy Owen to find them so he hastily closed the safe. However, he knew that he had to grasp the nettle of the sealed tenders so he took a piece of paper from his file and without a second thought he culled five prices out of the air and wrote them on a piece of memo paper. His five prices ranged from £13,345,072.85 to £18,793,065.98 and just for good measure he made two of them exactly the same giving the impression of collusion. A nice touch, he thought, and poured himself a Glenfiddich. He did not like to drink during the day but he was living on a

The Lodge Meeting

knife-edge these days. At the precise moment of raising the antique rhoemmer to his lips the bell of his private telephone line rang and it was Cheryl snatching a moment to 'phone from Cornwall to make his day with a few loving words. Of course, he harked back to his previous sharing of Glenfiddich after the Special Council meeting and the rest of the day he walked on air.

The taxi called at half past six. Celia had laid out his Masonic regalia and although she was not allowed to be present at the ceremony she was pleased for him. Their marriage had gone smoothly over the years and she felt that the support she had shown him had enabled him to attain his potential. That it had been slightly boring for James Pickering-Eaden did not occur to her and as their long years together had not been threatened she gave no thought to her husband's equanimity. Had she known the Town Clerk was utterly devoted to his nubile Administrative Assistant Grade III and was in terrible trouble occasioned by cavorting on the Mayoral 'Chez Lon Gue' and that he was on the brink of a major breach of local government law in relation to sealed tenders did not enter her Wella permed head. She merely set out his regalia in impeccable fashion, daringly added a spoonful of Curacao to the cocoa that she had prepared for his return and settled down with a good Jeffery Archer novel to await his return. She knew the order of things for Lodge Night. The Town Clerk would arrive home at any time. He would never drive. He left by taxi. If the meeting finished early or late – or he was detained talking either complicated Council business or complete rubbish he would make an instantaneous decision as to his method of return. If the evening was fine and he felt fit, he would walk home via Brentford Woods, over Girton Top, skirting Sunflower Hill Estate and drop down to their home at the bottom of Cunningham Hill. If he felt tired, or the weather was inclement, he would 'phone for a taxi. So, the Town Clerk's departure taxi arrived and he went off to the Masonic Hall. Celia settled down with her knitting and her Jeffery Archer novel and, just to be daring, put a teaspoonful-and-a-half of Curacao in the cocoa ready for James' return whatever hour that might be. That this whole performance of Freemasonry was arcane and anachronistic occurred to the Town Clerk from time to time but he put it to the back of his mind. It was merely a gentleman's club and the Social Committee did some fine works in deprived areas of the Borough.

The Town Clerk enjoyed the celebrations and the pomp of his installation

The Town Clerk

as Worshipful Grand Master. He did not put any great truck on it but he had a good regard for the principles of freemasonry and the fact that great good was done in a covert way by his Lodge. Unfortunately, though, there were some members of his Lodge who used the brotherhood for their own ends, a small minority perhaps but it sometimes left a bad taste in his mouth when members tried to use other brothers to influence their own business. One of these pests was Alfred G Page, the franchise holder for the Majolta car builders, a new government subsidised cheap car from, unbelievably, Moldavia. The Town Clerk used to get the hard sell from Alfred G Page each week at the Lodge but easily resisted Alfred G Page's attempts to inveigle the Town Clerk into assigning the Town's fleet of vehicles – Mayoral limousine, dustcarts, building works lorries, official cars into the economy of Moldavia, wherever that might be. He had once had the misfortune to ask Alfred G Page what the G stood for but was told that it did not stand for anything but was inserted for emphasis, rather like (and the Town Clerk unfortunately instantly forgot) a famous film personality. Try as he may he could not remember who the famous personality was and, although intrigued, he did not relish asking Alfred G Page. Later he thought that film personality might have been David O Seltznick but he wasn't sure and he did not want to ask Alfred G Page as it certainly would have resulted in the hard sell followed up by a visit by the area concessionaire groaning under a welter of leaflets concerning everything from the Majolta whirlwind to the Majolta dustcart. Also he knew that Mr Page would then regale him with the tyrekicker's tale. Apparently Alfred G Page used to flout the law (which was unfortunately administered by the local authority) by trading on the Sunday. Already fined many times he nevertheless continued trading hoping that the number of sales of the new Moldavia Majolta would outweigh the fines imposed. Unfortunately, though, Alfred G Page had more 'tyrekickers' than genuine punters on a Sunday and continued to lose money. For anyone who cared to listen, Alfred G Page would inveigh against tyrekickers – the lookers and touchers and dooropeners of the car industry – whose sole occupation, it seemed was to visit as many car salesrooms as they could on a Sunday and kick tyres, without intending to spend even a penny, and certainly not on a Moldavian Majolta.

It was the Town Clerk's misfortune that it fell to Alfred G Page to propose him for the office of Provincial Grand Master and in his supporting speech

The Lodge Meeting

there were a few transparent hints that the worthy burgers of Middlethwaite would do well to consider the fleet of the Moldavian Majolta. Uncorrupt as ever, the Town Clerk (who was wrestling with his inner conscience at the time regarding the sealed tenders) promised Alfred G Page that although he could not promise anything and was supremely grateful to Alfred G Page for taking one of the new units at the second phase of Water's Edge Business Park, he would, at least, visit one of his showrooms one Sunday and 'kick a few tyres'. This part of his acceptance speech brought the house down, quite unexpectedly and the Town Clerk surmised that most of his fellow brothers had been similarly canvassed on behalf of the Moldavian Majolta. He visualised an army of masons descending on the Majolta car salesrooms at the first opportunity, feverishly kicking tyres. He liked the vision for Alfred G Page was not well-liked at all.

The evening flew by. He enjoyed the company of his fellow masons, especially his Council officer-colleagues, most of whom were members of the same lodge. He spent some considerable time with Alan Unwin, who had been his pupil and articled clerk many years ago in his former authority. Alan was never quite cut out for the dry-as-dust legislation of the Council Solicitor's Department but the Town Clerk had mothered him through his articles and, on qualifying, Alan had left and had set up and built up a flourishing criminal practice with many branches in the North of England. Alan knew that without James Pickering-Eaden's sympathetic handling and encouragement, he would never have qualified and gone on to such a satisfying and diverse legal practice. So the two men spent a long time swopping legal anecdotes and the Town Clerk was able, with the help of many glasses of liquor, to put the thoughts of his 'little local difficulty' with the Mayor on the back burner.

He had a happy time talking to the Rector of St Mary's, the Reverend John Savage. Before the Mayor's Sunday he had not been aware of the Rector's relationship to 'Bramble the Ramble' and, as they chatted, he found out how she had inveigled the Rector in selecting the Mephibosheth reading at the Mayor's Sunday. Together they relived the memory of the Mayor's bottom set sliding along the aisle after the fifth Mephibosheth. It was even more amusing with each telling of the story for the Rector was ideally positioned in Church that day to see the course of the projected missile.

"Jim," he said, "I was sitting directly in line behind him," he said slurring slightly for he had been no stranger to the wine that night, "the bottom set

The Town Clerk

shot out, hit the kneelers by the pulpit and it seemed to gather speed as it shot down the centre aisle. It was like the pinball machine that I used to play when I was a boy as it clattered into the pew-ends, pinging each one, as it seemed to gather speed as it got halfway down the aisle although it was going slightly uphill. I must admit I had many un-Christian thoughts after the service especially as I knew I was a bit naive in allowing my Aunt Eunice to talk me into the Mephibosheth reading. But quite honestly, Jim, I don't think that I am Bishop material – all I want to be is a parish priest so I don't think any great harm has been done. I also don't think that our Mayor will ever become a scion of the Christian church but I also don't think there were any great odds on his recruitment even before Mephibosheth."

Clearly this was a story that would become more embellished over the years. Nearby Barnsley Town Hall was opened by the then Prince of Wales in 1936 and it was said that he asked the then Mayor how many people worked in the Town Hall and the Mayor replied "About half of them..." but this story has been told about most of the public buildings that he – and successive royalty – have opened over the years.

Later in the evening the Town Clerk was buttonholed by Doc Slack, the Medical Officer of Health, "I was pleased with your condition, Jim, he said but there is just one small point. I sent your specimen straight down to the laboratory and according to the analyst there are one or two little buggers swimming around in the milky stuff. I did tell you at the time that it wasn't always one hundred percent effective but as I know Celia has since had a hysterectomy, I don't suppose you'll want me to do anything about it. If you do, let me know." The Town Clerk was assured that chances of fertilisation were minimal as there were only 'a few little buggers' swimming around but it did raise another aspect for him to consider.

"Just what are the chances, Josh?" he queried.

"Well I was going to say none at all, Jim," was the reply, "but there are more swimmers than I would have thought and, had Celia not been 'doctored', I think I may have had you in for another look but I don't think there's any chance of a junior James making an appearance so I'll just tell you that you are an extremely healthy man and keep on ... not ... taking the tablets." He seemed to think this was a very funny joke, laughed uproariously, spun on his heels and went to the bar to replenish his glass.

The evening wore on and the convivial atmosphere relaxed the Town Clerk

The Lodge Meeting

to the point that his foreboding over the sealed tenders, due to be revealed to the Mayor at the imminent cricket match had been subdued by the many and varied drinks that had been bought by the brothers for their new Worshipful Grand Master. One by one the brothers took their leave of him until there was only Colin Turner, the Director of Transportation and Technical Services (he used to be called the Borough Engineer) left. He lived in the same direction as the Town Clerk and they usually shared a taxi home, or accompanied each other home if they decided to walk. It was nearly midnight. They took a look at the balmy evening and decided to walk the evening's excesses off. It was only about two miles for each of them as they eventually set off. They strode purposefully through the dark back streets of Middlethwaite, breasted Girton Ridge, talking all the time of their jobs, their families and the evening's happenings.

"Look at this, Jim," said Colin and produced a small silvery cylinder barely a half-inch in diameter and three inches long. There was a mesh at the top. "What do you think it is?"

The Town Clerk took it and examined it closely. He could feel calibrations down the side but would make no guess as to its use. To tell the truth, he was not terribly interested in technical matters and handed it back to the Borough Engineer. He still thought of Colin Turner as the Borough Engineer and, although he had had a major expansion of his title, his duties were the same as the Borough Engineers of old. He was a small fat man who was enthusiastic about his job. He lived and breathed his work as Director of Transportation and Technical Services. Unlike the Town Clerk who liked to retain his old-style title, Colin Turner was excited by every new innovation and development in the technical field. It was said he took his Sewer Manual to bed with him and for 'light' reading switched easily to Street Lamps, their Development and Control. He would speak enthusiastically of pollution control and liked nothing more than squeezing his inappropriate frame down a manhole cover and having a tour underneath Middlethwaite. Once in the middle of Middlethwaite Market he had got wedged in a manhole whilst descending the sewers and his ganger had been sent down a nearby manhole on the same circuit to either shove him up or drag him down. Eventually he popped like a Laurent Perrier champagne cork but successive tellings of the tale could not be certain whether he went up or down so it's probable that the tale is apocryphal anyway.

113

The Town Clerk

It had been a matter of extreme disappointment to Colin Turner when responsibility for sewers had been taken from him and handed over to the newly privatised Water Companies and the National Rivers Authority. He had to liaise closely with these bodies and still liked a 'sewer tour' as he called it. He was very helpful to the Town Clerk in the development of the infrastructure of Water's Edge Business Park and shared the Town Clerk's enthusiasm for filling it. He could not wait to get on with the detailed work in respect of the Second Phase and his keen grasp of the problems and their solutions were vital to James Pickering-Eaden. He was like a boy with a new toy with anything new in the field of technology and, if the Town Clerk sometimes found him slightly boring, he was patient with him for he valued him as a friend and colleague.

Colin Turner took the small metal object from the Town Clerk, flicked it imperceptibly in a downward manner and all of a sudden the still night air was filled by the sound of a man speaking. "Although I may visit one of Alfred G Page's showrooms one Sunday and kick a few tyres..." and the man's voice being drowned by hearty laughter. It was, of course, a recording of the events earlier in the evening and the Town Clerk was amazed at the clarity and volume of the device.

"It is frightening, Jim, about today's technology. I was three rows from you but still managed to record this. Impressive isn't it?" He showed Jim how it worked.

"Can I borrow this, Colin?" said the Town Clerk.

"You can have it, Jim. A representative gave one of my technical officers a demonstration this week, and although we were impressed, there was no way we could use it. It smacks of Big Brother slightly but I thought I would record you tonight, especially when you made those pithy comments about Alfred G Page, that obnoxious prat. Funny thing, Jim, it's probably obsolete by now for already I've seen two more sophisticated devices. Soon technology will be able to read your mind, in fact bank scanning machines can already verify your palmprint and eye input. It's frightening, Jim, isn't it? I bet that long-legged Mrs Oldroyd will soon be able to slap your face when she can tell what you're thinking!"

Initially shocked by the accidental perception by his colleague, it set the Town Clerk thinking of his love languishing in Cornwall.

A germ of an idea was beginning to seed in the Town Clerk's mind and as

The Lodge Meeting

he laughed at Colin Turner's description of Alfred G Page he rightly surmised that he too must have been canvassed by Alfred G in respect of gully-emptiers and dustcarts which no doubt could be made better by the Majolta Company of Moldavia.

By this time the two men had reached Girton Top and had skirted Sunflower Hill Estate. Their routes diverged at this point and they bade each other goodnight. The Town Clerk was only about half-a-mile from home, dropping down the ridge and into the valley where he lived with Celia. As he breasted the rise he was aware of rustling in some nearby bushes. He quickened his step but it was no good. Within moments he was surrounded by about a dozen youths, dressed in garish clothing, baseball caps worn back-to-front, and with an assortment of hairstyles ranging from mohican to pineapple. One had an aerosol can and he squirted it in the direction of the Town Clerk.

"Have a sniff of this, suit!" he said.

The Town Clerk threw himself sideways and diverted the aerosol squirt over his shoulder. He was frightened but did not want to show it, he was grateful for his military training but he was heavily outnumbered. The Town Clerk reeled backwards and caught the second squirt full in the face. Another youth came out of some bushes and lashed into the Town Clerk with a karate kick in the ribs which took all the wind out of him. There was a small bonfire lighted nearby and another youth took a stick from the fire, holding it above him as he lay writhing on the ground.

"What 'ave we got 'ere," he said, as the flame illuminated him, "a proper suit. Don't he look bleeding silly in those striped trousers."

Two young girls came out of the bushes, barely fifteen and wearing microskirts. One, very high on solvents or dope, hitched her skirt high and sat plumb on the Town Clerk's face as he writhed on the ground. "Fancy some young crumpet, do you – you dirty old man?"

"Kick him in the bollocks," said another and another youth tried to do so but the Town Clerk parried the blow and took it on the top of his thigh. The aerosol can was back again and squirted full into the Town Clerk's face. Momentarily he passed out. Karate Kick had another go at him and James Pickering-Eaden lay distraught on the ground. He decided to stay put as he lay on his small attachÈ-case which carried his Freemason's chain and medals. He pushed the gadget that Colin Turner had given him down his

115

The Town Clerk

trouser pocket for safety. He played dead and the gang of gluesniffers were beginning to bore at having brought him down. Most of them drifted off, not at all concerned at any grievous damage they may have done to him.

The two young girls shouted to the rest of the gang "Come on, back into the bushes, we'll have some more sniffs, we've got some E and some shit. We'll go down to the Sunflower, nick a car and torch it."

The boys were no doubt attracted to this menu put before them and as he lay prone, the Town Clerk thought of the Mayor's tirade at the golf course and, bleeding from many cuts, tried to work out the Mayor's theory that the Town Clerk was responsible for this social deprivation. No doubt the Mayor was at that moment either watching some rubbish on television or throwing ten pints of Tetley's down his throat at Hollowdene Working Men's Club. Meanwhile, the Town Clerk lay bleeding on Girton Top.

"Look at that stupid bleeding suit laying there, let's leave him and go torching," said Pineapple Haircut.

The Town Clerk heard all this and thought about the depravities of youth. Despite his injuries and pain from every part of his body he knew from his experience that these youngsters were not representative of youth in the Borough of Middlethwaite for he was involved with many considerate and talented youngsters. He lay on the ground smarting from his injuries. He had heard about these yobs and knew there were conclaves throughout the Borough. It had been impossible to do anything for them. Scores of apologists had made excuses for them over the years but the problem was as intractable as ever. The Council had spent vital funds converting a pub that had been closed through lack of customers and had then been vandalised. They had converted it into a drop-in centre for young unemployed and local businesses had donated a considerable amount of money in fitting it out. Within a month it had been burnt out and had returned to being a gluesniffers' den. The Town Clerk knew of many other places but did not realise that there was one so close to his route home. The Council had had trouble with vandalism and wanton destruction and he thought that the ghettos of Middlethwaite were becoming an eyesore but he could see no solution to it and, truth to tell, he had skirted around the problem regarding it as insoluble and distancing himself from it. Now, as he lay on the ground he was more closely involved than ever he thought he would be or wanted to be.

When everything had been quiet for about half-an-hour he took stock. He

The Lodge Meeting

could not open his eyes, the squirt from the aerosol can had temporarily blinded him. His ribs ached, his testicles were sore and he had bruises all over his body. Slowly he sat up but as he did so Karate Kick came back, together with Pineapple Haircut. He put his foot again into the Town Clerk's ribs but this time the Town Clerk had had time to get his breath back and, with odds a bit more even, he managed to catch Karate Kick's foot, although the leather case in which he carried his Masonic regalia slipped out and snapped open. His chain glistened in the moonlit night, the shields of the previous holders etched in script on the silver-gilt embellishments. Pineapple Haircut picked it up and swung it round his head but as he did so the Town Clerk swivelled round and caught his ankles in a vice-like grip between his own. Pineapple Haircut pitched forward onto his face into a holly bush, got up and ran out of sight. The odds were now too much against him and he wanted no more of it. The holly bush had made a mess of Pineapple Haircut's face. Not only were there concentric bloody tramlines across his face but a hundred or so single piercings of his face, each being mapped by a large globule of blood. Karate Kick now had hold of the Masonic chain of office but the Town Clerk, although injured, was fit from his Territorial Army training and a one-against-one situation was now definitely in his favour despite his injuries. He rolled over, grabbed Karate Kick but the Masonic chain broke and fell into two halves. There was now just the two of them. The Town Clerk at forty-eight filled with moral indignation at his treatment was one-to-one against Karate Kick who "couldn't give a fuck." It was now no contest. The Town Clerk sat astride him, his knees on the youth's shoulders pinning him helplessly to the floor.

"No mister, please don't..." he pleaded, but the Town Clerk, resentful of his treatment that had by now lasted all of an hour, clenched his knuckles and hit Karate Kick straight on the nose and mouth, blood, bits of teeth, flesh splattered all over. It was just one punch but it settled the score. He then proceeded to give Karate Kick a bloody good hiding, a good hiding the Town Clerk thoroughly enjoyed meting out. His final act was to put his foot into Karate Kick sending him spinning down the copse and Karate Kick landed aching from every part of his body a hundred feet below.

The Town Clerk gathered up the two halves of the ceremonial chain as Karate Kick rose, spitting blood and chipped teeth and colourful mucus all over the place. With renewed energy the Town Clerk bounded down the

The Town Clerk

copse and grabbed hold of the slobbering Karate Kick. The Town Clerk was now in the ascendancy and he pondered his next move. Would it be the police? The next few moments decided him.

He heaved Karate Kick to his feet. "Police, for you," he said, "and you can get ready to tell them the names of all your associates," he thought quickly that Karate Kick would not understand this word so he said, "all the yobs and scrubbers that infest this sniffing den with you." To his surprise Karate Kick remonstrated.

He was having trouble talking, his nose was broken and his teeth had been forced into his tongue, "I don't fink so, mister," he said, "I'll get my granddad onto you." Karate Kick tried to identify 'suit' but couldn't do so as by now the moon had been obscured and Karate Kick's vision had been blurred by blood and sweat.

"Why, what's your name?" said the Town Clerk putting the youth's arm up his back until he responded.

"My name's Craig Ullathorne and my granddad's got a bigger chain than you have. He's Mayor of Middlethwaite and he'll do for you. He's got control of this town and if I find out who you are, my granddad will see to you."

This took the Town Clerk temporarily off his guard and Karate Kick wrenched free of him and was gone running down the hillside at the speed of the wind.

Fate had conspired against James Pickering-Eaden. Slowly he got himself together and felt his aches and pains. He found the broken chain of office and restored it to its leather case. Painfully he limped the last part of his journey home and let himself in. Celia had long since gone to bed. There was an empty bottle of Curacao on the dresser and Celia was snoring deeply as he eased himself in beside her. At least he would not have to fulfil the duties of husband tonight.

He eased into bed and lay flat on his back. It was painful to turn over but sleep came quickly although throughout the night he was awoken every time he moved.

In the morning he looked a mess. Celia wanted an explanation. She got one but it was far removed from the truth. The truth had rather gone by the wayside in his marriage recently and he was not proud of it. She had been a good wife to him and he did not like the evasions that from time-to-time he had had to employ to continue his affair with his Administrative Assistant

The Lodge Meeting

Grade III. When they awoke in the morning he told her that he was ashamed of himself. Every one of the Lodge members had wanted to buy him a drink to congratulate him on his installation. He had had too much both in quantity and variety of drink. At the end of the evening he did not want to take a taxi home for fear of spewing up in the back. He decided to walk it over his usual route but when he reached Girton Top he had staggered into a low wall and plunged down the embankment. He was lucky to be alive. As the story unfolded he felt proud of it and almost believed it himself. He must write a novel, he thought. With his talent for embroidering the facts he would win the Booker Prize. His chest swelled but there was a sharp pain in his side from the kicks of Pineapple Haircut and Karate Kick so he decided he would stick to Town Clerking.

Celia believed him and was most solicitous. Every time he moved something hurt. When he looked in the mirror he saw there was a mess of blotches and bruises all over. "Kinell," he said.

CHAPTER TEN

THE L.V.A. CRICKET MATCH

The Town Clerk was dreading the day. He ached all over, he had a large swelling in the groin, he was sure that at least one of his ribs was broken. Fortunately his face was unblemished by the solvent attack and outwardly he looked alright but the Town Clerk hurt. Nothing hurt more than his feelings, to be assaulted by a gang of yobs, one of which was in the family of The Worshipful the Mayor of Middlethwaite, Councillor Leslie Ullathorne. He expected more pain today, considerably more pain, although there seemed to be a silver lining appearing. It was – thought the Town Clerk – a very dim silver lining, the un-hallmarked kind of silver. More pewter than silver.

He reached down his old cricket bag and filled it with the equipment that he had garnered over the years. Incredibly, his bat was now forty years old. His father had bought the Dennis Compton bat for his eighth birthday and there was a picture in the family album of James Pickering-Eaden playing an immaculate forward-defensive shot. The angle of the photograph coupled with the fact that the bat was far too large for him contrived to totally obscure him behind his 'Dennis Compton'. The bat remained his prize possession and he intended using it today.

The Mayor's side contained a few officers who could play a bit and some of the Mayor's cronies. The day dawned cloudless so the Town Clerk's hopes that the fixture might be washed out proved unfulfilled. Robin Armstrong, the Mayor's Secretary, still not happy in the service of The Worshipful the Mayor of Middlethwaite, had written a speech for the Mayor and was sitting with the Town Clerk as the Mayor rose to say the introductory words that he had written. The Mayor threw the prepared speech away and spoke verbatim, lambasting the government. Despite the fact that government money had been poured into the 'deprived' areas of the borough – especially the

121

Sunflower Hill Estate – they might just as well have given tuppence for all the credit they got for it. The Mayor tore into them, unmindful of the fact that it was supposed to be a sporting and non-political occasion.

Halfway through the speech, Robin Armstrong turned to the Town Clerk and said, "You know this speech reminds me of Gilbert and Sullivan written all of one hundred years ago about 'the idiot who praises with enthusiastic tone every century but this and every country but his own'." The Town Clerk agreed wholeheartedly but dutifully applauded at the end of the Mayor's tirade.

The Town Clerk had witnessed another tirade by the Mayor. He had hardly been aware of Councillor Leslie Ullathorne before he became Mayor of Middlethwaite. He thought he was just an inoffensive time-server who would glory in his year of Mayoralty and then submerge back into obscurity. He never imagined that he would be capable of tirades such as this. He had obviously nursed these grievances for years and now the swift conversion from Barnsley Bitter to gin had loosened the Mayor's tongue. Robin Armstrong remarked on this to the Town Clerk. The Town Clerk thought back to the Mayor's recital at the eighteenth hole at last week's Sidney Hebblethwaite Trophy match and he wanted to tell the Mayor's Secretary of his amazing précis of the foibles and fallibilities of the Council officers, but regretfully he could not do so without letting the whole situation out of the bag. He actually chuckled as he thought back to the Mayor's invectives against the council officers. He had just about lashed every department with his spiteful tongue and used about every invective in his summing-up of their worth.

The Town Clerk had enjoyed previous matches against the Licensed Victuallers Association. The Licentious Villains had a few old professional players who had taken pubs after retiring from the game and, like all old professionals in most sports, played the game for real. There was no such thing as a friendly. Similarly the Council team had the nucleus of a good side, particularly from the Leisure Services Department. There was, of course, a new Leisure Centre on the drawing board which, the Town Clerk thought, just might figure in the day's conversation. The make-up of the teams included a previously agreed mix of nine good players and the figurehead players of the Mayor and Town Clerk on one side whilst the President and Secretary of the Licensed Victuallers Association on the other side could

The L.V.A. Cricket Match

hardly hold a bat, let alone swing it. After the introductory speech the Mayor and the local President, tossed the coin for the start of play, the Mayor won and the Council team was to bat.

It was tradition that the Mayor opened the batting. Since he had beaten the Town Clerk in the golf match for the Sidney Hebblethwaite Trophy he now looked on himself as the Ian Botham of the cricket world. He even gave a team talk beforehand, theatrically locking the dressing room door behind him in case the Licentious Villains should be listening. He took the field immaculately attired, his whites held up by the requisite old school tie.

"I'll give you a laugh, Jim," said the Mayor's Secretary to the Town Clerk, "when Ullathorne arrived today he had got together his whites, lovely sweater, long cream trousers held together with cream belt and cricket boots and cap. When he arrived he saw all the others with trousers held up, as is tradition, by a tie. So he threw off the cream belt and demanded I supply him with a striped tie to hold his trousers up with. I could only go along with his wishes so I lent him mine. He was as pleased as punch as he went out to toss up. I wonder if he realised he was wearing the tie of an Old Etonian? You know how he feels about privilege especially after today's tirade, it'll be a laugh watching him today. I think I may tell him after the match about the tie. On second thoughts I may tip the wink to the reporter from the Middlethwaite Gazette, he could get a bit of lineage payment from Peterborough of the Daily Telegraph – don't you think it would make a nice little story? Did you know the tie was handed down my family by my father and grandfather who were both Conservative M.P.'s? Wouldn't he be ragged at Hollowdene Working Men's Club – the Mayor wearing an Old Etonian tie?"

As the Mayor opened the batting the first ball was delivered by his opposing captain, the President of the Licensed Victuallers' Association. It was a full toss designed to give the Mayor a run to get off the mark. Unfortunately, the Mayor missed it completely and his stumps were spread-eagled but the umpire was quick off the mark as he foresaw the implications of the Mayor being bowled for a duck, "No ball," he shouted, just in time. He had been treated to one of Ullathorne's fiercest glowers and even the world's number one umpire, Dickie Bird, who was born in nearby Barnsley would not have had the courage to give the Worshipful the Mayor of Middlethwaite, Councillor Leslie Ullathorne out first ball. The next ball was duly despatched for a four by the Mayor due to a timely misfield by the Secretary of the

123

The Town Clerk

Licensed Victuallers' Association. Councillor Leslie Ullathorne was bowled neck and crop by the next ball but strode back to the pavilion having scored four runs, his trousers hoisted aloft by the Old Etonian tie.

"You're in number six Town Clerk, and I want you to play straight down the line and let Bill Aylward score the runs from the other end." He then gave his instructions to Bill Aylward (who had had three seasons in Surrey Colts as a youth) for the Mayor was playing the game for real and these Licentious Villains had to be beaten today.

Eventually the Town Clerk batted at number six. He scored twelve and was well satisfied with his efforts, especially in view of all his injuries, for his Dennis Compton bat had flicked a couple of leg glances for four. The ex-pro's of the other team were bowling well but at 86 for 4 the Mayor's XI was in a position to make a decent score. As he ached all over he was satisfied, he couldn't swing the ball to leg due to his pain from the ribs whilst his off-drive was curtailed by the bruises in his fore-arm caused by the attention of Karate Kick and Pineapple Haircut. As he came off the field his captain met him on the pavilion steps.

"I think you were a bit too soon with the shot, Mr Eaden-Pickering," getting the Town Clerk's name the wrong way round as usual. "If you had had your elbow higher and had played forward instead of playing back you could have thrashed that long hop through the covers instead of getting a nick and being caught behind."

The Town Clerk was astounded. Here he was getting a reprimand from the Mayor who had been out first ball, reinstated courtesy of the umpire's "No ball" shout, been gifted a four second ball and had been out third ball. And the reason the Town Clerk had only scored twelve was because he had been given a good kicking from the Mayor's grandson the night previous.

He tried to ameliorate the situation, "I'm sorry, Mr Mayor. I'll do better when we field," he said. He was feeling the humiliation.

Before the Mayor batted James Pickering-Eaden had lent the Mayor his bat. "This is the bat, Mr Mayor, with which I scored 131 for the Combined Universities in 1970 against the Free Foresters. You are welcome to use it." The Mayor looked at it closely and, after it passed the most stringent examination had gone out and scored his four runs. "Not much of a bat, I am afraid, Town Clerk," he had said on his return from the crease. "I think it is slightly warped, or I would not have played the shot that I did, Town Clerk," he said.

The L.V.A. Cricket Match

The Mayor's XI innings had progressed steadily and after the Town Clerk had been dismissed the Mayor said to the Town Clerk within everyone's hearing, "I think we ought to have a few moments alone to plot the downfall of these Licentious Villains. What do you say about a stroll round the boundary?"

It was the moment the Town Clerk had dreaded. "Here, Mr Mayor," he said, throwing his bat to him. "We must look decorous on our perambulatory stroll round the boundary. Take Dennis Compton as a walking stick." The Town Clerk foraged in his cricket bag for his second bat and the two men strolled around the boundary ropes in tandem, the Mayor (resplendent in Old Etonian tie) acknowledging his cronies by a deft wave of the Town Clerk's bat, as if he had just scored a century at the Adelaide Oval. He was enjoying every moment and milking the office of Mayor.

Eventually they reached the sightscreen. "Now, Town Clerk, we've been fucking around long enough, 'as tha got the prices of the sealed tenders for the new Sports Centre?" Without a word the Town Clerk handed him a scrap of paper with five prices ranging from £13,345,072.85 to £18,793,065.98 – two of which were identical down to the last penny.

The Mayor glanced swiftly down the list of five prices noticing immediately that two were identical. "You know, Town Clerk, there is no morality these days in local government," said the Mayor.

The Town Clerk was astounded at this switch of moral rectitude but the Mayor continued, "Have you noticed that two of these tender prices are identical down to the last penny? There must have been collusion. I think it is disgraceful. You can't trust anybody in local government these days.." he said it without blushing and the Town Clerk was amazed at the gall of the man. The Town Clerk was feeling uncomfortable and wanted to get away from the embarrassing situation, but the Mayor had not finished with him.

"Right we've got that out of the way. This is the next thing. Marston's Brewery have been very good to me by sponsoring my Mayoralty at various functions. I want them to have the liquor licence for the new Sports Centre and while they are about it they may as well have the licences for all the other Council bars as well. See to it ..." So, that was it, thought the Town Clerk. That was why we were drinking Marston's Light at the Mayor-Making. This Mayor was going to milk the Mayoralty for all he could during his year of office.

He tried to remonstrate but he knew he would be wasting his breath, "Mr

The Town Clerk

Mayor," he said, "the tender will be advertised publicly and there is no way I can influence it. As for the other facilities they are tied up with existing contracts and ...."

The Mayor cut him short, fixed him with the weasly look that the Town Clerk new well by now, "Just fucking get it done," he said simply.

The Mayor was not finished, he launched into the Town Clerk again. "This bloody lone Conservative Councillor, Mrs Bramble. You've got to get her off my back. She's a vicious old cow. You've got to get her off my back, do you understand? If I go down, Town Clerk," he said ominously, "I'll take thee with me. Do you understand?" The Town Clerk had been silent all the time and kept his equanimity under the force of the Mayor's latest tirade but he was about to receive another one as vitriolic as the golf course lambasting. They had by now reached the elm tree opposite the pavilion. The Mayor sat on the rustic seat in the shade of the spreading branches. "Sit down," he said, "you've got more to come." The Town Clerk joined him and they sat together hands resting atop their respective cricket bats.

"Alright, Town Clerk, this is my chance to get even with you lot. You lot at the Town Hall who are pinching money, getting good pay for no effort. Us Mayors have always had our fingers in the pot. I could tell you a few things about my predecessors. One of them treated all his pals for years afterward with all the money he made, another used his Mayoral limousine as a passion-wagon. He told me he had had twelve bits of local crumpet in the back seat of the Mayoral car. Well, Mister Bloody Town Clerk, I am making sure that this Mayor will come out made for life. And you can't do anything about it since my Solicitor has got that video of you a-shagging on my Chez Lon Gue." The Town Clerk had been silent throughout the latest tirade, he looked across at the Mayor and was filled with distaste for him, he was a sniffling little runt he thought. As the wickets fell the Mayor and Town Clerk resumed their slow perambulation around the boundary. The tirade continued but the Town Clerk still did not rise to the bait and kept quiet.

Eventually the Mayor could stand it no longer. "I know I've got you by the bollocks, Eaden-bloody-Pickering but I didn't have you down as a quitter. We've walked round this boundary and I've goaded you, I've teased you and I've insulted you. And you've said nothing ... have you nothing to say?"

The Town Clerk had bided his time, "Yes, I have, Mr Mayor. I want you to look at this and listen to it also." He took his cricket bat, pressed a lever by

The L.V.A. Cricket Match

the handle, there was a slight whirring noise and – clear as a bell – came the voice of the Mayor, "I want Marston's Brewery to have the licence for the new Sports Centre, see to it ... get that old cow Bramble off my back ... one of my predecessors as Mayor had twelve bits of local crumpet in the back of the Mayoral car ..." The Town Clerk deftly pressed the calibrated switch and was adept in selecting by fast forwarding to the very best of the "Incriminating Ullathorne" tape.

"Quite a clever device this Mr Mayor, I had it installed into the handle of my cricket bat. I have to think that we are just about square, don't you, Mr Mayor?" It was not ideal, he pondered, two local government figureheads at each others throats but he knew that he was dealing with someone who was determined to capitalise on the office of Mayor and would not brook any interference. At least he had something on his adversary and knew that the Mayor could not play his hand without endangering his own position. He had known thirty Mayors during his local government, of every shade of political hue and with varying degrees of intelligence. Some had got carried away by being installed as First Citizen. Some had only just about managed to get through their year of Mayoralty without any scandal breaking but the Town Clerk knew that this man Ullathorne was a different kettle of fish. He was devious and cunning and greedy and had learned from his first taste of Mayoralty and must not be underestimated.

Slowly the two men resumed their perambulations around the boundary in complete silence save for a few barely audible "Kinells," from the Mayor. It was the Town Clerk's turn to feel his opponent squirm and he was quite enjoying it, despite being in considerable pain from his assault at the hands of the yobs in the hills above Sunflower Hill Estate. The Mayor's XI was all out for 168 and the Licensed Victuallers had little difficulty in knocking off the runs. Throughout their innings the Mayor as captain ordered the Town Clerk to field at the far extremities of the boundary. He did not let him bowl even one over. At the end of the innings he ached all over but had a deal of satisfaction that he and the Mayor were perhaps level on points. The Mayor was not pleased and the celebrations afterwards hosted by Marston's Brewery were muted.

127

CHAPTER ELEVEN

LIEBFRAUMILCH

The following day things took an unexpected turn. James Pickering-Eaden was headhunted. Marked "Private and Confidential" the morning post brought an application form from New Elms Development Corporation. The advertised post of Clerk and Chief Executive suited him down to the ground as it was a position combining the administration of the legal complexities of a new corporation and the brief also stressed the importance of some entrepreneurial capabilities to entice national, local and multi-national firms to the newly developed-area of New Elms. Flushed with the success of Water's Edge Business Park in Middlethwaite and coupled with the fact that he had for some considerable time guided successive local authorities without any hint of malpractice or scandal, the Town Clerk rightly considered he was a major candidate for the post which was advertised in a salary range from £105,000-130,000 per annum. It seemed they wanted someone with the panache of Richard Branson and the dry-as-dust personality but administrative skills of the Governor of the Bank of England and whilst not allying himself with personalities of that level, James Pickering-Eaden thought that he must have a favourite's chance of being appointed. The Town Clerk had seen the post advertised in "The Municipal Journal" and had thought it suited him down to the ground. But this was different for the invitation to apply came from a firm of Recruitment Consultants and the covering letter gave him the impression that he only had to apply and the job was his. Obviously the Recruitment Consultants knew nothing about the Chez Lon Gue video or the Rebuttal Dennis Compton Cricket Bat tapes.

He was tremendously flattered by the invitation and he did not think for one moment of how he was to reconcile his problems, responsibilities and intrigues in Middlethwaite as he buzzed for his Administrative Assistant

129

The Town Clerk

Grade III. Mrs Oldroyd, of course, represented the major obstacle to his application and as she appeared the first doubts were entering his mind.

"Mrs Oldroyd," he said. He was imagining gremlins in the form of concealed video cameras and bugging devices to be present in every nook and cranny. He could not subjugate his feelings completely as she swung towards him wearing the yellow hipster panties, so clever was the Town Clerk on the subject of the Oldroyd Underwear as a study of pantie lines had made him an expert. An illicit kiss followed, the Town Clerk placing his hands firmly round the gracefully curved buttocks of his Administrative Assistant Grade III. She responded eagerly and he could feel himself rising. And so could she. She tenderly traced the form of his erection with her index finger, a beautifully cuticled nail tracing every form of the Town Clerk's manliness. He put his head in his hands.

"Kinell," he muttered under his breath in a tone usually reserved for the twin 'delights' of cocoa and Musk. "Mrs Oldroyd," he said, "please ensure that I am not disturbed for an hour and a half – say I am in a meeting. Even if the Mayor wants me – especially if the Mayor wants me! I have something very important to attend to."

"Certainly, sir, if that is what you want," a smile played around her lips as she wheeled around speedily and swayed her way across the Town Clerk's office. He was quite right about the yellow hipsters, she thought, but then he had had intimate knowledge of most of her lingerie drawer.

He was beginning to take chances in his flirtations with his Administrative Assistant Grade III and he made a mental note to behave himself. If any member of his staff caught him with his hands around the Oldroyd bum the talk would go through the Town Hall like wildfire. If his assistant, Roy Owen, had caught him there would be no problem as the pedantic old barrister would promptly drop dead on the spot.

It took the Town Clerk a few moments to regain his equilibrium. It was always the same when she entered the room. It was always the same whenever he saw her, he was completely besotted by her. But things had to be done and James Pickering-Eaden was never one to abdicate responsibility so he took his pen from his pocket and set about the application form. He fulfilled every requirement for the post in relation to age, experience and qualification. He must get away and make a new start, away from Middlethwaite, away from the Bloody Mayor and away from who? Away from

Liebfraumilch

Celia or Cheryl Oldroyd. He could hardly take both with him. Or perhaps he could embrace the Moslem faith and take two wives with him. But, then he had probably been headhunted for the New Elms job by the Recruitment Consultants because he was a pillar of the establishment so if he turned up with two wives it would hardly square with his curriculum vitae. And, if he were to remuster as a Moslem, why stop at two wives, he was allowed three so why not take 'Bramble the Ramble' with him? After all the Mayor had told him to "get this bloody woman off my back!" He was being silly now but as he re-read his curriculum vitae he thought that New Elms Development Authority might create more problems than it solved. One problem that it would not solve was the Mayor's ace card – his video of the 'Chez Lon Gue'. He carried on with the application form, signed it with a flourish and – just like an examination paper when the candidate had been given one and a half hours to complete the paper – the office door opened at the stroke of completion. It was not the invigilator, it was his inamorata Mrs Cheryl Oldroyd, Administrative Assistant Grade III. She was carrying a briefcase. His mind was on other things.

"Are you available again, sir?" she said.

"For what?" he enquired.

She knew exactly what was in his mind, she knew about his double-entendres and she encouraged them. It turned her on, just as it did him. "Sir," she said in mock humility, "I come here at the behest of the Mayor," she said, "you left your briefcase," putting it down beside the bentwood hallstand, "in the pavilion after the cricket match yesterday. The Mayor asked me to return it to you, personally. He was very charming, Mr Town Clerk, isn't he a charismatic person? He always has a twinkle in his eye when he talks to me." Dropping her voice slightly she continued, "You promised me that we would return for that bottle of Liebfraumilch to the Strines Valley. When?"

Without thinking, and eager for her company, body and out of his mind despite all the problems he immediately said, "Next Thursday." It was a trait he had evolved from the 'ask a busy man' syndrome. He often made instantaneous decisions and worked on the principle that anything was possible and if he said 'Thursday' then Thursday it would be and nothing would come between them. If anything were already fixed for Thursday it would be unfixed and if anything came up that required fixing it would be fixed for any time bar Thursday. It was one of the traits that Cheryl Oldroyd

131

The Town Clerk

admired about the Town Clerk – if he said Thursday it would be Thursday and barring the revelation of the 'Chez Long Gue' video, the death of the Queen or the commencement of the Third World War, it would be Thursday. And she could look forward to it for the intervening days.

And what of the Town Clerk? He picked up his application form and read the eleven pages. It read very well. He must be a strong candidate for the appointment. He re-read every word, thought of the challenge of a new appointment and the prestige of a job of that nature. He thought of the salary of c£100,000 a year. He then thought of the knicker-legs of Cheryl Oldroyd and the way she swayed as she left his office. He thought of the impending return to Strines Valley. He thought of the pendulous breasts and the nipped waist and the Charnos underwear. He took the application form and fed it into the shredder.

He picked up the letter from the Recruitment Consultants, telephoned the principal on his direct line and told him he was not interested. The principal was obviously taken aback and his immediate reaction was to say that if money was a problem he had authority to offer above the minimum starting salary, say £120,000. He also listed some more perks as a sweetener. The Town Clerk said he was tremendously flattered but his mind was made up and if the situation changed he would contact the principal of the Recruitment Consultants again. When pressed for the reasons for refusal he could hardly mention the Dennis Compton tapes, the salacious video or those neat little panties with the hand-stitched gusset .....

He felt better as he watched his application form slowly feed into the rollers and emerge in fine shreds at the other end of the machine. He thought that he had received a back-handed compliment from the Mayor when he had said that he did not think he was a quitter. If he had accepted the New Elms job he would not have been happy leaving so many loose ends. He was sure that some or many would have come back to haunt him and he recalled some occasions in the past when local authorities for which he had worked had appointed officers whose past just did not reconcile with their curriculum vitae and had caught up with them and had come back to haunt them. On one occasion a Leisure Services Manager had been appointed by the name of Ronald Jones and his job application form was so impressive that it got him an interview. At the selection committee there was just one man for the job. He had done everything, had all the right qualifications and had the sort of

Liebfraumilch

personality that fired everybody on the committee with enthusiasm. He was way ahead of all the other candidates and his references were impeccable. Ronald Jones started work in due course but within a short space of time anomalies started showing up, not least when the new Leisure Services noteheadings were received from the printers. It was noticed that Ronald Jones had become Roland Jones, just a printer's error thought the Town Clerk until other things came to light. It transpired after a little in-depth investigation that Ronald (or Roland) Jones had recently come out of Parkhurst after five years sentence for fraud, false accounting, counterfeiting and similar offences and this was the first job he had applied for. He was sacked immediately but the Council paid compensation to Roland/Ronald to hush the matter up and the Town Clerk nearly lost his job for being hoodwinked. Fortunately James Pickering-Eaden was Deputy Town Clerk at the time and escaped censure but he admitted that had he been the Town Clerk he too would have fallen for the Roland/Ronald syndrome as well.

So he watched the shredder chew his application form and thought that he must exorcise his ghosts before even thinking about anything similar. He wondered what would have happened had the offer been made a couple of months previously when he was untainted. No doubt he would have taken the job but how would he feel if he had lost these moments of joy with Cheryl Oldroyd – the matter was hypothetical and unanswerable. As he sat glassy-eyed watching the shredder his mind was exercising abut exorcising but, he thought, this play on words was doing nothing to clarify the matter, so he was pleased to be interrupted by his Administrative Assistant Grade III. This time she was very businesslike and there was to be no penile stroking as she was accompanied by the Head Messenger.

"Would you sign for this sealed tender, sir," he said.

The Town Clerk did so, watched the delightful bottom depart and thought that, as he did so, the 'poncified Cultural Officer' Adrian Watts might just as intently view the disappearing rear of the Head Messenger. Come to think of it, had not Adrian Watts been instrumental in designing the new uniforms for the Messengers and was not the Head Messenger mincing somewhat? Perhaps his mind was wandering – and it was – it was wandering ahead to Thursday and the thought of Strines Revisited, hope it does not rain or we shall have to shelter in the bothy, although that might be alright anyway cuddling up for some hours ....

The Town Clerk

All of a sudden he had a thought. The sealed tender that had just been delivered was the last that was outstanding for the new Sports Centre. The Mayor had not been very clever for it was obviously the one for which he had been canvassed and, no doubt, adequately rewarded. It was a weak point which the Mayor had overlooked although he had to wait for the other tenders to come in. So the Town Clerk dropped the latch on his door, told his Secretary that he did not want disturbing for ten minutes and went to his cupboard for the electric kettle that was kept for his afternoon tea visitors on occasions. He filled it, waited for it to boil, took his paperknife and as the steam elevated the flap on the Sealed Tender, slid the knife under the flap and flicked it open. He switched off the kettle, put down the paperknife and was just about to withdraw the Tender and Bills of Quantities when he thought 'fingerprints'. He was getting paranoid about security so he took his linen gloves he wore ceremonially as Town Clerk and withdrew the Tender. He was getting excited about all this intrigue for he was about to learn a few answers about the duplicity of Councillor Leslie Ullathorne, the Worshipful the Mayor of Middlethwaite. He purposely did not look at the tendered figure on the bottom line as it bore no relevance to the others he had already received as he did not know the true figures on these and he had simply plucked the other figures out of the air. He folded back the letterheadings and was astounded when he read MAJOLTA LEISURE (Consultant Alfred G Page) on the mast-head of the letter. So that was it, curiouser and curiouser, thought the Town Clerk, what strange bedfellows greed breeds. But his surprises in this direction were not yet over. He reglued the envelope, sat on it for a few moments to ensure a firm seal and placed the envelope in the wall safe, still wearing his gloves. He shut the safe, took off his gloves and then realised that there would be none of his fingerprints on the outside of the envelope. So he re-opened the safe, picked up the sealed tender and put his fingerprints all over the outside of the envelope. He then stood back and wondered exactly why he had gone through this charade so he just shrugged and walked across the room and lifted the latch of his inner door. He sat silent for a few minutes considering this latest twist in his affairs when his 'Nemesis' – the girl who had been instrumental in his slippery slide entered again with some more business for his attention. He looked briefly through the papers and decided that he would dictate some letters to clear his file.

"Ask Miss King to come in, please Mrs Oldroyd", he said, "I want her to

Liebfraumilch

take something down..."

"She'd better not," was the rejoinder and the Town Clerk wondered if this double-entendre had touched a raw nerve with his Administrative Assistant Grade III for her cheeks coloured instantly and she clonked out a lot more noisily than she had clonked in. Not the slightest bit jealous surely...?

The Town Clerk worked hard dictating to his secretary. Not for him the latest technology, he liked to have his papers before him, his mind fully engaged and his secretary taking his instructions down in shorthand. He had to clear his desk as he was missing a day in the office this week and work was tending to pile up. Firstly he had to lay a smokescreen for Thursday by dictating a letter to the Sewage and Purification Sub-Committee of the Association of Metropolitan Corporations saying he would be at their meeting on Thursday. He asked Laura King to type it out straightaway, which she did and returned with it at once. The Town Clerk asked her to get the file from the outer office and whilst she was away fed the newly-typed letter into the shredder. That was his alibi for Thursday duly laid. In the middle of his repetitive work through his in-tray he thought back to how much of a compliment it had been to be headhunted. Had he done the right thing? Who knows? How would it turn out? His next job was to find some reason to delay the opening of the Sealed Tenders at the next meeting of the Leisure Services Committee. That would be harder as the building of the Sports Centre was due to start in the current financial year or else the Middlethwaite Metropolitan Borough Council would lose its government grant and also its grant from the Sports Council. It was imperative that he had this breathing space for the latest bombshell via the Mayor and Alfred G Page had to be considered. He knew it would be all up if the tenders were opened and his false figures supplied to the Mayor were discovered to be not worth the paper they were written on. He knew that the Mayor would be at the meeting as he was an ex-officio member of all Council committees and, short of murdering the man or introducing bubonic plague into his morning coffee, he could see no way out of that problem either. He had a brilliant thought. He would contact Alan Brannan, the Member of Parliament of his former Authority. He had already asked his help in trying to influence the Honours Committee to get an inclusion for the Mayor's Secretary in the next Honours List. This was in hand and he had high hopes that Alan could fix something. He now needed another favour. He would ask Alan who was now a Junior Minister at the

The Town Clerk

Department of Trade and Industry to send some sort of 'waffling' letter from Whitehall asking for more information in respect of the new Sports Centre. It would be a 'something and nothing' letter but the Council could not go ahead and open sealed tenders unless everything was tied up for they might be sued for breach of contract. Later in the day he made a telephone call to Alan Brannan who said that he would arrange it. Alan was a very good friend. He did not ask the reason why James Pickering-Eaden needed the breathing space, he knew that he would tell him all the details when he next saw him. Early the next week the letter duly arrived from Whitehall so the Town Clerk contacted the Chairman of the Building sub-committee of the Leisure Services Committee and the Opening of Tenders was duly deferred another month. That was two favours he owed Alan Brannan and he had to be careful he did not overstep the mark.

The Town Clerk was pleased with the way he had fixed things in that direction. He was very good at it. He used to look at the mountain of his 'IN' tray as a challenge. He would allocate a certain amount of time to it and plough through it at speed, dictating to Miss King or instructing Mrs Oldroyd on practical remedies to the problems emanating from the pile. He would tackle each one as it came to the top of the pile – sometimes his decisions did not come off but those were rare occasions and he always observed the principle that a wrong decision that could be righted was better than a no decision. He leaned back in his chair and thought what a very good Town Clerk he was. He then thought what a bloody mess he was in and then thought he wasn't so good after all.

Meanwhile he resumed dictating to Laura King and, as the adrenaline was flowing in expectation of Thursday ahead, he cleared a lot of outstanding matters. It was just as he dictated the last letter to Miss King that he noticed the briefcases in his office by the bentwood hallstand. There was not one briefcase there. There were two... he froze but did not know why. As he had just about cleared his 'IN' tray, he dismissed his Secretary after dictating one final letter to the Sports Council. Miss King always simpered when he said "Two balls and a bar," meaning a colon and a hyphen and it was just about the nearest he got to being salacious with her and, truth to tell, he had led an exemplary life with his staff until Mrs Oldroyd came along. And then it had taken him eight years to get round to appreciating her fine form. So, James Pickering-Eaden, although not quite a pillar of rectitude was never likely to be

Liebfraumilch

fodder for the legion of 'abuse discoverers' who seemingly found different ways of defining abuse every day. One day a handshake will be defined as manual thumb abuse, he thought, as he sat motionless in his office chair and pondered the existence of two briefcases nestling under the bentwood hallstand.

He remembered that the Mayor had returned a briefcase via Cheryl Oldroyd and she had set it down by the bentwood hallstand. At the time he remembered how she had simpered about how charismatic the Mayor was and how he was so friendly towards her. That's because the mucky sod of a Mayor had viewed her on the video, the Town Clerk thought how wise he had been not to tell his Administrative Assistant Grade III about the Mayor's video, she would have known instantaneously the reason for the glint in his eye. But, unless his reading glasses were creating a double image, there were two briefcases there. All of a sudden that familiar sense of unease was back.

He could stand it no longer and crossed his office. He had very great difficulty in springing the top lock of the invader briefcase as it was bulging. It was almost identical to his own and he could quite understand why the Mayor had delivered it to him via Mrs Oldroyd but the Mayor had made a mistake for it wasn't his. He opened it up and wads of currency sprang out. He was taken aback. There were wads of notes of every denomination, twenty, ten, fifties, even fivers and all in used notes. There must have been fifty thousand pounds there. The Mayor had made no mistake. His Town Clerk was now to be included in the Kickback Stakes but what was he to do about the Faginesque hoard of loot? If he tried to implicate the Mayor it would just mean the peremptory appearance of the video. The briefcase would not fit in the wall safe for which he had the only key, it was only big enough to contain such important items as the Sealed Tenders and the soiled pants of his Administrative Assistant Grade III. So he went into the walk-in safe which contained the council seal and reams of important documents and neatly hid the briefcase behind piles of documents that had been there since the creation of Middlethwaite 108 years ago. So long had some of the old ledgers lain there that they were covered in layers of dust. The Town Clerk moved a pile of ledgers and shoved the briefcase amongst them so it would never be found. It would have to stay there, he thought, until he could work out what to do with it. He then had another thought, went back, took it out again, wiped it clean of fingerprints, put on his white ceremonial gloves and returned the

The Town Clerk

briefcase to its hiding place, thinking that, if necessary, he could lie about it as there were other keyholders of this safe. So that was another one up for the Mayor – previously he had thought him a thicket but he was certainly scoring plenty of points over the supposed intellectual Town Clerk. "Kinell," he thought to himself, what a bloody liability this Mayor is.

Thursday dawned cloudless and there was hardly a breath of air. He had arranged to meet his Administrative Assistant Grade III in the car park of the Waggon and Horses and everything went according to plan. Once again he put all his problems to the back of his mind, there was now one extra, a bulging briefcase full of currency. She was there, looking lovely, slightly before him and slipped easily into the passenger seat of his car. She took his left hand into hers, pushed it upside down between the tops of her legs and made the Town Clerk drive one-handed through all the twists and turns of the Strines Valley. She hitched her skirt high and the Town Clerk could not take his eyes off her milk-white thighs. When it was time for a gearchange he said "third" and Cheryl changed gear with her vacant hand. Once or twice they did not de-clutch in harmony and the car stuttered all over the road but they laughed happily together and the Town Clerk certainly did not complain about the proximity of his hand to the fount of his inspiration and perspiration, the luscious thighs of Mrs Cheryl Oldroyd. Too soon they reached the parking point when it was time to head on foot across the rough terrain. Once again they were the only people in the world and they reached the limpid pool without the intrusion of the hikers this time. They saw the same dog-fox who seemingly recognised them for he made no effort to run as if he knew he was not threatened. They had agreed beforehand that Cheryl would provide the food this time and her selection was more eclectic than the Town Clerk's but still required a fire so he set off to bring the bracken. He had already admitted that he was second-best in the fire-lighting stakes. They had brought another two bottles of wine but the Liebfraumilch was easily retrievable and was chilled to serving temperature. The stone fire-circle that had been built before was still in existence and was lit easily this time due to the firelighters that the Administrative Assistant Grade III had brought.

They were both busy when she said, "How do you see this affair progressing, is there any future to it?" It took the Town Clerk by surprise.

The Town Clerk pondered. There were tears in his eyes as he took her hands in his and over the smoky bonfire he said, "I don't know, I really don't

Liebfraumilch

know. All I do know is that you have given me a pinnacle in my life that I did not envisage ever scaling. I live for the moment I see you every morning, I count the hours when you are away from me. Weekends are worse, when I think of you and your husband together and I count the hours until Monday morning when I see you again in the office. If you don't come in at nine o'clock exactly I am counting the minutes until you come through the door. By nine-fifteen I am a nervous wreck and my mind is in torment thinking how long will you make me wait to see you. I cannot think that I have ever thought this way before. I can only think that because you are on my mind at all times I am deeply in love with you. Sometimes I wake in a cold sweat at night being transmitted down a tragic road with you which has no end and I wake up frightened that you will say "no more." I live just for moments like this and one day I shall tell you exactly how this affair with you has altered my life from a clear well-trodden path to a mountain pass, full of highs and lows and twists and turns, of excitement and desultory moments. I can't think that I have ever had feelings like this and I would not want to have them again with anybody but you. I re-live again our first moment of lovemaking. I know exactly how long it took, every moment of passion that I felt from the moment you entered the room to the final ejaculation. If I live to be an old man I shall remember and cherish every moment of that first embrace. I also can vividly trace every other moment of our lovemaking and I have not the remotest regret that these things have happened. I am not an immoral man but I had no way of resisting the feelings that have flooded through me since our affair and I have not the slightest thought that what I was doing was wrong. I respect my wife and your husband but I have felt a bond between you and I that has transcended any barrier. I cannot tell you some of the hurdles that have come my way since that first remarkable day with your yellow underwear but I want you to know that, not for once, have I considered that our relationship was, in any way, cheap and I have also thought in the depth of night when I have tossed and turned in my bed with my somnolent wife at my side that, if some day I am to be made to pay for our affair then I shall pay, keep my shoulders back straight and emphasise to myself that whatever the price, then you have been worth it and it is a price that I shall willingly and proudly pay..." The Town Clerk had trouble saying the last few sentences. His eyes were red-rimmed, his voice trembling and he had trouble in keeping tears trickling down his cheeks. It was an emotional outburst but he felt that

139

The Town Clerk

the girl was entitled to know his innermost thoughts and he kept nothing back.

It was so emotional that the girl sobbed. She had never realised that her feelings were so intensely and so completely reciprocated. She lay atop her man and they kissed for an eternity. "Please..." she said, "take me now."

He rolled her skirt up and her pants down. He had never had an erection the like before. She lay straddled across him and her vagina was awash with stickiness before he entered her. So fluid was she that he, despite the size of his erection, slipped from her. His hand went down between her legs, retrieved his penis and re-inserted it. As soon as he entered her she came with a climax that was heightened by his descriptions of his feelings for her, the sun on her back and the bottle of Liebfraumilch that they had consumed hastily whilst he had poured his heart out to her. She worked astride him and came again instantaneously.

"Your tits," he said, "your tits". She arched her back, deftly flicked the bra-clip open and her rose-tinted breasts spilled out. He took one in his mouth and sucked the nipple hard, drawing a sharp intake of breath from her, he was still in her and she came again.

Under the hot midday sun there was no controlling her emotions. "Do it, do it," she said, "do it," not knowing quite what she meant.

He flicked her over in one movement keeping himself well entrenched in her as he assumed the top position. He put one hand under each buttock and, not being able to sustain himself any longer came with such a mighty explosion that the red mist behind his eyes deepened to a crimson fog and would not abate. For an eternity juices were spilling from them until they both subsided, the culmination of forty-eight years and twenty-nine years respectively satisfied by this one immense spontaneous demonstration of interaction between male and female perfectly in tune with each other...

The dog-fox laughed atop the nearby hillock. The crows, magpies and hawks wheeled together above the couple. They made an unlikely carousel. The sun blazed down upon the couple as they lay interlinked and as one with the world.

As they walked back at nightfall the words fucking, infancy and Barnsley entered the Town Clerk's mind.

140

CHAPTER TWELVE

THE MAYOR'S PARADE

On the Sunflower Hill Estate an urban fox tried to assail a chicken coop which started the cockerels crowing early on the allotments that proliferated around the perimeter. The cocks aroused the whippets who wanted a walk and the lone donkey, kept illegally in an outhouse of a Council dwelling, added to the urban cacophony.

The Mayor woke early. This was to be his finest hour. He was to be the figurehead, all eyes were to be on him at the head of the procession and that was just as it should be. It was the culmination of his years on the Council, whatever followed didn't matter, a year as Elder Statesman, Deputy Mayor and then finish, he had achieved everything he wanted to do. He lay in bed beside the supine form of the Mayoress and likened the day to the old Roman Gladiatorial days when he was Caesar and everyone was to do his bidding, particularly that 'bloody hyphenated Town Clerk' and his own Secretary who, the Mayor reckoned, did not quite have the degree of servility that the office of Mayor demanded. As he lay there he thought of all the times he had cultivated his electors on the Sunflower Hill Estate by his promises that he would serve them faithfully and that all he was interested in, by being on the Council, was representing them to the best of his ability. What a load of bollocks, he thought, all I am really interested in is becoming Mayor, securing as much cash as I can whilst I am on the Council and buying a caravan at Chapel St Leonards that I can retire to.

He dug the Mayoress in the ribs and she turned towards him, "Come on, old love," he said, "this is our big day. Take thee rollers outa tha hair, do me a big breakfast and we'll go and show the people of Middlethwaite that they have a Mayor and Mayoress to be proud of. And, at the same time, we'll make a bob or two for ourselves and secure our future. We'll show those suits at the

141

The Town Clerk

Town Hall that we're as good as them any day! We are there as representatives of the Sunflower Hill Estate, I know some of them are rough love, but they rely on us to be their ambassadors on the Council."

He looked around his Council house, furnished in teak room dividers and units that had long become unfashionable. His pride and joy was his eight-feet long teak Schreiber sideboard in 'the room' – as Northerners describe their best parlour. It had cost him nearly three hundred pounds, twenty-five years ago, and he thought it was worth a fortune. It was only when he passed the local house-clearance yard and saw a similar one priced at five pounds that he was brought down to earth. He had gone into the yard and seen the proprietor Alec Appleyard.

"That sideboard," he said, kicking the leg like one of Alfred G Page's tyrekickers, "is that all it's worth, a fiver?"

"Can't sell 'em, mate," Alec Appleyard had replied, "everybody's getting shut of 'em," he said, "I try it for a fiver, the passing buses splash it, the passing dogs piss on it and by Saturday it's falling to bits so I put the chainsaw to it and it goes on my woodburning stove at home. They're no bloody good at all ..." he said, then added as an afterthought, "burn well, though. Oh, I'm telling a lie, sold two last month. One for a garage workbench and the other for a rabbit hutch!"

So the Mayor had returned home, looked at his furniture which was all of the same ilk and totted up the worth of it. It came to under one hundred pounds so he was rather deflated.

"Bloody government's mad," he said to his Mayoress to whom he had told the tale of the sideboard in Alec Appleyard's Tat Place, "letting a sideboard go for a fiver." Councillor Leslie Ullathorne, Mayor of Middlethwaite blamed everything onto the government.....

His chauffeur came early. Early in his Mayoralty he had tried to travel home in the full rig of vivid scarlet and ermine robes, tricorn hat and Mayoral regalia but Robin Armstrong, his Secretary had put his foot firmly down. "Suppose you are burgled, Mr Mayor?" he had said.

"Nar," had been the reply, "they're only after fags, beer and videos." He seemed an expert on the burglarial selectivity of the Sunflower Estate criminal fraternity but so insistent was he about wearing his trappings that his Secretary took out special insurance to enable him to wear just the chain for the journey between the Town Hall and Sunflower Hill Estate. He was

The Mayor's Parade

unhappy about it but it seemed to be a reasonable compromise. So the Mayor and Mayoress boarded the Mayoral Daimler, if it had been any Daimler other than the Mayoral Daimler it would have been stoned on entry to the estate but the Mayor had instructed his grandson Karate Kick and his friend Pineapple Haircut that there was to be no interference with his transport and, besides, there was a job for them today at the end of the Parade which just might give them a bit of pleasure. Today for the Parade he would be in his robes. If he had his way he would have been in his robes every day but, most events just necessitated the wearing of chain or badge. When he wore the chain on his journey to the Town Hall Councillor Leslie Ullathorne liked the residents of the Sunflower Hill Estate to realise the luminary that they had living among them and he made sure that he saw many of his electors acknowledge him as he weaved his way through his estate. Quite early in his Mayoralty he had devised a good 'wheeze'. As he sped through his estate he would purposefully look for his old ladies who were laden down with shopping in both hands. As they trundled through the estate heavily laden he would instruct his chauffeur to 'pip' his horn and he would wave to them. Laden down and unable to respond to the wave, the only way they could acknowledge the Mayor was by inclining from the waist in a ceremonial bow and the Mayor used to get great pleasure from seeing the genuflections of his flock.

So he was one of the first to arrive at the Town Hall. Early on in his Mayoralty he had had to decide the theme of the Parade which he declared to be 'Middlethwaite is fun.' He had had to do nothing in the organisation of the many and varied arrangements that the occasion demanded. He was the figurehead. He was the man everyone wanted to wave to. It was up to Robin Armstrong, his Secretary, the hyphenated Town Clerk and the poncified Cultural Officer to do all the work. All he had to do was take the credit, which was just as it should be, after all these years on the Council. He opened the Parlour, went in and made straight for the drinks cabinet. He surveyed the rows and rows of cans of beer but settled, as usual, on his new love.

"I think we'll have a gin," he said to his Mayoress.

"I don't mind if I do," she replied.

It was barely ten o'clock in the morning and the Mayor's Secretary wondered if he would ever revert to the taste of Barnsley Bitter again.

"Ring for the Town Clerk," he told his secretary, and the Town Clerk duly

The Town Clerk

responded immediately, immaculately attired in his morning suit of black half, striped trousers and wig.

The Town Clerk, too, had arrived early, bearing some trepidation of the day to come. As he had made himself ready for the festival ahead he had thought back to the equanimity he had felt prior to the installation when he had gone through from his office to meet Councillor Leslie Ullathorne as Mayor-Elect. Now every meeting was filled with an upcoming dread and today was no exception. Rather earlier than he expected or wanted he was summoned into the Mayor's Parlour.

The Mayor looked him straight in the eye, "Sit thissen dahn ont Chez Lon Gue," he said, "art thou comfortable?" He was turning the screw and the Town Clerk knew it.

The Town Clerk kept his composure although he was not quite sure how he managed it. He could see no way out of this impasse and could only wait for the fates to intervene to get him out of it. And, at that moment in time his outlook was decidedly bleak for whereas he was worried sick about the cavorting on video with his Administrative Assistant Grade III on the Mayoral chaise-longue, the First Citizen of Middlethwaite seemed ambivalent about his tapes from the cricket bat. The Mayor rightly knew that James Pickering-Eaden had a lot more to lose than he did and if it came to the showdown the biggest loser would be the Town Clerk.

"Have a gin, Town Clerk," he said, but the Town Clerk gracefully declined. "I would like to introduce you to Martin Marston of Marston's Brewery who has very kindly sponsored today's Parade and has been very kind in providing the hospitality for many of our occasions. I have told Martin that you will have a word with him after the Parade. He has a tight schedule but I know that you want to talk to him..." he looked the Town Clerk straight in the eyes.

The Town Clerk knew what he meant and the Mayor knew that the Town Clerk knew what he was expected to discuss with Martin Marston. The Town Clerk also knew that he had vastly underestimated the Mayor's cunning and, save for the cricket bat victory, each run-in that he had with the Mayor seemed to bring fresh problems. However, he maintained his dignity and thought that he had about three hours to come up with a solution to the Martin Marston situation.

In the meantime he checked through the arrangements for the Parade

The Mayor's Parade

which tended to fall familiarly into place year after year. Unfortunately, one imponderable was the weather but there was nothing he could do about it except offer a silent prayer that the threatening clouds would retain their contents at least until the conclusion of the Parade.

Earlier in the week he had lent his Administrative Assistant Grade III to the Cultural Services Officer, Adrian Watts. The Town Clerk would have been unhappy at seconding her to Edgar Fox, the Industrial Development Officer, who he considered rather 'raffish' and Mr Fox certainly had an eye for the ladies, but he considered Cheryl Oldroyd would not be any way at risk with Adrian Watts. Mrs Oldroyd was very capable in organising the procedural aspect of functions such as this and, whilst he missed her from the office, he was happy that she would do a good organisational job with Adrian Watts. She was happy also that Mrs Oldroyd would hold no attractions for Mr Watts, although the same could not be said for her husband Darren. Adrian Watts certainly liked young muscular men although he always seemed to be surrounded by fey, lithe young things of uncertain gait and carriage. In fact Mrs Oldroyd and her husband were riding on one of the floats as the local amateur operatic society's theme was 'Carousel' which was to be their autumn production. She looked stunning in her brief leotard but, as the Town Clerk drooled over the apparition of her beautiful face and figure he also questioned his sanity when he looked at Darren's rippling torso. Darren Oldroyd was cast as Billy Bigolo in Carousel and the years of physical work in the quarries had given him a magnificent body, perfectly in tune with the Billy Bigolo role and whilst he was aware that Adrian Watts was looking at Darren in rather a different light than the Town Clerk, James Pickering-Eaden could not help but speculate that if Darren ever found out about the relationship between his wife and her employer, then that said employer might be due for a good hiding that would make the kicking he had got from Pineapple Haircut and Karate Kick pall by comparison.

He also could not help but analyse the situation of how he had managed to be held as an attraction by Cheryl Oldroyd. She had a husband whose torso was magnificent whilst his own body which had been good in his younger days had slipped a lot in recent years due to his desk job. He just did not understand how Henry Kissinger seemed always to be surrounded by lithe young ladies young enough to be his grand-daughters. Perhaps it was an intellectual attraction? Whatever it was he was content and proud and happy

The Town Clerk

to be the lover of Cheryl Oldroyd and as he looked at her lithe thighs in that leotard he reiterated that if she were married to Arnold Schwarzenegger or Sylvester Stallone he would still take the chance of illicit union. After all, didn't he fall asleep most nights dreaming of those beautiful thighs...?

Earlier in the week, Mrs Oldroyd had come back for a day into the Town Clerk's General Office. Halfway through the day she had sought an interview with the Town Clerk to alert him about a task that the Mayor had given her.

"Mr Pickering-Eaden," she said, playfully passing her breast within kissing distance of the Town Clerk's cheek.

The Town Clerk succumbed and kissed her protruding nipple albeit through the shot-silk white blouse she wore. It made no difference. To him she was standing there naked, he knew every contour of her body.

"I thought we were going to behave ourselves at the office," he said, "this nipple kissing and penile stroking have got to stop." He did not sound at all convincing... "I have your briefing report for the Mayor's Parade. It seems much the same as in previous years. Is there any problem I should be aware of?"

"Nothing I can put my finger on," she had replied and although she had no inkling of the Town Clerk's problems with the Mayor, she felt she had to warn him as she was a trifle uneasy. "The Mayor has asked me to find out the officials, sympathisers, patrons, sponsors of every float in the Parade. It has been a very hard task but I have managed it, but I think you ought to know that something somewhere does not feel quite right."

The Town Clerk could not guess what the Mayor was up to but early on in the morning of the Mayor's Parade he was about to find out. The Mayor was calling his markers in. He had a good memory, despite being gin-fuddled and was about to get even.

But before this he had to host the reception of all the local businessmen and dignitaries in his Parlour prior to the judging of the floats and the award of the prizes. Marston's Brewery had arrived early to set up the hospitality bar and the Mayor had locked his own drinks cabinet so none of his own liquor could be consumed by his cronies. The panelled partition had been drawn back against the wall and the chaise-longue now formed an integral part of the Parlour furnishings.

The Mayor had a video camera. Quite unashamedly he was squinting into the focusser and videoing everything and everybody. Mostly of course it was

The Mayor's Parade

a source of fun and pride for the visitors to the Parlour but James Pickering-Eaden knew that by continually videoing him on the 'Chez Lon Gue' he was milking the situation for all it was worth. Perhaps he was making a before-and-after compilation, a clothed-and-naked production. Resignedly he went along with it, he could not do anything about it and he just thought, and hoped and trusted that one day – and, please God, may that day be soon – he would have the chance to strike back.

Perfectly to time with the schedule of events, the Mayor, although coping better with the gin than on his induction, rose unsteadily to his feet. "Before we commence the judging, my words of thanks to some very special people." He then proceeded to list just about everyone in Middlethwaite, although pointedly omitting the Town Clerk. "Finally, my best thanks must go to Mr Alfred G Page, local concessionaire of Majolta Motors who has kindly arranged another 'first' for Middlethwaite. I am pleased to announce that I shall be leading the Parade today, not in a traditional manner but in the new open-top Majolta Whirlwind, a car capable of one hundred and sixty five miles per hour." He halted his speech abruptly so all present could imbibe the full majesty of his momentous announcement. He was unashamedly promoting it. He had deviated completely from the schedule. He had been due to lead the Parade in the Mayoral Daimler but that was now demoted to number two vehicle containing the Deputy Mayor, Councillor Cairns. In the past the Mayor had led the Parade in a succession of dignified vehicles notably vintage Rolls-Royces, Daimlers, open-top landaus drawn by four sleek horses, and, even on one occasion, by the Tetley Dray Horses. On another occasion he led the Parade in the Mayoral Granada of neighbouring Barnsley Metropolitan Borough Council which had the registration number ' THE 1'.

But this year the lead vehicle was to be the Majolta Whirlwind. And to cap it all the Mayor said with suitable gravitas, "It would have been impossible for me to organise today's Parade without the immense help of Mr Alfred G Page of the Majolta Motor Company, and" added as an afterthought as he caught sight of the groaning hospitality table, "Mr Martin Marston of Marston's Brewery."

Nice touch, thought the Town Clerk, he had managed to give himself the credit for organising the Parade when, in effect, he had done bugger all.

After the pause the Mayor continued, "Unfortunately, Mr Norman Wisdom has been unable to accept my invitation to be present today. My very good

147

friend has engagements at home in the Isle of Man."

The Town Clerk had his own thoughts about the Mayor's 'very good friend' for Norman Wisdom had been 'top of the bill' for 50 years and was not now going to play second fiddle to Councillor Leslie Ullathorne.

The Majolta Whirlwind was promoted by Alfred G Page, the Town Clerk's sponsor when he was inducted as Provincial Grand Master at the Lodge Meeting and now the Mayor boarded it to go the short distance to the judging field at Valerie-Alice meadows. Taking their timing from the excellent arrangements compiled down to the second by Robin Armstrong, the official party arrived at the collecting ring to judge the entries for the Parade exactly on time. It was then that the party – indeed, the world, was privy to the first sight of the Majolta Whirlwind. The Town Clerk was no aficionado with cars but even he could see that the Whirlwind owed nothing to originality but everything to plagiarism. It had the bonnet of a Rolls-Royce, was about ten metres long like a Studebauker Stretch limousine, it had dainty sidelights like a Wolseley and a front bumper cribbed straight from a best-selling Volkswagen. It had a soft top like a 1940's Humber and wheel trims sporting a big MW logo that gave you vertigo when you watched them turning. In short, it was the bastard car to end all bastard cars and the Mayor, escorted by the cadaverous Alfred G Page took his seat with the Mayoress who was practising her 'Queen Mother' wave to the assembled dignitaries.

The Mayor was milking the occasion for all it was worth but not to the extent that Alfred G Page was. He was handing out leaflets offering a 'Test Drive in the New Majolta Whirlwind' as introduced to this country, endorsed by and driven by the Worshipful the Mayor of Middlethwaite Alderman Les Ulathorpe. That he had spelled his name wrong and had named him an Alderman – an office that had been abolished fifteen years previously – hardly seemed to matter for the whole affair had descended into farce. The Town Clerk had to go along with it although it saddened him but he had now to look on the matter as a damage-limitation exercise and hope that the Mayor would not overstep the mark. Watching the Mayor shamelessly promoting himself and the Majolta Whirlwind filled the Town Clerk with trepidation for the Mayor was surrounded by his cronies and, had they got the requisite £49,999.99 would have been in a queue the following morning to purchase a Majolta Whirlwind.

Worse was to come. This was to be the Mayor's "tour-de-force", his

The Mayor's Parade

St Valentine's Day massacre, his night of the long knives.

The official party adjourned to the collecting field at Valerie-Alice Meadows for the judging. The Town Clerk was now to find out why the Mayor had assiduously instructed Mrs Oldroyd to find the connections and antecedents of all the floats in the Parade. It was the Mayor's job alone to judge the floats and with twelve trophies to assign, previous Mayors had diplomatically ensured that most floats had been adequately rewarded for their hard work in mounting and equipping a float to grace the parade. Not Councillor Leslie Ullathorne – or Alderman Les Ulathorpe according to the Majolta Motor Company. He 'had a little list'. Like the Mikado his little list gave him an opportunity to square matters for it was after only a little while that the Town Clerk noticed that the Awards List did not contain 'elliptical billiard balls' like the Mikado's but was more notable for its exclusion rather than its inclusion. For excluded were all the floats that had anything to do with Councillors Bramble, Harlow, Scott, French, Grainger, Scourfield, Lomas, Pepper, Turnbull and Redgrave – all the dissenters that had forced the Motion of Censure on the Mayor after the unsavoury incidents early in his Mayoralty. They did not have a chance. If any float was remotely connected with the ten dissidents it was proscribed. The Mayor was wielding a huge blue pencil just as the Lord Chancellor did in the days of Theatre Censorship before abolition of these particular duties appertaining to the Lord Chancellor. Whilst most floats retained their virginity in respect of rosette awards, others were groaning under their collection of cups, plaques and badges.

The results were not comical, they were hilarious. Almost forty floats were excluded by reason of association with the dissidents and the Mayor was hard put to get some sort of Honours List from among the remaining untainted floats. For example, the Crematorium won the Duggie Chapman trophy for the most amusing entry. The Computer Industry Prize was won by the Alec Appleyard's Tat and Antique Yard, the Most Decorative Prize was won by the local concrete company and of course Hollowdene Working Men's Club was mentioned in nearly every category and won the Mayor's Prize for best overall float. The Chamber of Trade and Commerce Trophy for the best commercial entry was won by the Majolta Whirlwind although nobody could ever remember the Mayor's carriage ever being mentioned in the Honours List before. The Mayor's Special Prize was awarded to Marston's Brewery

The Town Clerk

who did not even have a float. When the amounts were counted from the collecting tins, it seemed at first that Councillor Pepper's wife would win the prize for the most money collected until the Mayor intervened and put ten pounds in a rival tin to ensure that an untainted collector would be rewarded. The local Hosiery and Underwear factory was awash with awards as the Mayor, scarcely able to contain himself from drooling at the scantily clad participants made sure that they were adequately rewarded for their efforts and, of course, the Mayor found time to arrange with the Works Director a future visit to the factory to see the undergarments being made.

"All-in-all a satisfactory morning," the Mayor said to no-one in particular as the party adjourned for lunch. This was held in the top local hotel, The Freeman's Arms, before the afternoon Parade which was to be headed, of course, by the Mayor and Mayoress in the new Majolta Whirlwind.

The Town Clerk was speechless. Once again the Mayor of Middlethwaite, Councillor Leslie Ullathorne, had taken the wind completely out of his sails. He had been warned that the Mayor was up to something but the scale of his fixing had amazed him. He could scarce forebear a chuckle. The Town Clerk thought he was quite a proficient 'fixer', he had admired Harold Wilson who as Prime Minister was reckoned to be a fixer-without-a-peer but this Mayor of Middlethwaite had them all beaten. The Town Clerk knew he had vastly under-rated this man but now he was wondering if he was ever to be beaten. He could not hide some grudging respect for the man. He thought, in retrospect, how lucky he had been to obtain The Compton Tapes. The Mayor seemed to have had everything covered and he wondered if anything could bring him down. When he thought back to the Mayor-Making he regretted that he had not let him sink then. But hindsight is a dangerous beacon, he hoped, perhaps the gin would do for him in the end? But he was by no means confident ....

The Town Clerk felt himself rather an outcast at the lunch. He had no wish to sit near the Mayor who was entertaining expansively on his Hospitality Account. At all costs he had to keep away from the man from Marston's Brewery for, as yet, he had no clear idea of how he was to conduct the forthcoming interview with Martin Marston that the Mayor had so kindly arranged for him. He certainly did not want to talk to Alfred G Page for there would be concerted lobbying for the new Majolta Whirlwind and there was also the uncertain matter of a briefcase bulging with currency at the back of

The Mayor's Parade

the Documents' Safe. So the Town Clerk and Celia got ensconced with Robin Armstrong and his wife and talked about nothing in particular, just hoping that the afternoon parade would go off uneventfully. Some hopes.

At 2 pm prompt the Mayor led off the Parade from the collecting field. The route was the usual one that had been evolved over the years to minimise going up or down the many hills in this Pennine Borough. There had been an awful occurrence one year when a sharp shower had caused chaos on Hyde Hill with a float running into the one in front and the many majorettes and marching bands becoming amalgamated. The Parade had subsequently been re-routed and the Mayor's Secretary and the Cultural Officer were reasonably hopeful that no disaster would happen. Adrian Watts, the Cultural Officer, was over-attentive to his float from the Civic Theatre which was packed with lithe young men from 'La Cage aux Folles' which was playing the Theatre that week. This float immediately followed the Central Band of the Royal Air Force which was the premier band after the Mayor and his entourage in the Majolta Whirlwind. The Moldavian government had certainly gone to town on sponsoring the Whirlwind. It was festooned with ribbons, flowers and glitter-slash, it looked like the bridal car for an Elizabeth Taylor wedding. It housed the Mayor and Mayoress along with twelve of their cronies with ease. That it could speed at one hundred and sixty five miles per hour was probably beyond dispute. The only problem was that, at three miles per hour the car was underperforming. It coughed and spluttered, groaned and wheezed, jerked and ejaculated, swerved and swayed along the crowded route. If the Most Amusing prize could have been re-awarded, the Majolta Whirlwind would have walked off with it. By dint of good luck and several helpful pushes from the Central Band of the Royal Air Force and the cast of 'La Cage aux Folles' (most of whom did not have a push in them), the Mayor arrived back at the saluting base in order to view the rest of the passing Parade. The crowds gathered at the kerbside were wet eyed with laughter. The Mayor had lost some of his dignity as he mounted the saluting base.

The Mayor was livid but fortunately his hip flask was at hand and as the Parade snaked past him equilibrium was restored by a few slugs of gin, swigged under cover of the voluminous robes. The Mayor had been practising his dais wave and had come up with something akin to a revolving wrist that King George the Sixth had used at Buckingham Palace on VE Day. The Mayoress was content with her Queen Mother impression and the rest

151

The Town Clerk

of the dais, including the Mayor's extended family seemed also to think that it was their duty to acknowledge the passing participants and were waving also. The Town Clerk found himself alongside Karate Kick, now looking uncomfortable in the smart suit which had replaced his street-cred clothing and who was not wearing his usual baseball cap pointing backwards. The Town Clerk thought back to the night of his installation at the Freemason's Lodge but it was obvious that Karate Kick had no recollection that he and the Town Clerk had met before outside his gluesniffing den. The Parade was an eclectic collection of amateur and professional. There were six regimental bands resplendent in gold braid, stepping out and playing superbly as they passed. There was the Moose Jaw Lions Band from America, touring the country and who made a splendid and unusual addition to the participants. There were the colliery bands, still in existence despite the diminution of the coal industry marching in front of the proudly-borne banners of the miners, there were the cubs and scouts and territorials all ragged and out-of-step but proud to be there. There were the commercial floats although the Town Clerk reckoned there would not be so many next year due to the Mayor's withdrawal of prizes. There were the playgroups and schools and there were floats from the working men's clubs, notably Hollowdene Working Men's Club who were dressed as oversized Bamfordesque women from the comic postcards who were squirting water onto the crowd from Fairy Liquid bottles, despite being asked not to do so.

Then the Mayor's luck ran out. Three-quarters way through the Parade the heavens opened. It had been threatening all day but the fates had conspired to keep the deluge off until now. Within seconds the streets were awash and everyone threw themselves for cover. Some hardy souls kept on parade but their participation only highlighted the farce that the parade had now become. The Mayor was under a sheltered dais and had remained dry until Karate Kid pushed the overhead canvas up and the trapped water cascaded down onto the Mayoral ermine. He looked like a drowned rat and the Mayoress had not escaped either. The Mayor duly berated and cuffed his grandson which would have been a picture for the papers except that the local reporters and photographers had led the charge from the deluge. The Town Clerk had managed to remain dry and had sprinted to welcome the official party at the Reception in the Mayor's Parlour.

It was certainly a motley crowd that assembled in the Parlour. The Mayoral

The Mayor's Parade

ermine smelled. It stank. Previously the Mayor could not wait to get into his ermine but now he could not wait to get out. He just threw it into an ante-room and donned more formal attire. The gin bottle was used again to calm him down although the douche that he had just received had sobered him up and had forestalled any possibility that he might have gone over the top. He looked around for the Town Clerk to blame him for the downpour but saw him talking to his Secretary in the corner and decided to blame him for it later.

Robin Armstrong had sought out the Town Clerk for a word "I have a feeling of unease," he said to the Town Clerk, quizzically. "Is there anything you want to tell me about?" he said. The Town Clerk seemed happy to talk. "There are a few things about which I am not happy but I cannot tell you about them. I do value your enquiry, though, and if there is anyway I need you to help me, I shall ask you. I value our friendship, I value the way that you are keeping this," he dropped his voice to an almost imperceptible whisper, "this fucking idiot (meaning the Mayor) under control. I have a feeling of doom but it is not something that, at this moment, I am able to address. It has caused me a lot of worry but it is something that I alone have to work out. It is very complicated, it involves my personal life but, with it, is tied up a web that pertains to my Council life. What we must do is to make sure this," he dropped his voice again, "fucking idiot Ullathorne is kept under some measure of control or he'll drag the Borough – and us – down. He's drinking far too much, I calculate that he's had at least a bottle and a half of gin so far today and it's only early afternoon. We are only three months into his Mayoralty and it is going to take a major feat of vigilance, mainly by you and I, to get him through the next nine months. As I say, Robin, I appreciate your solicitude.." His eyes moistened and it was as near that he got to unburdening himself. He would have liked to tell someone about his troubles – the video, the kicking he had received, the briefcase, Marston's Brewery, Alfred G Page, his Administrative Assistant Grade III but he could not. They were all problems of his own making and he must make his own solutions. The Mayor's Secretary felt, for the first time, a desperate sorrow for his colleague. He had felt for some time that the Town Clerk was under some sort of pressure but the Town Clerk was a strong man and not the sort to engender pity so the fact that he had hinted that he was in a deal of trouble meant to him that it was serious.

The Town Clerk

"I'm sorry, Jim, but if there is anything I can do, you know you only have to ask. My discretion is absolute..."

"Just let's try to keep the Mayor in order," was the reply from the Town Clerk, a smile of resignation flitting across his lips.

It was now time for the Town Clerk to cross another bridge. The reception had settled down, the stink from the Mayor's robes had assuaged somewhat and local personalities were beginning to drift off. The Mayor buttonholed the Town Clerk. He took him by the hand and led him like a little boy to Martin Marston the owner of Marston's Brewery.

"Come into the ante-room, Mr Marston. Sit on the 'Chez Lon Gue' with the Town Clerk. He wants to have a word with you.... Town Clerk," he said, "Mr Marston has only twenty minutes as he has to catch a train to London. He'll be very interested in what you have to say to him."

The two men sat together on the Mayoral chaise-longue.

"Well, Mr Marston," began the Town Clerk, "I want to tell you about the Sanitary and Sewage Sub Committee of the Association of Municipal Corporations, especially its responsibilities and the implications of the latest government Directive on pollution." He spent three minutes going down this road before switching onto the latest legislation on the stopping-up of highways, he veered onto the Clean Air Act that was being instituted for the western part of the Borough, he touched on the new traffic scheme for Cunningham Avenue, he went on at length about the new Hygiene Regulations governing eating establishments in the Borough. He told him about the possible provisions of the Financial Services Regulations (Middlethwaite) 1996 as enacted to involve the Water's Edge Business Park. He then went on to describe the possible outcome if the Middlethwaite Development Corporation Act (Area and Constitution) Order were enacted along with the Non-domestic Rating (Chargeable accounts) (Amendment) Regulations. He touched briefly on a Bill he was promoting in Parliament dealing with the Hypnotism Act. He paused briefly for breath and the Marston's Brewery man looked at his watch. Just as the Marston's man was about to interject the Town Clerk launched into a detailed and all-embracing synopsis of the Furniture and Furnishings (Fire Safety) Regulations 1988 which although enacted some years ago had just started being stringently enforced by his Consumer Protection Officers after a moratorium to allow the furniture trade to bring itself into line with the regulations. He went on at

The Mayor's Parade

great length about the provision of urinals in public places and traced a brief history from Victorian times and the duties of the Boards of Guardians in this respect.

Martin Marston could not get a word in. Exasperated he tried to interject but the Town Clerk was too quick for him and launched into the ramifications of the new issue of Building Regulations but Martin Marston was not interested, got up, flew through the door and without a goodbye to either Mayor or Town Clerk was off to catch his train to London.

The Town Clerk slipped back in his chair. He had spoken non-stop for nearly half-an-hour, it was an effort worthy of the best filibustering techniques of the House of Commons. Whether it was merely delaying the consideration of the licensing arrangements for the new Sports Centre he did not know but he did think that the Marston's man was shell-shocked and would not be in too much of a hurry for another lecture on local government law, custom and practice by the Town Clerk of the Metropolitan Borough of Middlethwaite.

As he sat back he was suddenly aware of intense activity in the ante-room between his office and the Mayor's Parlour. He looked through the door jamb. The Mayor had obviously forgotten the Town Clerk was still in the building but had managed to disperse the rest of his guests after the post-Parade reception. What to do with the remaining hospitality fare provided by Marston's Brewery held no problem for Councillor Leslie Ullathorne, the Worshipful the Mayor of Middlethwaite. A rented Transit van had been backed into the Mayor's private car park and the back was already half-full of crates and cases. The Mayor was taking everything that was left – half-emptied packets of cigarettes, half-full bottles of spirits, even spirit bottles with just one or two tots left were being loaded into the Transit. For youths who spent a lot of time in a glue-sniffing den, Pineapple Haircut and Karate Kick were certainly moving fast. Within half an hour all the hospitality provided by Marston's Brewery had been loaded. And what had Marston's got out of it? Just a dry-as-dust lecture on local government law by the Town Clerk.

The Town Clerk did not go to the Presentation Dance in the evening but apparently the Mayor enjoyed himself. He was into his third bottle of gin for the day when midnight came and all the guests went home. When he heard later the reports on the Presentation Dance there was one major factor that, to the Town Clerk's relief, came out of it. It was uneventful.

155

The Town Clerk

The Town Clerk was at home with his wife. That he was thinking of his Administrative Assistant Grade III goes without saying. Celia was embroidering a firescreen and the Town Clerk was praising every stitch. He nodded off a few times in front of the television. At ten o'clock Celia put the cocoa on and the Town Clerk pondered shall he do his marital duty or plead a headache. He did his marital duty but it did involve a few false climaxes. Celia seemed happy enough and snored lightly as James Pickering-Eaden pondered the events of another day orchestrated by the Worshipful the Mayor of Middlethwaite, Councillor Leslie Ullathorne. That this man had blighted his life, there was no shadow of a doubt.

As the Town Clerk lay in bed the Mayor was having the last waltz with the Mayoress at the end of the, fortunately, uneventful Presentation Dance.

The Town Clerk thought that by his filibustering he had averted, or at least, delayed another crisis but things were due to get worse before they got better.

CHAPTER THIRTEEN

THE TWIN TOWN VISIT

The Town Hall clock struck the half hour. The men huddled together on the Town Hall steps shuffled nervously and checked their schedules for the umpteenth time. They had been there for nearly three-quarters of an hour and had watched almost the full complement of Town Hall staff arrive for work.

The Town Clerk looked impatiently at his watch again. It was now well past nine-thirty and already the party was half-an-hour behind schedule.

"Where the bloody hell are they, Robin?" he said to the Mayor's Secretary.

"I don't know, Jim, I gave him a tight timetable and Bill Hutchings his chauffeur left on time to pick them up. I can't think what's delayed him."

Adrian Watts, the Cultural Officer, confirmed that the Daimler had left in plenty of time to collect him. The three men were standing outside the Town Hall awaiting the Mayor and Mayoress. They were due to set off for the Council's twin town of Schleigvighausen in Holland for a goodwill visit. It was a public relations exercise that took place every year and involved a high-profile visit to the twin town's attractions and the party also took the opportunity to slip over the border into Germany to pay a visit to the Royal Hussars whose regiment recruited in the Middlethwaite area. The party used the Mayoral Daimler to travel via the M1, M18 to Hull to catch the ferry to Rotterdam and although the route was easy and direct there was not much margin for delay. So tempers were getting frayed as time slipped by and when the Daimler eventually came into sight they had lost nearly three-quarters of an hour. And it was a big surprise when they saw that the Mayor was dressed in full robes and unaccompanied.

"Why have you got your robes on, Mr Mayor?" said his Secretary, "You know it is ultra vires to wear robes outside the Borough Boundaries. And where is the Mayoress?"

157

The Town Clerk

"She's not coming, got some shopping to do," said the Mayor, tapping the side of his nose in the manner that usually foretold doom, "and I can soon slip out of these," and he did so, making a pile of ermine in the corner of the limousine. The robes still smelled from their drenching at the Mayor's Parade.

"Tha sees, my people like to see me as a proper Mayor when they wave me off to something important."

The Mayor's Secretary stiffened. He had told him time and time again not to go home in his robes but it was like talking to a brick wall. He decided not to comment, looked across at the Town Clerk and raised his eyebrows.

The Town Clerk fumed for the Mayor had obviously delayed leaving so that he could go slowly past the Post Office queues at Sunflower Hill Estate as his constituents drew their dole, but he resisted commenting on the Mayor putting the day's timetable at risk by his antics. And why wasn't the Mayoress coming? No doubt they would find out later.

The three men, tempers fraying, slipped into the Daimler and joined the Mayor. As the Town Clerk's eyes got used to the darkness of the interior caused by the tinted windows he blinked as he focused onto the Mayor. He looked, well, different and it was only after a while that he understood why. The Mayor was wearing a new ill-fitting hairpiece, it was awful, the fair tight curls contrasting vividly with the grey sideburns that poked down each side. He was drenched in Brut aftershave and he wore an expensive pair of Armani sunshades. He was dressed in an ill-fitting Versace suit that had obviously been borrowed from Pineapple Haircut. The Town Clerk had contemplated about this Versace suit when he saw it worn at the Mayor's Parade. He had speculated as to how an unemployed gluesniffer managed to afford such a suit but had concluded that it had been acquired by social security fiddling, pinching videos or drug dealing. Later events put into the equation that such style might be obtained from his share of the Marston's stash after the Mayor's Parade. So he was surprised to see the reappearance of the Versace suit, albeit now fitting where it was touching around the Mayor. He looked a dog. No wonder he was late, it must have taken two hours to get dressed. There was a strange clicking sound when he spoke and his smile was all lopsided.

Out of the side of his mouth the Town Clerk said to the Mayor's Secretary, "He's treated himself to a new set of teeth."

The Twin Town Visit

"More likely bought the bloody things at a car boot sale," came the reply. Everything went wrong on the journey to Hull. They had only just gone out of the Borough boundaries when the thing that the Town Clerk feared would happen, did happen. There is a stretch of open road with greensward at each side and no houses within sight. It looks like a speedtrack and most motorists treated it as such, there were no thirty miles per hour restriction signs on it because there was no mandatory need for the local authority to signpost it but the whole stretch of road was limited to thirty miles per hour. Chief Superintendent Colin Murray used to say to the Town Clerk at their Lodge meetings that if the crime figures were down, he used to send a couple of panda cars up to Aylward Road to catch a few speedsters and improve the monthly figures. So when Bill Hutchings chanced putting his foot down there was the sight of the inevitable panda car emerging from an obscured lay-by, a wailing of a siren and the Mayoral Daimler was waved down. Appropriately, the Mayor could read the word ECILOP in the mirror as the Daimler was waved down.

"It's the police," said the Mayor, "I can read ECILOP in the mirror." He sounded more than a little triumphant and seemed to expect a round of applause for his dexterity in reading words backwards.

It seemed like an eternity as the officer got out of the car and walked slowly back to the Daimler. Deliberately he took out his notebook and said "Do you think you're Stirling Moss, sir?" he said to Bill Hutchings, "Documents, please."

Huddled in the back the Town Clerk, Mayor, Secretary, and Cultural Services Officer were in no mood to speculate why speeding drivers were always compared to Stirling Moss who had retired some thirty years ago, whilst Schumacher and Damon Hill never figured in police patois.

"Better not say anything," said the Town Clerk, "we can still just about make the ferry. Let Mr Hutchings accept the speeding ticket and we can be on our way."

Unfortunately, his warning was not heeded by the Mayor who had already been at his hip flask gin. As the officer walked around the vehicle taking a look at the tyres of the Daimler and kicking them as if he was doing the Sunday shopping at the Majolta car showrooms, the Mayor wound down his window and shouted at the officer "Ey oop, shitface, does tha know oo I am?"

The officer did not rise to the bait until the Mayor unable to be restrained

159

The Town Clerk

by the others in the back of the limousine followed it with "I'm the Mayor of Middlethwaite and thy are a big ignorant pillock, now fucking let us go 'cos we're going to Holland. We're going to represent Middlethwaite," he said.

The other occupants in the Daimler slowly slid down in their seats trying to distance themselves from their First Citizen.

The officer was out of his depth. He was used to dealing with yobs and he could easily tackle a drunken driver, he was used to putting a front goose lock on the thumb of resisting criminals but being called a shitface and a pillock by the Mayor of Middlethwaite was one scenario that he had not been taught at Hendon Police College.

"Wait there," he said to Bill Hutching and he slowly turned on his heel and very very deliberately strode back to his patrol car.

The Mayor thought he was being very comical when he said to the other travellers, "Eh oop, he thinks he's on the casting credits of The Bill." Stony silence greeted this attempt at levity.

"Mr Mayor," said the Town Clerk, "I don't know if you realise the position we are in. We are late. We are very late. If we do not catch the Ferry we shall be in an almighty mess. There is a civic party waiting to welcome us, the Town Band will be on parade, the press will be there, a tight schedule has been prepared for us, the caterers will have timed their refreshments to the minute, there will be officials from the Ambassador and Consular departments and bunting will have been erected throughout the Town to welcome us. We should have left Middlethwaite at nine am, it is now ten am and in the intervening one hour we have travelled precisely one mile and have now been apprehended by the Police. We are now stationary one mile outside Middlethwaite and – to put it mildly, Mr Mayor, it is distinctly unhelpful for you to call the police officer a shitface and a pillock."

The Mayor slunk into the corner of the back seat of the Daimler and said, "Well, you sort it out then. That's what we pay you for! I don't know how you four have come to get us into the shit like we are. If you'd only left everything up to me we wouldn't be in this mess." The Mayor had neatly stood the whole situation on its head. The Town Clerk gave a resigned look across to the Mayor's Secretary which was reciprocated with interest.

By this time the police officer had reached the patrol car and was talking agitatedly to his colleague who had remained in the car. After what seemed an interminable time, the other officer unwound from the police car and

The Twin Town Visit

joined his colleague in a measured walk back to the Mayor's car. The Town Clerk looked at the approaching figure and a now-familiar feeling of foreboding came over him. It was Sergeant Lycett, an officer he had known for the whole of his eight years in Middlethwaite, he was an officer who had been in charge of liaison at the Traffic Department for official functions like the Mayor's Parade and Mayor's Sunday. He was a surly, grey-faced individual, entirely devoid of humour and looking for trouble at every turn. The Town Clerk once remarked to Mrs Oldroyd that living with Sgt. Lycett must be like a prison sentence with the key thrown away, it was like a jail sentence with permanent solitary confinement. So when the occupants of the Mayor's car saw the measured tread of Sgt. Lycett coming towards them they knew that their chance of catching the ferry had receded considerably. Sgt. Lycett was an officer given to getting immense satisfaction from the misfortunes of others. As he padded towards them they could feel he was extracting great pleasure from the situation.

"What have we here?" said Sgt. Lycett, pretending not to recognise the occupants of the Mayoral limousine, "My constable is upset that certain allegations have been made against him. Would you like to repeat what you called him? You, hiding under that pile of ermine in the corner!"

Things could have got nasty but the Town Clerk slipped out of the rear door, took the officers aside and using his best diplomatic skills apologised for the Mayor's behaviour and explained he had had to leave the Mayoress behind and because he was already missing her dearly it had caused him a lot of stress. The policemen appreciated the Town Clerk's courtesy and on being told that the Town Clerk would mention their efficiency to Chief Superintendent Murray, allowed the party to proceed. Unfortunately, the incident lasted twenty minutes and the party was further delayed by the Mayor insisting on a roadside stop "for a tiddle." Eventually what should have been an easy connection with the ferry ended with a frantic dash into Hull, just in time to see the Rotterdam ferry steaming sedately out of port whilst the Daimler and crew smouldered at the quayside. As the ferry pulled out of the dock it blew a loud and very rude raspberry at the occupants of the Daimler.

The Town Clerk was known for his equanimity but was in a difficult position as he couldn't castigate the Mayor because of the hold he had over him. So the four others worked out an alternative route to Schleigvighausen

The Town Clerk

which, as the last ferry to Holland had left for the day, involved crossing to Zeebrugge in Belgium and a complicated trip zigzagging across two countries. Eventually the Mayoral Daimler arrived in their Twin Town with its officers crass and dishevelled whilst the cause of their troubles, Councillor Leslie Ullathorpe the Worshipful the Mayor of Middlethwaite, was snuggled in the back of the Daimler, his ermine robes wrapped round him and hip-flask of gin at his lips. Although he smelled of a mixture of Brut and dead cat he was certainly the freshest of them and as they booked into their hotel half a day late it was left to the Town Clerk and the Mayor's Secretary to apologise to their hosts. The Mayor, wig awry, teeth clicking and still drenched in Brut was shown to his room by a delectable young lady from the Consular's office and he winked, tapped his nose and slipped his arm around the young girl's waist as they went upstairs. The Town Clerk was on hot bricks until the young girl returned immediately as he didn't want sexual harassment problems on top of all his other difficulties.

The Mayor dominated the first day's events. The guard of honour transported from the base in Germany was inspected by the Mayor who was saluted by the Colonel Commandant. The Mayor went along the lines of soldiers straightening ties, looking at haircuts and trying to see his face in the shining bulled toecaps. He was being insufferable. Councillor Leslie Ullathorne particularly enjoyed this duty as he had served as a private in the Pioneer Corps during his National Service and quite liked the idea of being saluted by a Colonel. The Town Clerk was a major in the Territorial Army and also had to perform his own genuflections to the Mayor. That the Mayor knew how to turn the screw was beyond dispute. The salute by the Colonel was photographed ad nauseam by the official photographers and the Mayor had absorbed enough about syndication of photographs that he insisted on the pictures being sent to all sections of the media. The Colonel was apoplectic as the Mayor made the most of the photo-opportunity.

The final event of the day was played out in the Officers' Mess with a dinner in honour of their distinguished visitors from Middlethwaite. The Mayor was at his most obnoxious. At the conclusion of the evening the Colonel took the Town Clerk aside and said, "Major Pickering-Eaden. I don't know where you have found this man, Major, but please ensure that you do not bring him back here." Any further promotion the Town Clerk may have envisaged in the Territorial Army were peremptorily ended. The dinner over

The Twin Town Visit

the Town Clerk relaxed and his eyelids were drooping.

He was interrupted by the Mayor calling for a "Gin all round, in celebration of the visit to cement the mix of the municipalities of Middlethwaite and Schleigvighausen and our hopes that they will always be one except when England and Holland play football." Everyone toasted this ideal, although no-one was quite sure exactly what the toast was.

Another thing no-one understood was who was to pay for the round of drinks. Only one person knew who was responsible and the Mayor gestured for the Town Clerk to pick up the tab and, as he shelled out, he thought that he just might have difficulties with the Borough Treasurer when he sought to get reimbursement for several hundred guilders. He sat in the corner and speculated how this ignorant, uncouth, uneducated, philistine of a Mayor had run rings round him. As he sipped his gin – and the Mayor called for a second round, no doubt also at the Town Clerk's expense – he thought back to his Administrative Assistant Grade III and wondered what he was doing half-pissed in Schleigvighausen, slumped in the corner of a bar, miles from home, having seemingly travelled halfway round the globe and being alternately insulted and berated by the Mayor and the Colonel at every turn. He tried to assess the situation, failed to come up with any logical analysis and went upstairs to bed. He slipped between the clean sheets, closed his eyes and was asleep within seconds. As he slipped into the beyond he thought to himself that he was fortunate that there was no function until mid-day and he could sleep for ten hours. He was wrong.

At four o'clock in the morning he was awakened violently by the Mayor's chauffeur. "You'll have to come with me, Town Clerk," said Bill Hutchings, "it's urgent, the Mayor's dropped a reight clanger this time." Surely this was a nightmare thought the Town Clerk and tried to turn over and go back to sleep. It was no good, Bill Hutchings shook him again and sat him up straight. The Town Clerk struggled to get his thoughts in order. He had fallen asleep content that all was cleared up but had reckoned without the enigmatic Worshipful Mayor of Middlethwaite. Half-conscious he slipped out of bed and attempted to shrug on his dressing gown.

"That's no good, sir," said the Mayor's chauffeur, "you'll have to dress and come with me – the Mayor's dropped a reight bollock this time."

Half-drunk and half-conscious James Pickering-Eaden dressed by remote control and followed Bill Hutchings down to the Mayor's Daimler which was

The Town Clerk

garaged at the back. Obediently he slipped into the passenger seat and Bill Hutchings set off. They had gone about a mile when the Town Clerk's mind cleared, "Just a minute, where are we going?" he said.

Bill Hutchings dropped down a gear, turned to the Town Clerk and said, "I don't know how to tell you this but when you went to bed the Mayor commandeered me and ordered me to take him to the red light district of Amsterdam. What could I do, sir?" he continued, "it's more than my job's worth to tell the Mayor I couldn't take him."

The Town Clerk realised now why the Mayor had not brought the Mayoress. The Town Clerk was now fully awake. He was slumped beside the Mayor's chauffeur but he could not understand why he was hurtling along Dutch roads so he placidly put his hand on the chauffeur's knee and said, "Please stop Mr Hutchings and tell me slowly why we are charging through the Dutch lowlands at eighty miles an hour at four o'clock in the morning."

The Daimler slowed to a halt. "Right," said Bill Hutchings, "the Mayor told me to take him to the red light district. I couldn't refuse, Mr Pickering-Eaden, he's a nasty man and I have a wife and three children and he would have made it bad for me if I'd said no. Honestly, Town Clerk, he's been a real shitbag to me since he came into office. You wouldn't believe it sir, he's only been Mayor five minutes and he's had me chasing around from arsehole to breakfast table. You'll have to excuse me, Town Clerk, but I didn't know whether I was having a shit or a haircut with this bloke. He's run the bloody legs off me."

"Get to the bloody point, will you, for God's sake get to the point, what's happened to the Mayor, is he lost, is he dead?" said the Town Clerk hopefully.

"No," was the reply, "he's not lost, but the Mayoral chain is."

"Christ," interjected the Town Clerk.

Bill Hutchings resumed, "He left it on after the function tonight. He was wearing it when I took him to the Thai quarter of Amsterdam but when he got back, he hadn't got it. He kept saying that he would bet anyone that he was the only one with a Thai round his neck that night, but he may have had a Thai round his neck but he came back without his chain round his neck. Whatever are we to do? It wasn't my fault, Mr Pickering-Eaden. Do you know what he said, Mr Town Clerk? You wouldn't believe it. I've been chauffeur to thirty Mayors and this bloke is the worst I've ever had. Do you know what he said, Mr Town Clerk?" He almost broke down as he was telling the tale, "he said he'd nail my bollocks up for chapel 'at-pegs if I didn't do as I was told. I

The Twin Town Visit

ask you, Mr Pickering-Eaden fancy talking to a Mayor's chauffeur like that!"

Once again the Town Clerk was thrown in the deep end by the Mayor. No doubt the Mayor was sleeping the sleep of the just at that moment whilst the Town Clerk was trawling the red light district of Amsterdam looking for the Mayoral Regalia of Middlethwaite. The situation was beyond belief. It was four o'clock in the morning.

"Which brothel did the fucking idiot go into?" said the Town Clerk.

"I can't say," said Bill Hutchings, "but I parked round the corner of the Lyndon canal and the Mayor was back within fifteen minutes so he couldn't have gone far."

"Park there again," said the Town Clerk.

He did and the Town Clerk got out. He knocked on the door of the first brothel and when the Madam opened the door he said meekly, "I am sorry to bother you but did our Mayor leave his chain in your establishment earlier this evening?" He drew a blank.

He was trusting the honesty of the Madams and was not even considering the consequences for him and eternity should his mission fail. On the fifth call he succeeded. The Madam produced the Mayoral chain of office complete with 108 shields as if she was producing a left umbrella. The Town Clerk thanked her and parted with one hundred pounds sterling. He knew he would not be able to bother the Borough Treasurer with a request for reimbursement of that one although as he paid the Madam she said, "Do you want a receipt?" It was obviously all in a day's work for her. The Town Clerk was relieved, but declined although he did count the shields to make sure there were 108 there.

"Is there anything we can do for you whilst you are here?" the Madam said. Like a dutiful News of the World reporter he declined her offer of services and left.

As he walked slowly down the street in the first light of dawn, the brothel door re-opened. The Madam was at the door, "Here you might as well have this as well ... there's no charge," and threw at the Town Clerk an ill-fitting blonde curly wig. The Town Clerk caught it and lobbed it with the dexterity that he chucked his own wig onto the bentwood hallstand in his own office towards a rat-infested food silo at the back of a restaurant. The last he saw of it a family of rats were fighting over it.

The following day the Mayor carried out another six functions. He had not

165

The Town Clerk

even noticed that his chain was missing let alone retrieved. He did not miss his wig. He still wore his Armani shades and Pineapple Haircut's Versace suit. The Cultural Services officer got friendly with a big guardsman and they were last seen swapping addresses. At the completion of the day's events the party got into the Daimler and this time managed to get the Rotterdam ferry. The Town Clerk was shattered when he reached home. He threw himself into bed.

Celia was pleased to see him and said she hoped he had had a good time. She told him he was very lucky to visit all these interesting places with all these interesting people. Cocoa was not necessary.

CHAPTER FOURTEEN

THE CONFERENCE AT SCARBOROUGH

The Town Clerk watched the diesel draw into Holmfirth station. He was parked on the hill overlooking the station. Just one person got off, his Administrative Assistant Grade III. She came out of the station, looked left and right and her eyes alighted on the Town Clerk's car which was parked unobtrusively some one hundred yards away. Her step quickened, the Town Clerk's heart quickened as he leaned over and slipped the catch on the passenger door. She slid in, threw a small attaché case onto the back seat and kissed her man. The kiss lingered for a minute or more. His temperature rose although it was by now a very hot summer's day.

"Any problems?" he said.

"No," she replied.

"Good," he said. He slipped the car into gear and very slowly cruised out of Holmfirth. They said nothing. He put a tape of Vivaldi's 'Four Seasons' on the car stereo, they smiled happily at each other and James Pickering-Eaden headed very slowly towards the Yorkshire Dales. He was in no hurry. All the complicated connivances to arrange this tryst had been done, now was the time to relax and enjoy the results.

He had been looking forward to this escapade for some time. And it had taken some organising. He was off as the Council's delegate for the two day Conference at Scarborough sponsored by the Council for the Preservation of Rural England. It was not one of the most popular conferences that the Council subscribed to for the papers were usually as dry as dust and the lecture tours not very inspiring. It was also to be held in Yorkshire and since Labour members had recently attended conferences in Orlando and Buenos Aires their home county held little attraction for them. It was part of Council policy that conferences such as this should be attended by one member and

The Town Clerk

one officer but the Labour members were not keen on the C.P.R.E. conference this year, no member was nominated by the Labour Party. Usually the officer nominated was of a lower echelon such as deputy or assistant Town Clerk. But the Town Clerk had decided that he was going to this one and invented a reasonable excuse that they would be considering some legislation that he was closely involved in drawing up.

That part was no problem. Neither was the persuading of Mrs Oldroyd whose husband had gone away on business to Cornwall. The thought of two days away with her had filled his heart and mind since he had first had the inkling of an idea. The arrangements had fallen neatly into place. One of his Lodge members owned a bungalow overlooking the cliffs in Filey, just near enough and just far enough away from Scarborough. It was perfect. All he had to do was to collect the keys which had also presented no problem. There was a slight hitch in that Mrs Oldroyd did not have a car available but he had arranged for her to catch the local diesel at Middlethwaite Station and detrain at Holmfirth. No problem there either. There was one thing that could be perceived as a fly in the ointment. His nominated member to the Conference was to be Councillor Mrs Bramble – 'Bramble the Ramble'. It was highly unusual for an opposition Councillor to represent the Council at a conference but not unknown. Not for nothing was she known as 'Bramble the Ramble'. She was interested in all things rural and did some good works. It was, in fact, a good decision by the ruling Labour group. For one thing, no Labour member was slightly interested in going to the conference – in fact not many knew what the initials C.P.R.E. stood for. For another thing, nominating her for this just might mollify her when the next year's Mayoralty came up for grabs and she would again qualify on a seniority basis. Whilst she was an opposition councillor the Labour people would not countenance her being Mayor but if they were appointing on a seniority basis it would be very hard to resist Councillor Mrs Bramble's claim on that basis. In fact, neighbouring Barnsley had appointed a Citizen Mayor, Councillor Frank Crow in recent years on the basis of seniority. So the appointment of Councillor Mrs Eunice Bramble as delegate to the C.P.R.E. conference was not as obtuse as it seemed.

The only trouble, thought the Town Clerk, was that she would be at every meeting, every seminar and would expect to see the Town Clerk there also. There was no love lost between the Town Clerk and Councillor Mrs Eunice

The Conference at Scarborough

Bramble. He had handled her Special Council Meeting in a strictly businesslike way but she felt that he had steamrollered proceedings and that the Mayor had escaped censure only because of the efforts of the Town Clerk. But the Town Clerk had worked out that, even if he were committed to spending time at the Conference, there was plenty of time to be spent with Cheryl Oldroyd and he was excited by the thoughts of being with her for two whole days (and more importantly three nights) and spending time in bed with her. Their lovemaking to date had been carried out everywhere but bed, primarily on the Mayoral chaisé-longue, but not lately – although at the Mayor's insistence he had passed a little time sitting on it on social occasions.

So the opening arrangements had gone easily to plan but they had gone only a short distance before the Administrative Assistant Grade III rummaged into her handbag and said, "Stop please, I have a letter to post." As the Town Clerk stopped she jumped out of the car at the adjacent letter box, posted it and they set off again.

There was no problem as they found the bungalow at the top of the cliffs. They had turned off the main coast road, skirted a neat hamlet, veered round what seemed to be a village green and gone half a mile down a track, almost to the cliff edge above Filey Bar. The Housekeeper had ensured that everything was in order for their stay. There was clean linen, all the rooms were aired, the wine cupboard was full and the larder was stocked.

It was heaven, they both wished that they could have stayed there all the Conference time but perhaps their stay would be heightened by the Town Clerk's responsibilities elsewhere at the Conference. They had arrived early enough to have a quick aperitif to toast their seclusion before, under a sun still high in the sky, they took a walk along the clifftop. It was idyllic. They met a few walkers but the chances of meeting anyone they knew was exceedingly slim and it was a chance they were willing to take. The scenario was perfect and James Pickering-Eaden pondered that he did not often take advantage of his freemasonry but had little doubt that he had been right to accept a few days hospitality from a brother mason. The weather was good, the Mayor and Mayoress were at their caravan at Mablethorpe, Celia had her mother to stay, Darren was in Cornwall, God was in His heaven, all was right with the world.

They said nothing as they slowly walked along the cliff-top arms around each other's waist and drawing each other so close together that they had to walk in military fashion, step by step together. They walked about a mile,

169

The Town Clerk

retraced their steps and then returned to the bungalow and their feelings having been heightened decided not to wait until the night-time to make love. They lay on the heavily carpeted lounge and made love to the accompaniment of Ravel's "Bolero" but were unable to time their climax to match the music. They clung together tightly and told each other how near heaven this was. They were so much in tune with each other despite being a generation apart and the Town Clerk's troubles seemed distant and he resolved to try not to think about them in the two days they would have together. Dusk was beginning to fall and they realised that neither had eaten since they had met some hours previous so they walked over the cliffs to the nearby village and found a small restaurant where they had a candlelit meal. Everything fell into place again, they found that the sea air had given them a huge appetite so they ordered and got through easily the full four courses supplemented by champagne and, although, a red wine would have been more in keeping with the menu the choice of Liebfraumilch was appropriate as at their last meeting in the Strines Valley. They even lingered over the brandy until it was time to wend their way back under the stars of a cloudless night, arms drawing each other in tightly and gelling together as one. It was straight to bed where their first night together was spent relishing each other's body in many different ways. It was heaven.

The following morning the Town Clerk woke first and went out onto the veranda. If the sea is slightly murky off the Yorkshire coast he did not notice it, preferring to dwell on the boats working out of Whitby fishing in the grounds off Filey Bar. The shimmering sea sent up a heat haze even that early in the morning. There was scarcely a wave or ripple and James Pickering-Eaden felt very happy as he leaned on the balcony rail. He was in a relaxing mood and the touch of Cheryl's hand on his elbow startled him.

"Penny for your thoughts," she said.

Straightaway, without thinking he said "I wish this could last for ever."

She said nothing but clinged to him and wept. Tears seemed inappropriate and yet so appropriate. He felt that she was strangely quiet. Was there anything he could do? No there wasn't, let's just enjoy our time together she had said. They had a light breakfast on the veranda and discussed the arrangements for the coming day.

It would be dangerous for her to come into Scarborough to meet him for lunch, especially as Councillor Mrs Bramble was just about the last person on

The Conference at Scarborough

earth that she would want to bump into. So the Town Clerk kissed her goodbye, drove to Scarborough, parked some way from the Conference Hall and walked from the car park. As he strode along he thought about the coming events of the day but, more specifically, anticipated the evening's reunion with Cheryl. He went into the Conference Hall and duly signed in. He met his elected member and sat through the opening ceremony. The Labour members of Middlethwaite Metropolitan Borough Council had judged this one right, he thought, for there was nothing inspirational about the under-Secretary of State that the government had earmarked to make the opening address. The Town Clerk felt it was going to be a long hard slog and he was to be proved right. A glance down the morning fare on the conference menu filled him with foreboding. He knew exactly what would happen and his worse anticipations were realised. If there was any worse place on earth to be at that precise moment it could only have been at Mablethorpe with the Mayor and Mayoress of Middlethwaite.

Obscure legislation was examined clause by clause in the morning session. It was dreadful and he found it very frustrating knowing that the object of his affection was only ten miles away looking gorgeous and awaiting his return. How he got through the morning session he did not know, if there had been a quiz on the contents he would have been a complete dunce. Councillor Mrs Bramble, by his side, made copious notes on every little thing and was obviously relishing the report that she would take back to the Council as delegate. She was proud to have been chosen by the Council for this Conference and was determined to make her mark, assimilate every fact and make telling contributions in any way possible. There was no escape for the Town Clerk, he had been in some tedious places in his time but this conference, huddled close to seventy year old Eunice Bramble, would surely have won the gold medal. After an eternity he looked at the clock and noticed it was nearly lunch time so he did the noble thing and invited Councillor Mrs Bramble to join him for lunch.

That was a mistake. She spent the whole lunch analysing everything that had happened in the morning session. The Town Clerk could hardly raise a fork-full of food to his mouth before she was in with the next question, relentlessly pursuing every small point that the Town Clerk could not even remember, let alone comment on. He got through lunch with just about the same enthusiasm as he had got through the morning session but the food had

171

The Town Clerk

only fuelled Councillor Mrs Bramble's enthusiasm for the afternoon session. She insisted on paying for her own meal. She even gave the Town Clerk a lecture on graft and corruption in local government remarking that sometimes a bought lunch could lead to more sinister things. The Town Clerk agreed but thought it inappropriate to mention sealed tenders, a bulging briefcase, the Mayoral 'Chez Lon Gue' or Marston's Brewery. He thought that at least he had saved a tenner, although he had had to endure a lecture to do that. If his life depends at some later stage of any public disclosure of briefcase et al he could certainly rely on no support from the Leader of the Opposition.

And so it was back for the afternoon session. A scion of the Ramblers' Association took the platform and did not leave it for nearly two hours. He traced the aims and ideals of his Organisation and his interpretation of the events of the Kinder Trespass made World War One seem tame by comparison. He detailed every piece of legislation from Victorian times onwards and gave a detailed synopsis of it. Councillor Mrs Bramble sat transfixed, head-cupped-in-hands, taking in every point and asking for the Town Clerk's evaluation of it. He was bored out of his mind but could not slide out of the meeting for fear of upsetting Mrs Bramble. At last the Rambling Man was finished but the Council for the Preservation of Rural England trawled up more earnest speakers who would not relinquish the rostrum and defended it against interlopers, just like the British Army in the Boer War clung onto Rourke's Drift and Mafeking. The meeting ran hopelessly overtime and the Town Clerk slunk deeper and deeper into his hard and uncomfortable chair which made his bottom ache. The last speaker harked back to the Kinder Trespass. We have heard all this thought the Town Clerk, surely they are not going to do a lap of honour. But the loquacious bearded speaker was merely preparing the conference for his climax. "We must trespass the world," he shouted, punching the air. "Kinell," thought the Town Clerk.

At long last it was over and a bright-eyed, eager-faced Councillor Mrs Bramble who obviously had not been similarly inconvenienced turned to the Town Clerk and said, "There is only one word to describe today's event, Town Clerk."

The Town Clerk was tempted to offer the word 'excruciating' but before he could blot his copybook Mrs Bramble came up with her own interpretation of the day's events, "Stimulating," she said, "very stimulating."

As they left she said to the Town Clerk, "I trust we shall make an early start to the morning's business, Town Clerk, when we shall make another attempt to put the world on the right path."

It was her attempt at a joke and the Town Clerk laughed feebly and not very convincingly said he was looking forward to the next day's events. He could not wait to dash to his car but it was a dash that took him past the local Charnos concessionaire so he abruptly halted his dash and went into the shop. He knew every colour of his Administrative Assistant Grade III's underwear and was besotted by it. But there was a new colour out and he was happy to spend two hundred pounds buying the complete range of the newest colour – chocolate. He produced his Barclaycard and then hurriedly returned it to his wallet as Celia always paid his personal bills and just might query a large amount spent on Charnos ladies underwear, especially as she had been favouring sensible locknit knickers for some time. So he paid cash and was away quickly to his car with his packages.

He drove like the wind back to the bungalow at Filey Bar. Cheryl was beginning to get worried as the Town Clerk had been expected back an hour earlier. They kissed enthusiastically.

"Tell me all about it," she said.

"I'm telling you nothing about it," he replied, "the complete day's business went in one ear and out of the other. The only thing I can remember is an earnest bearded young man punching the air and exhorting us to Trespass the World! What a load of bollocks!"

He produced his present for her and proceeded to try each piece on her willing body. It was a relief of frustration for him as they made love on the deep pile carpet of the lounge. Naked, they lay together on the floor and he reached for the local paper in the Canterbury by their side.

"What is your taste in music?" he said.

"Well I like some pop, a few light classics, a good musical for remember I am in Carousel .... oh and I like folk music."

"Great," he said, "for I noticed that Reighton Gap Folk Club have a 'Singers' Night' tonight with a guest in the local pub. Instead of having a meal at home, how about a hike across the fields – it's a lovely evening – and having lots of different drinks, a bar meal and listening to the music. I'd like to get out after sitting with that bloody woman for eight hours in that oppressive

173

The Town Clerk

atmosphere today. Is it alright with you, please say that it is?" He was like a schoolboy and she was happy – very happy – to go along with it.

"Just one moment," she said, producing a Parker pen, "This is my present for you. I've bought you this to remember this Conference and the woman who was by your side, Councillor Mrs Bramble!, and also to help you take notes at tomorrow's session," she said with a smile. "You could even send a card to the Mayor and Mayoress at Mablethorpe. Councillor Mrs Bramble will be very impressed with your dedication..." he took the pen and said something trite like he would remember her every time he used it. But it was not trite, he would remember her for the rest of his life, she had made an indelible mark on him and he knew that whenever he used the pen in the future it would bring back memories of her and Filey Bar, long after the thoughts of Councillor Mrs Bramble and the excruciating conference had faded from his mind.

The two lovers set out over the stile and across the fields that led to Reighton Gap. If they were taking a chance of being seen together, it was a remote chance and they were happy to take that chance. So when they arrived to find the Folk Club in full flow and packed out it was great, it was a lovely atmosphere and everybody was out to enjoy themselves. The subdued lighting suited them down to the ground, but all seats were taken so they had to lean against the wall in one of the nooks adjacent to the stage. He took the girl close to him and they sang along with the Wild Rover followed by "Lizzie Wan", a lament of a young girl cast out pregnant. The words seemed to hit the girl hard and salty tears appeared. "Let's have a drink," said the Town Clerk to break the spell.

"It's my turn to pay," Cheryl said, "you bought the last round, Laurent Perrier champagne, wasn't it?"

"No," said the Town Clerk, "let's play a game I used to play at University. We each write the name of five drinks separately on a piece of paper and put the ten slips in a glass. We each then draw one slip at each round and, even if it's inappropriate, we are honour-bound to drink it. At the end of five rounds we'll have mixed our drinks just enough to be merry without being too drunk. At University we used to find that with five we were merry, six we were wobbling, seven we were falling over and eight it was honking stations behind the pub. I don't think we ever got to nine – or if I did I can't remember it."

So they cut a cigarette packet into ten sections and each took five. The

The Conference at Scarborough

Town Clerk used his new Parker pen for the first time. As he picked it up he said, "You see I am using your present and I am delighted to see that you are wearing mine," he said peering down her cleavage like a lecher. Modestly she drew her blouse together.

He looked across at the bar and wrote the first five bottles of the spirit shelf – brandy, Drambuie, Advocaat, chartreuse and Glenfiddich, which was cheating really for the Glenfiddich bottle was a little bit farther along the shelf but it reminded him of the first time they had made love three months, three weeks, three days, one hour and six minutes ago. He told her this and his quick mental arithmetic impressed his Administrative Assistant Grade III. They folded the cards into a glass – Cheryl had written pint of Stones, pint of Guinness, pint of Heineken lager, a Special Brew and a pint of Barnsley Bitter. The first draw was made, the Town Clerk drew chartreuse and his Administrative Assistant drew a pint of Guinness! So it was a rather mismatched pair that lounged against a wall – the urbane man fingering a small liqueur glass whilst his slim companion clutched a foaming pint of Guinness. But all games have rules that must be obeyed so as they sung "Johnnie Mackeldo" with gusto, Cheryl swigged her Guinness whilst James Pickering-Eaden sipped his liqueur. Fortunately the second round was a bit more conventional with the Town Clerk's drink being a pint of Barnsley Bitter and Cheryl's an Advocaat. But this was only because the Town Clerk palmed the card that he drew whilst Cheryl was away at the ladies, well, he thought, all rules are meant to be broken. She leaned back against him as they joined in all the traditional songs that they both seemed to know so well and he could feel his manhood rising as she arched her backside into him. He ran his hands down her hips, spread the fingers wide around her haunches and gently rocked her to and fro. She took up the motion and things may have got out of hand had not the interval lights gone up.

"Fancy slipping round to the bike-sheds?" he said in her ear.

"Behave yourself," was the instant rejoinder.

"Be careful, I just might ..." he replied.

"No chance," she countered. She was dead right. He knew it, she knew it.

The mix was working. After three rounds they were happy and singing as loudly as anybody. The evening was slipping by, it was setting a tingle into their cheeks, they sang lustily and loud and not always in tune. The guest was introduced and the Town Clerk was pleased to note that it was Dave Burland,

175

a singer whom the Town Clerk had known from his University Folk Club days. He sang a couple of songs that they both knew well and then he sang 'The Barnsley Anthem' which began 'We're reight dahn in't cellar oil wit muck-slats on winders' – the Town Clerk remembered the opening line well but whether it was the passage of time or the fact that he had now drunk Chartreuse, Barnsley Bitter, Special Brew, Brandy, his memory was not all that it should have been and he got no farther than the first line. He took out his new pen and sent a message to Dave Burland via the Club Organiser and for his second session Dave announced that he had been requested to sing 'The False Bride' – shielding his eyes from the spotlight Dave tried to see who had requested it but James Pickering-Eaden slipped deeper into the shadows with his girl seemingly part of him as she laid back into his contours. He did not think that Dave Burland would have recognised him but did not want to chance it.

He kissed her on the forehead. "Listen to this song," he said, "listen to every word, and if you remember nothing more of me, remember tonight and the words of this song." He was getting emotional. He knew every word of the old ballad and the feelings he had with every verse were strong and vivid and these feelings were getting through to the girl.

The Folk Club was hushed. Dave introduced it with a five bar introduction and then into the lyric:

When first I saw my love in the Church stand,
With a ring on her finger and a glove in her hand,
I stepped up beside her to kiss the false bride,
Sing adieu to false loves forever.

When first I saw my love out the church go,
With her bridesmen and bridesmaids she made a fine show,
And I followed after with a heart full of woe,
For I was the man should have had her.

When first I saw my love sat down to meat,
I sat myself by her but nothing could eat,
I valued her company sweeter than wine,
Although she was wed to some other.

So dig me a grave both wide long and deep,
And strew it all over with flowers so sweet,
And I lay me down for to take a long sleep,
And maybe in time I'll forget her.

Well I loved a lass, and I loved her so well,
That I hated all others who spoke of her ill,
But now she's rewarded me well for my pains,
For she's gone to be wed to some other.

She sobbed gently. She turned to him and sobbed into his chest. It was the culmination of a perfect evening. After the five mixed drinks the salty sea air hit them like a hammer as they left the club and made their way back across the fields. They stumbled as they climbed the stiles, slipped a couple of times on the uneven surface and had difficulty in fitting the key into the doorlock. They swayed into their lovenest and even went straight to sleep and the first birds of morning were tuning up when their second night together was consummated.

The second day at the conference mirrored the first even to the extent of taking Mrs Bramble to lunch. That she hated the Mayor was more and more apparent to the Town Clerk and he was subjected to a vitriolic tirade about Councillor Ullathorne again over lunch. So spiteful was the attack on him that, at one point, he found himself defending the Mayor, a course of action that, in retrospect, felt laughable with the Mayor having such a hold over him. He dutifully sat through the morning session and even made a telling contribution to the debate in an attempt to foreshorten it but he was glad when the truncated afternoon session ended early. He could not wait to get back to Filey although it was perfectly possible to return to Middlethwaite the same afternoon being only a couple of hours drive away. He had told Celia that there was a reception in the evening and did not want to chance driving after alcohol so the arrangements for a further night with his Administrative Assistant Grade III had been laid. He bade farewell to Councillor Mrs Bramble who told him she was continuing her holiday on the Yorkshire coast and they parted in mid-afternoon. It had seemed an eternity that he had spent in her company and they were no friendlier at the end than they were at the beginning. 'Bramble the Ramble's' social conscience had been massaged and she was well pleased and certain that her involvement with the C.P.R.E. would lead to lasting good coming out of it for Middlethwaite, Yorkshire, Great Britain, Europe, the world and the universe, not necessarily in that order. The Town Clerk sighed a deep sigh as they shook hands but there was a steely look in her eye and he knew she could not be trusted. She was, in short, a bitch, but the Town Clerk felt that he had handled her well, well above the call of duty. He had listened to her character assassination of all and sundry and had refused to be drawn, even finding himself mumbling at one time that he hoped the Mayor and Mayoress were having a good time in Mablethorpe.

The Town Clerk could not remember when he had been so assiduous. He had been at 'Bramble the Ramble's' every whim for two whole days. He had not shirked his responsibilities. If he had gone for a coffee in mid-session he had felt her neck swivelling and her eyes boring into the nape of his neck until he returned with the beverage. No officer had ever engendered such a devotion to duty as she had, he thought of himself as one of the cannon fodder privates of the First World War, so good was he at obeying her every whim. That he had an ulterior motive she was not to know but he thought at the time that had he just left her to her own devices at the Conference instead of being attentive to her beck and call all the time, he might have been better thought of. But he got no credit from her for being such a dedicated officer and 'Bramble the Ramble' was rapidly becoming a clone of the Mayor of Middlethwaite in her treatment of the Council's Clerk and Chief Executive. He was tempted into launching into an Ullathornesque tirade but he bit his lip, said he hoped that she had enjoyed the conference, hoped that many positive points would come from it, looked forward to her report to Council and can he pay her the fifty pence he owed her for the shandy she had bought him in mid-morning as he recognised and accepted her interpretation of local government corruption. He stopped short of implying that this fifty pence shandy might entail a good 'seeing-to' for the delegate by the Town Clerk. The delegate from Middlethwaite Metropolitan Borough Council was not aware of the latent sarcasm in the Town Clerk's manner so she said goodbye to him and said that she would send him her draft of the proceedings of the Annual Conference of the Council for the Preservation of Rural England for him to study and assimilate.

"Can't wait," said the Town Clerk.

The leader of the opposition of Middlethwaite Metropolitan Borough

The Conference at Scarborough

Council was unaware of the heavy sarcasm and departed the Conference shaking hands with all and sundry and congratulating the man from the Ramblers' Association in a manner that gave him the impression that he had just won the Kinder Trespass Award for the Millennium.

"Don't forget," he told her, "'Trespass the World' – let that be our watchword." Councillor Mrs Bramble looked at him in awe, he was her kind of man. The Town Clerk had told Cheryl that he would be back early. As he entered the bungalow he had a surprise – she was standing waiting for him in a winceyette nightie and a steaming cup of cocoa in her hand. He laughed uncontrollably for he had told her about the connotations of cocoa and winceyette with Celia but, just to go along with the charade, he picked her up and carried her to the bedroom, cocoa and all. A quick climax was achieved by both whereupon they rose and as it was still only early afternoon they found a sunny spot on the clifftop and lay together until the sun went down. They watched the blood-red orange of the sun slip down over the horizon, a fishing smack silhouetted on it as it passed the skyline and they were both romantic about the setting and the occasion and the fact that they only had another night together before their return to the Town Clerk's office in Middlethwaite Town Hall.

As the sun disappeared nightfall came quickly and seemed all the darker to contrast the brightness of the early afternoon. In fact it was beginning to cloud over but they were content in their love-nest and returned for a grilled meal with wine, brandy and liqueurs. As they settled down they were both full and were beginning to doze off although the hour was not late. From across the bay came a slight rumble of thunder and sheet lightning lit up the bay. They went out onto the veranda and watched nature in her many moods at once violent and active and then passive and still as the storm passed over. One moment the hailstones were rattling the roof, then the wind had veered and a slight spray was swirling around, next the storm had moved away and everything was still save from the dripping trees nearby.

"Get those plastic macs from the lobby," said the Town Clerk.

"You're mad," replied the girl, "what do you want to do?"

"I want to walk along the cliff path with you, I want to feel the wind in my hair, I want to feel you by my side, I want a few lung-fulls of this marvellous salty air, I want to walk our excesses off and I want to return with you in one hour and join you in a steaming shower, that's what I want."

179

The Town Clerk

"Sounds good, put like that," she said and they giggled together as they put on the plastic macs and also found two pairs of wellington boots in the lobby. Hers were too big and his were too small but they managed to get into them and it was a motley pair that set out on the cliff path, swerving dangerously close to the cliff-edge at times and walking like a pair of the old time music hall comedians due to their ill-fitting footwear.

"Here look," the Town Clerk said as he tried a sand-dance, "how's this for an impression of those two music hall greats Wisdom and Ullathorne at the opening of the Middlethwaite Hippodrome?"

"Alright, it's very good," she responded, "but I don't think the Mayor would countenance that billing, it would have to be Ullathorne and Wisdom, remember you told me that Norman Wisdom declined to come to the Mayor's Parade because he knew he'd have to take second billing?"

"You've got a good memory, Mrs Oldroyd," he said and they shared a few other occasions in their memory as they sashayed along the cliff path.

They had gone all of a mile clinging closely together when they agreed that they had better retrace their steps for fear of getting lost, it might look slightly obverse if they had to call the coastguards out. They put this point to each other, did a quick about-turn and bumped slap-bang into a rambler coming up behind them. It was Councillor Mrs Bramble.

"Christ," said the Town Clerk. What a cataclysmic thing to happen. So astounded were all three at this unexpected meeting that, mouths agape, they just froze and stared at each other.

"Oh dear!" said Cheryl.

"This is disgraceful!" said Councillor Eunice Bramble, "I can see it all now, I can see all the double-dealing that you have both been up to. Not for you to show any kind of moral lead to the Council, Mr Town Clerk..." she looked at him evilly, "this will finish you, I shall make sure of it," she said, turning onto her heel and heading along towards Filey Bar.

The Town Clerk caught her by the shoulder and swivelled her round. "Please," was all he could say.

"Take your bloody hands off me," she said.

It was the first time that the Town Clerk had heard her swear. "Look," said the Town Clerk, "we are in love."

It sounded so trite. It sounded like Noel Coward at his worst and it was similarly treated by Councillor Mrs Bramble, "Love," she said, "you don't

The Conference at Scarborough

know the meaning of it. Here you are with that prostitute from your office," she clearly remembered the dealings she had had with Cheryl Oldroyd and her husband, especially the dynamiting of her path, "this is the end for you, Town Clerk."

The Town Clerk drew a deep breath, for two days he had waited on her hand and foot and a fat lot of good it had done him. She was at her evil worst. Nothing could have mollified her. She got free of the Town Clerk's hand on her shoulder and headed down the path, the mazy path along the clifftop. For a woman of seventy she was amazingly agile and the Town Clerk, despite his twenty-two year advantage in age, was wrong-footed and she broke free and headed down the cliff path. The Town Clerk saw her disappear into the mist-shrouded cliff-top. Just for one moment, he thought, what possible pleasure could bloody Councillor Mrs Bramble get from this walk down a rain sodden path in semi-darkness unaccompanied? The question remained unanswered, there was no answer, ramblers were a breed all of their own and logic just did not apply. The question was put to the back of his mind. What was he doing asking himself such stupid questions at such a crucial time in his life?

It was time for instantaneous action. The girl was already weeping having at once taken in the enormous possibilities that discovery would entail.

"Go back home," the Town Clerk said, "I'll catch her up and plead with her .... perhaps she has a better nature," he said, without too much hope. Mrs Bramble was almost out of sight. She had splashed through Belinda Beck that dropped into the sea at that point and she was speeding along the cliff top path. He had to hurry to catch her before she reached Fiveways Hamlet for she would be gone beyond recall by then. His army training came into play, he gulped a huge mouthful of air and yomped after her. It took him some time to catch her but he came alongside her at the top of the knoll and as he did so she increased her pace in an effort to leave him behind. For seventy years of age she was incredibly agile. As he chased after her brambles rent his skin, he turned his ankle over but felt no pain. He just had to get to her.

"Please," he called out, "please, talk to me."

"I don't want to talk to you. I am altering my holiday plans to go back to Middlethwaite and do my worst. You are finished, Town Clerk. I want to say nothing more, Town Clerk," she spat, "I want nothing more to do with you .. or that trollop that you are with." She turned on her heels and ran.

The Town Clerk moved towards her but when he was a yard from her, her

181

The Town Clerk

heels caught the uneven surface and she spun round, her arms flailed out straight like a scarecrow, she made a grab at a cliff fence that was not there and, with a seeming ballet-like pirouette was gone over the cliff. As the Town Clerk saw her disappear the wind seemed to hold her in mid-air for just a moment before she plunged. Like a sky-diver the eddying currents seemed to bear her up and she made eye contact with James Pickering-Eaden. For only a split-second she was held immobile in mid-air but it seemed like an eternity before nature took the cushion away and she was gone. With a sickening thud she hit the rocks below and lay still like a rag-doll.

The Town Clerk looked over the cliff and felt a well of sickness engulf him. She cannot survive that, he thought, so he spun on his heels, kicked the wellington boots off so he could walk properly and returned to the bungalow. The girl was weeping uncontrollably.

"You'll have no trouble with her," he said simplistically, "she's dead." He explained that he had not touched her and she believed him.

"What will happen to us?" she said, facing up to the fact.

The Town Clerk was decisive, as ever. "She's dead and nothing is going to bring her back. No-one knows we are here. If our affair is exposed it will not help her one jot. It will ruin both of us but it will not help her one jot. I think we should put it out of our minds and hope for the best. If it is discovered that we are involved we shall have to make a clean breast of it, but I shall probably be able to shield you for although it is known that I am in Scarborough, there is nothing to locate you here." He was being strong and she appreciated it.

He looked at her and a smile flicked across his face, "Ullathorne said 'you'll have to get that bloody Bramble off my back'.... but I didn't think I'd end up murdering her! That's a figure of speech, darling," he said. "Honestly, my love, I didn't touch her. She tripped over some gorse and smashed onto the rocks below. There is no way she could have survived it. If I'd got the RNLI or the coastguards out they couldn't have done anything for her. But I couldn't call them out, I had to think of you and me and try to protect us."

It was the first time he had called her darling and he felt passionate towards her. He made up his mind that he would keep her out of this sordid business at all costs. He analysed the position in his mind and then spelled out the situation to her.

"This is how I see it. In the morning they will find her body, or if the tide has washed her away into a gully it could be a few days. It could be even longer and with the vagaries of the tides she could end up miles away. She is a widow but I don't know where she is staying so they may not miss her as she has taken herself off before many times on the Pennine Way and the Lyke Wake Walk. So if she does not show up no-one will raise the alarm immediately. We must not panic – although I do intend having a very large whiskey now and I should be obliged if you would now pour it for me." He grasped the tumbler but as he raised it to his lips his hand shook uncontrollably.

He tried a joke, "I don't drink much," he said, "spill most of it." Somehow it was not the time for levity.

The girl was sad. She was very subdued. No wonder really, their affair had brought him nothing but trouble but fortunately she did not know the half of it. He took her into his arms and she sobbed. He kept saying "I'm sorry," and trying to reassure her but she remained sad.

"I'm sorry," he tried yet again, "if only I had thought there was a chance of meeting that bloody woman on the cliff path I wouldn't have suggested a moonlit stroll, honestly, the bloody woman did not come into my calculations any more than she did in the Strines Valley. Remember how we laughed and joked that lovely afternoon if one of those ramblers three miles away had been 'Bramble the Ramble'?"

She put one hand at each side of his head and drew him to her in a passionate kiss, "Look," she said, "it's nothing to do with the demise of Councillor Mrs Bramble. She means nothing to me. I have already put her out of my mind. I have only known you a short while but I know you as a kind and gentle man and if you say she went over by accident, then that's enough reassurance I need. Now, take me to our bed."

They spent their third night together locked in a passionate embrace which lasted all night. The Town Clerk woke once and she was still clinging tightly to him. He had awoken with a start but had not disturbed her. In his nightmare he had seen Councillor Mrs Bramble prone on the rock, her eyes staring to heaven. She looked just like one of those Pre-Raphaelite maidens so beloved by Burne-Jones, Rosetti and Millais. She was moulded to the rock, her shroud flapping around her, her locks straightened by the breeze. There was a seraphic smile on her lips. As he peered over the cliff-edge laser beams jetted from her eyes into the unlit leaden sky. Her body was then washed from the rock and eddied into a whirlpool like Charybdis (or was it Scylla, he never

The Town Clerk

could remember which was which). The blood from the body stained the sea and – suddenly – Mrs Bramble came to life as Lady Macbeth speaking Macbeth's soliloquy from the play "Will this sea wash the blood from my hands? No my hands will rather the multitudinous seas incarnadine turning the green one red." It had been thirty years since he had studied Macbeth but he could see the parallel that night on Filey Bar.

His nightmare lasted a long time. Still locked in an embrace, he finally went to sleep again but, not unnaturally, it was a troubled sleep and he greeted the first rays of morning with relief. He strained to hear the wailing sounds of emergency services and was not quite sure whether he was glad or sorry when all he could hear was the lapping of the waves on the shore below.

The hall clock struck five o'clock. He was wrapped round her bicycle-fashion as if they had slept together for thirty years. He was wide awake so he traced his finger between her legs and she responded. She pushed her bottom at a more acute angle so he could caress her clitoris. At once all thoughts of 'Bramble the Ramble' were gone. She was very sticky and he marvelled at his capacity to excite her. He thought she was still fast asleep but as he put two fingers now in her furrow she responded by throbbing at an even tempo. Not sure she was even awake, he could wait no longer and he inserted his throbbing member into her. She sighed deeply and then generated a rhythm that accelerated until a frantic climax was achieved. After detumescence they subsided into each other. At last the Town Clerk slipped into a deep somnolence. He woke again at eight o'clock and listened once again for the emergency services. Once again he could hear nothing. All was still. He wished things could be different but, unfortunately, Councillor Mrs Eunice Bramble was just as dead as she had been nine hours previously.

Surprisingly the girl slept until nine o'clock. The Town Clerk was puzzled as to why she had seemed only slightly affected by the demise of Councillor Mrs Bramble but was quiet and withdrawn although loving towards him. They got together their belongings and made towards the car. She was to be dropped off at Holmfirth station where they had met and with her husband being away, the Town Clerk had omitted to enquire what alibi she had concocted for the three days away. They drove slowly and not much was said. At Holmfirth station it was time for them to part and the Town Clerk parked out of sight halfway up the hill where he had picked her up three days previous. They turned to each other and a moist kiss lasted an eternity.

The Conference at Scarborough

Finally she spoke. "James," she said.

The Town Clerk shuddered for he knew something momentous was going to happen. She had never used his name before.

"James," she repeated and her eyes were red rimmed with weeping, "James," she said, for the third time. "That's it."

He recoiled. He passed his dry tongue over drier lips. He throat was parched and he could not talk.

She put her finger onto his lips and said, "James, please don't say anything. Please listen. This is the last time I will ever see you. That letter I posted when we met three days ago was to you. It is my resignation. There is a doctor's certificate in it. I am three months pregnant. I leave Middlethwaite on Tuesday. Our house is sold and we are moving to Cornwall where Darren has been appointed Operations Manager in Bodmin at the English China Clay Operation for Rio Tinto Zinc. Although I have given myself to you completely since the start of our affair there have, of course, been times when Darren and I have consummated, to use no better word for it. I know I cannot become pregnant by you due to the vasectomy and now that Darren and I are to have a child I must devote all my time and energy to it. I will always think of you. I will always have a place in my heart for you but, James, there is no alternative and I must make this break and go away from Middlethwaite for ever, without you. It is my only chance. I could not see you every day and be unaffected. I don't want to do it but I must. Goodbye ..."

She opened the door, swung her legs out of the passenger seat and was gone, breaking into a trot as she saw the diesel approaching the station as if aware of the stage timing of the drama that was being played out.

The Town Clerk watched her out of sight, he could just see her as she boarded the diesel and he watched the diesel wend its unsteady way around the hillocks in the direction of Middlethwaite. For some moments he sat motionless and took stock of his situation. It was grim. But everything else palled into insignificance in relation to what he had just been subjected to. He put his head in his hands and stayed immobile for a long time. He drew several deep breaths and his shoulders heaved convulsively. He felt awful. He wanted to call her back and tell her what Doc Slack had told him about the "few little buggers swimming about in the milky stuff." But this sounded just what it was, a desperate ploy.

He felt as if the bottom had just been pulled out from his world. He could

The Town Clerk

not imagine any worse scenario. The trials and tribulations of all the Mayor's triumphs over him did not matter a light in comparison with the fact that Cheryl Oldroyd had just pulled the rug from under him and effectively ended his life. Whatever the future had for him now it just would not stand up against the past. However would he get through life without Cheryl Oldroyd, his Administrative Assistant Grade III? There was no chance, he may just as well end it there and then. He was shell-shocked, his mind was in a turmoil, he could not think straight. He was finished. He stayed there for an eternity. Successive travellers from the railway stopped to ask if he was alright. He was grateful for their interest and solicitude. He was broken. He was a barren man. He felt dreadful. He had had it. He closed his eyes and slept a nightmarish sleep for three hours. At the end of it he put the car into gear and drove home. Slowly, very slowly.

CHAPTER FIFTEEN

IN MEMORIUM

The Town Clerk was in a black mood, an all-pervading cloud of doom enveloped him and nothing could lift it. He threw himself into his work, he drank too much, he could not sleep at night and every day comprised twenty-four black hours. He tried not to communicate his abject state of despair to his staff in case they guessed a connection with the leaving of Cheryl Oldroyd but after a while he just withdrew into his shell and was almost incommunicado. The letter with the Holmfirth postmark duly arrived and the Town Clerk came into the office early to intercept the post. He need not have bothered – there was no coded message, merely a formal letter of resignation enclosing a Certificate of impending motherhood and thanking the Town Clerk and his staff for the happy years spent working for the Metropolitan Borough of Middlethwaite. That was all. That was it. The Town Clerk felt a broken man and whilst he had hitherto been aware of his feelings for his Administrative Assistant Grade III he had no idea that her departure would leave such a mortal stain on his whole being. If time was supposed to be a healer, it had done precious little to heal anything so far. The Mayor had returned from Mablethorpe and things were obviously the same in that direction. He could see no hope anywhere.

It was the day of the Memorial Service for Councillor Mrs Eunice Bramble and St Peter's Church was full for the Requiem Mass being conducted by her nephew, the Reverend John Savage. There was an overflow congregation in the adjoining church hall and the service was relayed to it. Every organisation that Mrs Bramble had been connected with – and there were many – was represented in the Parish Church.

As the coffin was borne into church the Town Clerk said, "Thanks be to God," and crossed himself exaggeratedly with the sign of the crucifix for it

187

The Town Clerk

seemed that he had got away with any suggestion of involvement with the death of Councillor Mrs Bramble.

Her body had been found three days later washed ashore at Reighton Gap and the subsequent Coroner's Court recorded death by misadventure. The three days awaiting the finding of her body were the longest in the life of James Pickering-Eaden, Town Clerk of the Metropolitan Borough of Middlethwaite. He reckoned that the longer it took to find her, the more chance he would have of distancing himself from events. He was right in his surmising that she would not be missed for a while and, in fact, the body was found before she was reported missing. He had prepared a full report on the Conference of the CPRE and had very cleverly left some items blank noting that Councillor Mrs Eunice Bramble wished to give a verbal report on this matter. His first draft he had hurriedly fed into the shredder as the wording of it implied that his co-delegate was no more and no-one at that time suspected that she was even missing, let alone dead.

He thought endlessly about Cheryl Oldroyd – endlessly – all the time – and reckoned that she would be having an interminable time in Cornwall waiting for press coverage of the missing councillor.

On the third night back from Filey he woke with a start and shot bolt upright in bed in the middle of the night. Those bloody wellington boots that he had cast off at the cliff top. They would have his fingerprints on them. He must find them. He was in a cold sweat. He remembered how diligent he had been to wipe the fingerprints from the resealed sealed tender and how he had donned his white linen ceremonial gloves to handle the briefcase. Christ, he thought, if they find my fingerprints on those wellington boots they will connect me with the death, the Council will suspend me and someone will find a briefcase stuffed with money in my safe. They will also find a pair of soiled panties in the other safe...... He must go to Filey straightaway and find those bloody boots. But no, supposing the police had found them and had posted a look-out in the bushes around them, waiting for the wearer to reappear? In the early hours of the morning he had got into his car and was reversing out of the garage en route to Filey when he said to himself, Jim. Hold on. Her body may be miles away from Filey Bar by now. If anybody finds a pair of discarded Wellingtons how can they be connected with the disappearance of Mrs Bramble? And how can there be any fingerprints on them after three days exposed to the elements and the sea-spray? And, if

In Memorium

there were fingerprints, how could they trace them to me? I've led a blameless life without so much as a parking ticket. That is, he reckoned, until this year's Mayor-Making since when he had been guilty of corruption, blackmail, forgery, adultery, drunkenness, debauchery, sniffing knickers without a licence and causing death by dangerous chasing. He took the keys out of the ignition and returned to Celia's side. Celia had not stirred. She was full of cocoa. The Town Clerk looked down at her somnolent form with the seraphic smile and thought, I wish I was normal. He then dwelt on the times and cavorting with Cheryl Oldroyd and thought, I'm glad I'm not. But how am I to get out of this bloody mess? Perhaps God will help. He recited the creed under his breath and prayed for God's help and guidance. If He could see His way to helping the Town Clerk sort out his mess he would be eternally grateful. For all his misdemeanours he figured that he had only transgressed one commandment so he apologised profusely for shagging Cheryl Oldroyd.

The cortège procession came slowly down the aisle. The organist struck up the introit hymn, Jerusalem, commencing with 'And did those feet in ancient times'. How appropriate he thought. He found himself singing at full voice, "And did those feet in ancient times, walk upon England's mountains green," and paraphrasing it to "walk upon Yorkshire's coastal path," – he was so active with his mind that he was paraphrasing every line. But when he came to the "and did that countenance divine," his mind became a mess of red and orange spears as he thought of the last time he had seen that "countenance divine." It was as she was plunging off the cliff path at Reighton Gap and when the downdraft seemed to hold her in mid-air and he made eye-contact with that countenance divine. And it was not a countenance divine. It was an evil steely look full of bitterness and moral indignation. But he must not think ill of the dead.... although it was difficult for him not to.

The Mayor of Middlethwaite entered the Church. Councillor Leslie Ullathorne was definitely going over the top. His garb resembled that of the grand Edwardian funerals of East London. He wore black all over complete with a stovepipe silk hat. His measured gait faltered as he walked behind the coffin and he took a large linen handkerchief and wiped a tear away from a tearless eye. As he passed the Town Clerk's pew he looked sideways at him and brushed another tear from a tearless eye. Bloody hypocrite, thought the Town Clerk. He could see the bulge of a hip flask appropriately enough in the hip pocket of the tailcoat that he wore. Robin Armstrong had told the Town

The Town Clerk

Clerk that he was now up to two and a half bottles of gin a day with the Mayoress lagging not far behind at about one and a half bottles. Just recently they had converted to litres and convinced themselves that their intake had not increased. They had taken to having it delivered by the case direct to the Parlour and Robin wondered in a conversation with the Town Clerk where the Mayor was getting the money from. The Town Clerk knew for just along the pew was his paymaster, Mr Alfred G Page. The Town Clerk would have liked to tell Robin Armstrong about the Alfred G Page connection but he knew that one thing would have led to another so, with difficulty, he kept silent.

The eulogies of the life and work of Mrs Eunice Bramble were long and profuse in their praise. The representative of the Ramblers' Association who had spoke long and loud at the Scarborough Conference of the Council for the Preservation of Rural England said that it was "as though Councillor Mrs Bramble had died on active service striding out to mark, emphasise and enjoy the footpaths of England." Quite a nice touch thought the Town Clerk and he was now coming round to the fact that perhaps he had done 'Bramble the Ramble' a favour for if she was looking down from heaven – or even up from the murky waters of Filey Bar – there is no doubt that she would be enjoying every minute, particularly she would like the notion that she had died 'on active service'. The Ramblers Association man told the hushed congregation that "Trespass the World" should be the epitaph on her tombstone but the Town Clerk thought that was bloody silly. He thought RIP would be sufficient for everyone could use the "requiescat in pace" initials for their own summation as a mnemonic for Councillor Mrs Eunice Bramble. His own acronym would perhaps be "rapacious interfering prissy" and his mind was really drifting now and he came up with "relieved insoluble problem" by her death. While she was alive she "ritually inflicted poison" whilst perhaps taking her final flight off the cliffs at Filey Bar she would have "required insulated parachute." Whilst the Town Clerk's thoughts were travelling along these lines, there must have been a modicum of thought transference for in his eulogy the Ramblers Association man took up the theme of RIP on the tombstone and told the packed and impressed congregation that Councillor Mrs Eunice Bramble would be "Rambling in Perpetuity." The congregation could scarce forbear to cheer.

The Mayor, swaying slightly, departed from the text, as usual, that Robin Armstrong had prepared for him to add that although Mrs Bramble had been a political opponent he had had enormous respect for her and enjoyed the cut-and-thrust of debate with her. Yes, thought the Town Clerk, about as much as you enjoyed saying Mephibosheth at Mayor's Sunday. The Town Clerk noticed that even the Mayor was restrained and did not launch into a political invective.

He had given thanks to God many times during the service but it was now time to take communion at the Requiem Mass. Councillor Mrs Eunice Bramble had stipulated in her will that she wished to be commemorated with a Requiem Mass so about half the congregation filed slowly in line to the altar to receive the bread and the wine of the holy communion. There was certainly an air of gravitas hanging over the proceedings, much of it genuine, some of it false. Whilst the congregation took communion many appropriate hymns were sung including the 23rd psalm which the Town Clerk proceeded to paraphrase. When he got to the verse about thy rod and staff he could see her, backpack amid her shoulderblades and shepherd's crook to sustain her. He hurriedly switched off and watched the Mayor in his Edwardian splendour.

The Town Clerk found himself next to Chief Superintendent Colin Murray in the choir stalls as they lined up to take communion. "I want to see you afterwards.." he whispered as they knelt at the altar rail. The bottom fell out of the Town Clerk's world, his legs went weak at the knees and the prayers that he said as he went down at the altar rail and took the bread and the wine most certainly were the strongest ones winging their way to heaven that morning.

At last the service was over. The coffin was hoisted aloft and the congregation filed out in procession behind the bearers for Mrs Bramble to be laid at her final resting place, appropriately enough just slightly off the footpath adjacent to Middlethwaite Beck.

The Mayor followed the party but veered off when he came adjacent to the Town Clerk and said, "In the Parlour afterwards, Town Clerk, I thought we might just have a gin or two to celebrate – I'm sorry, I mean commemorate – the sad demise of Councillor Mrs Bramble." Whether it had been a Freudian slip or not the Town Clerk was unable to gauge but he did not take the Mayor up on his offer. He was thinking with trepidation of the "I want to see you afterwards," instruction that he had received at the altar rail from Chief Superintendent Colin Murray. He did not have to wait long as he looked and saw the head of Middlethwaite Police striding towards him. This is it, thought

The Town Clerk

the Town Clerk, ten years in Wakefield jail.

Murray came by and said out of the corner of his mouth, "I shouldn't really tell you this but, sometimes as a brother Mason, I can let loyalty intervene with my police duties. As you pulled away from the Freemason's Hall the other night I noticed that your nearside rear brakelight wasn't working and as I know that you must have been just about on the limit for drink-driving I wouldn't want one of my boys in blue to stop you for a breath test. There's one particularly ..." his timing was immaculate for as the bearers carried the coffin they had just stepped outside the church and Councillor Mrs Eunice Bramble was resting on the stone plinth just under the lytch gate. "There's one particularly nasty bastard by the name of Sgt. Lycett, I wouldn't want him to nab you."

The Town Clerk breathed a huge sigh of relief. "Thanks be to God," he muttered under his breath. He walked on his own back to his office. "Kinell," he said, "kinell."

CHAPTER SIXTEEN

COMMITTED

That he had got away with the 'Bramble the Ramble' episode was now assured. He had had a few days of unease when the local paper first published the news of the finding of her body. They led with the banner headline 'Did she slip or was she pushed..?' and at no moment did the Town Clerk consider picking up the telephone and telling the Editor the whole story. It remained a matter of speculation only for a few days before being superseded by the all-too-frequent story of youths killed whilst speeding in a stolen car. The Town Clerk felt un-Christian when he read it for he was secretly hoping to see Pineapple Haircut and Karate Kick – and those awful young scrubbers – mentioned in the press report.

There were, of course, many other avenues of disquiet for the Town Clerk but they were all considered insignificant beside the leaving of Mrs Oldroyd. No more could he look forward to her entrance in the morning with the day's post. No more the tossing curls, the half-smile playing around her lips, no more guessing the pattern of her underwear as his laserlike eyes traced the pantie lines over her rounded hips. No more tracing with his eyes that gusset leaving its imprint against that tantalising beige skirt. No more.. no more.. no more bloody anything thought the Town Clerk. Life was barren, let the Mayor do his worst, the Town Clerk did not care.

The balloon went up a week after Mrs Bramble's funeral.

Celia had persuaded him to take a few days off. He had agreed for he wanted to make up to his wife for being like a bear with a sore head. They took themselves off for a few days touring in the car and stopping at the best hotels. He had wanted to tour the Lake District but Celia wanted to go to Devon so Devon it was. The Town Clerk had no great interest in the matter. Life was dead for him but they had a pleasant time with pleasant weather and

193

The Town Clerk

the Town Clerk took solace in laying in the sun and drinking and eating to excess. He made himself bad tempered by looking excitedly at every auburn haired girl with tossing curls and shapely hips, thinking that he might just bump into his former Administrative Assistant Grade III in the west country. It was only when he realised that although in Devon he was still over one hundred miles from where she had moved to that he reconciled himself that any chance of a casual meeting was nil. He also tried to exorcise from his mind that beautiful flat tummy of hers. Now it would be slightly rounded. He wouldn't fancy her at all. He would. He would. He would.

For poor Celia even the cocoa and curaçao did not work and the Pickering-Eaden marriage had become a sexless one. He had left his mobile 'phone at home and no-one knew of his itinerary, he wanted nothing to do with Middlethwaite, anything he heard could only be bad news.

The highlight of his day was the arrival of the Daily Telegraph. Each morning he read it from cover to cover, obituaries, gossip, business, travel, everything. On the second Thursday he picked up the Daily Telegraph and, turning to the inner pages, his eye fell on the headlines 'One hundred jobs lost in South Yorkshire'. Another coal mine's closed he thought until he remembered that there were not many left. He read on. 'The Moldavian government has withdrawn its subsidy on the Majolta Car Industry following the putsch at the weekend of Colonel Subcheq. Heavily subsidised by the previous administration the spokesman blamed the international devaluation of the rouble and the fact that the new flagship the Majolta Whirlwind had failed to make any impact in the executive car market. All subsidy has been withdrawn from the activities in South Yorkshire and the company would not now go ahead with their plan to open a components factory on the second phase of Water's Edge Business Park in Middlethwaite. The Head of Operations (G.B.), Mr Alfred G Page said he was devastated to lose so many jobs including his own but he himself had managed to obtain a post in the City of London and, if he were able in the future to divert any finance and relocate other industries in Water's Edge Business Park he would certainly do so. He felt a commitment to South Yorkshire and was sorry to be leaving. He had left many things behind him that he had valued.' Yes, thought the Town Clerk, especially a briefcase!

The Town Clerk was astounded at his luck. In one whole swipe Colonel Subcheq had wiped out one of his biggest headaches. He told Celia to pack straightaway for he must be back at his desk. Celia did as she was told. Truth-to-tell she wasn't enjoying the holiday much, the curacao wasn't working at all and she thought her marriage might be revitalised in Middlethwaite. Besides there was the exciting prospect of taking cuttings from that new strain of polyanthus. There was also a certain matter of a certain briefcase that had to be attended to. The Town Clerk drove like the wind and was back in the office by early afternoon. There was a queue waiting to see him.

He first saw jointly Dr Joshua Slack accompanied by Robin Armstrong, the Mayor's Secretary. They had some momentous news. "The Mayor's been committed," they said in unison.

"Committed?" queried the Town Clerk, "What do you mean committed?" he followed up, "Has he been shoplifting or driving under the influence?"

"No, not that sort of committed," said Doc Slack. "He's flipped. Nutty as a fruitcake. He's in Storrs Garden Mental Hospital. He's gone completely. Talking backwards all the time. Daor Krap Ekoorbdik. Kidbrooke Park Road. What sort of rubbish is that? Shouting about videos and crumpet and gin and cricket bats and Chez Lon Gue and Public Heirs. Keeps yelling he's got a tie round his neck when the silly sod's not even wearing a collar to his shirt. The gin's got to him and he's gone to a point of no return. When we couldn't reach you we contacted your Deputy, Roy Owen, and he arranged for the last year's Mayor, Councillor Cairns, to be sworn in as Mayor. We've had to get the tailor to re-re-style the ermine but he said it stinks. Councillor Cairns says it smells somewhere between Brut aftershave and a couple of dead dogs, so we've taken an executive decision to make some new robes. It's been bloody hell-on-earth this past couple of days. I'm glad you're back, Jim, to sort out the mess..."

The Town Clerk took stock. He could see just a glimmer of light on the horizon. He said in measured tones to Doc Slack, "Josh. I want you to look me in the eyes and tell me one thing. Is he ever going to recover?" He spelled out the question one syllable at a time. "Is he ever going to recover?" he said again.

The Medical Officer of Health replied at once, "Jim, he's got no chance. I've spoken to the consultant psychiatrists, I've seen all the scans and I've seen Ullathorne personally. With a bit of luck he'll sit in a chair, stare blankly ahead and so long as he takes his medication he could live another ten years. Jim, you haven't heard him. He just talks – well, it's a load of bollocks – all the

The Town Clerk

time. It's quite funny really but we shouldn't really laugh, his mind has gone and we have to strap him down and tiddle him every couple of hours. I'll give you a laugh, Jim, he has to have Gilbey's gin on the National Health until we can wean him off it. But as for recovery, well ... there's more chance of you fathering a child," he laughed as he liked the analogy.

The Town Clerk thanked both men for so quickly acting and made an appointment to meet again in two hours time when the committal papers were expected to be available for filing with the Court of Protection. He sat back in his chair and put his feet on the desk and lit a rare cigar.

There was a knock at his office door. It was Laura King, his secretary. He puffed on his cigar and looked at Laura King's legs. They were nice legs ... no he mustn't think about them. "Sir, Mr Alan Unwin would like to see you. He says it is terribly important and could you spare him five minutes?"

"Of course, Miss King, please show him in straightaway."

Alan Unwin was his friend from years back who had been articled to him but unable to settle in local government had made a huge success of building up a private legal practice. He entered and the two men gave a Masonic handshake for they had last met at the Installation Lodge meeting when the Town Clerk was installed as Provincial Grand Master. Alan Unwin had a great respect for James Pickering-Eaden, he thought he owed him everything for the fruition of his career.

"I think that you should have this," said Alan Unwin, taking a package from his briefcase. He handed it to the Town Clerk. It was marked 'Council Business (funny business).'

Straightfaced, Alan Unwin said, "My instructions from the Mayor were that if anything happens to him this package was to be given to the Council Leader. Can I leave it with you Jim to do the necessary..?" and he spun on his heel and was gone.

The Town Clerk said nothing. He put his head in his hands but he could see that things that looked so black had a slightly less doom-laden look now. He must act quickly. The Town Clerk gathered up the package and made a quick exit through the emergency door and down the back stairs that led to the boiler. The Town Hall was still heated by solid fuel and even in summer there were boilers working to provide hot water. Solar panels had been tried and failed in Middlethwaite. The Town Clerk could feel the heat as he approached the bottom flight of stairs, package held tightly in his hand. He dwelt on the third step, spun round and retraced his steps upstairs three at a time. He went back into his office and took his 'cricket bat' audio recording from the Sealed Tenders safe. Regretfully, he also took a pair of brief panties from the same safe and retraced his steps down to the boiler. Halfway down he took one big sniff at the woman's secretions. As he did so his ankle turned over, he pitched headlong down the stone steps and ended up in an untidy heap at the bottom of the steps. So fast was the adrenaline flowing that he did not feel a thing, he gathered up Cheryl's knickers and was off again. He opened the bottom grille of the multi-fuel boiler and was almost seared as the blow-back of heat hit him. Without a second thought he threw the three items into the flames. They burned with a blue flame, appropriate, he thought. He shut the grille and went back to his office, his mind racing.... any more loose ends to tie up?

As he entered his office he thought of the bulging briefcase. He took it out and from his large Chippendale bookcase found an old law book with yellowed pages. He took Cheryl's fountain pen from his pocket and with an uneducated scrawl wrote on a yellowed page that he had torn from the book, 'PLEASE USE THIS MUNNY TO HELP THE INSANNE.' He slipped the note in the briefcase and rang for his Secretary.

"Miss King," he said, "I am just popping out for five minutes, hold the fort." He raced down the back stairs again and out of the Emergency Exit. He crossed Market Square and went into the charity shop run by Mencap, the mental health charity. He bought a paperback, paid twenty pence for it and kicked the briefcase under the rail of clothing so that it was just visibly sticking out a little bit. He went back to his office via the emergency stairs and took stock. Was that about all the ends tied up? He thought so. He hadn't felt as fired up as this since the first time he had slipped Cheryl's pants down.

It was now time to meet again to discuss the arrangements for Councillor Cairns to take over as Acting Mayor. The Town Clerk was summoned to the Parlour.

"Sit down on the chaise-longue Mr Town Clerk," said Councillor Cairns in his soft Scottish burr.

"Please, I'd rather stand," said the Town Clerk. He looked down at the upholstery of the chaise-longue. It was pristine, the nap was in perfect condition. It was a credit to its place in prime position in the Mayor's Parlour. He had had it cleaned along with the re-decoration of the Robing Room.

The Town Clerk

"I have to go to my car, Mr Town Clerk, to fetch some papers," Councillor Cairns said. "My Secretary will give you a drink, I think you have earned one."

"What would you like, Jim?" said Robin Armstrong, "A gin?"

"I don't mind if I do," said the Town Clerk mimicking the former Mayoress.

Robin picked up a bottle. His O.B.E. had come through and he had withdrawn all thoughts of resignation, he was comfortable with Councillor Cairns.

"You'd better not have it from this bottle, Jim," he said and poured the complete contents down the sink. "You see, it's pure alcohol. I could see the way things were going with that bloody idiot Ullathorne so I thought it wouldn't hurt if I hastened matters," he said.

"Kinell" said the Mayor's Secretary and Town Clerk together.

CHAPTER SEVENTEEN

JAMES

The next day the news of the Mayor's demise was headlines in the Middlethwaite Gazette. They could only say so much and the Editor, at the Town Clerk's behest, handled the matter sympathetically. The following day it was all forgotten as the Gazette made national headlines with a story about a briefcase being found in the local Mencap charity shop containing £125,000 in old notes.

In the Autumn the Town Clerk appointed a new Administrative Assistant Grade III, by the name of Hilary Burtoft. This Administrative Assistant Grade III also had a nice bum, the Town Clerk noted. But this Hilary Burtoft was a personable young man and the Town Clerk seemed to get rather a lot of visits from Adrian Watts, his Cultural Services Officer, who seemed to be very friendly with Mr Burtoft.

At the same time James Pickering-Eaden noticed that his secretary, Laura King's skirts were getting shorter. Next week's washing seemed to be on show all the time. Whilst taking dictation she dropped her pencil which rolled under the Town Clerk's desk. As her bottom was levitated in the search the Town Clerk could trace knicker-leg and gusset. Regretfully he looked away, took down Pitchfords book on the Provision of Library Services to the Disadvantaged and ignored the flickering bum.

The passage of time relieved the Town Clerk opprobrium somewhat but there seemed a void in his life. Around Christmas and New Year he took a cruise with Celia. Many exotic places were visited. Cocoa was served twice. The Town Clerk purposely got pissed most of the time. He looked at the calendar and worked out that a certain date was up-coming. He was very solicitous with Celia. She had known nothing about his peccadilloes but had supported him unwaveringly. She was also, unfortunately, the most boring person on earth.

The Town Clerk

In the second week of January the Town Clerk received a small white envelope marked 'personal'. It was postmarked Bodmin, Cornwall. The Town Clerk took it into his office, his hands sweated as he took the ivory paper-knife and opened the envelope. The card within read:

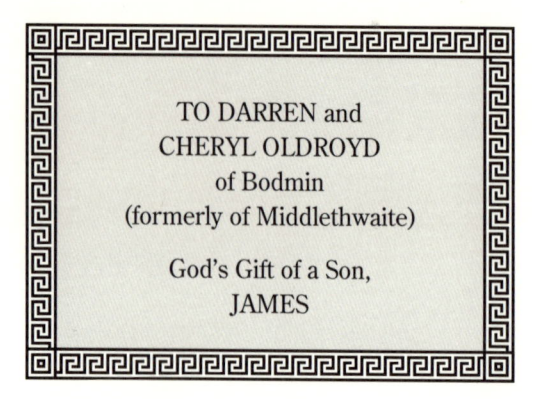

> TO DARREN and
> CHERYL OLDROYD
> of Bodmin
> (formerly of Middlethwaite)
>
> God's Gift of a Son,
> JAMES

The Town Clerk wept.